The Dissent

Laurel Solorzano

Published by Laurel Solorzano, 2024.

The Dissent

Book 3

Copyright © 2024 Laurel Solorzano

ISBN: 979-8-9884034-2-5

Cover Design by: Christine Savoie

To anyone who has ever felt defeated. Keep going. You may not solve the world's problems, but you can fix something.

Chapter 1

"Now that the asteroid has been successfully redirected, I will remind everyone that the Olympics will begin again tomorrow bright and early with the medical competition. If you would like to compete for a medal in this competition, please arrive at the medical center by 8:00." Roman, the leader of their small space colony, stood on top of the only table in the largest room of the space station.

Eden fidgeted, focusing more on one of her cuticles than on Roman's face. She couldn't look at him without a shiver going up and down her spine and the sharp memory of what it felt like to have his hands squeezing her throat.

Roman ran a hand through his longish, blonde hair and looked around, flashing his charming smile like some sort of celebrity. A couple of people in the crowd shouted out loudly.

"Why do we have to do this?"

"We should just get rid of the newbies!"

Roman addressed that one. "Now, now, that's not fair. We voted, and the majority decided to do our little version of the Olympics. No backing out now."

Then, Roman hopped off the table and marched from the room with his posse of henchmen following him. It wasn't until he had gone through the doors with a couple of shouting people following him that Eden felt like she could breathe again.

She reached up, rubbed her throat, and forced herself to take a couple of deep breaths.

"Are you okay?" Helena asked, her hand suddenly on Eden's shoulder.

Eden rolled her shoulder forward to escape the touch and took a deep breath. "Yeah, fine, but... I don't feel safe. I won't until..."

"You're right," Helena said, understanding exactly what Eden wanted to say. She pushed her braids behind her shoulder. She had been there when Roman went after Eden, trying to choke the breath out of her and silence one more person who wasn't in support of him. "We have to do something."

"But I tried," Eden said, hating the ball of tears that had formed in her throat and made it hard to talk normally. "I told everyone. I had the bruises."

"You *still* have the bruises," Helena told her, bending down to see Eden's neck more clearly and moving the neck of her shirt. "You need to tell your story. Roman can't stay in charge. It's too dangerous."

"But when he's there, talking..." Eden said, trying to explain why it felt impossible to talk when Roman stared at her, seeing all her secrets laid bare in front of him. She forgot what she had been saying as she imagined his piercing eyes predicting her next move and cutting her off before she had the chance. "I don't feel safe," Eden said, wrapping her arms around herself.

"Don't shout him down like his haters try to do," Helena suggested. "Just tell one person at a time. I will too. If they see you and know what happened, it has to mean something, right?"

Eden shrugged, unsure if it was even worth it. It felt like no matter how she told people, they ignored her or didn't take her seriously. If Xander were here, then he would have known what to do, but he had...perished saving them from the asteroid. She swallowed several times as she tried to push Xander out of her mind. He was gone, and she missed him. Crying about it wouldn't change anything.

"You okay?" Jazzy, one of Eden's three roommates, asked as she suddenly appeared beside them. Eden didn't know her well, but she recognized her from their blurry mornings getting ready in the dark to head to their shifts.

"Fine," Eden said, pasting on a smile as Helena squeezed Eden's arm encouragingly.

"You sure?" Jazzy's eyes fell on Eden's throat, and when she made eye contact again, Eden could tell that she had seen the marks.

Eden glanced at Helena, gathered her courage, then told Jazzy the truth. "It was Roman," she said, glancing over her shoulder like he might appear at the mention of his name.

"Roman did that to you?" Jazzy asked, her dark eyebrows lifting as she turned her head to the side to see Eden's throat more clearly.

"Uh huh," Eden nodded. "He..." She took a deep breath and told the full story. "I caught him strangling two others who didn't listen to him, after Derry was chucked off the ship. And when Roman saw me, he came after me. He choked me, and Helena smacked him with a chair. If she hadn't done that, then he would have killed me. I'm sure."

Jazzy's eyebrows had continued to rise until they disappeared into her hairline. Now, she glanced around to see if anyone was listening before she responded.

"Why is he still in charge?"

Eden shrugged slowly. "I think... I tried to tell people, but they don't listen."

"Uh uh," Jazzy said, shaking her head. "No, just because he's attractive and bossy doesn't mean he gets to do whatever he wants. I'm going to tell Avery what's going on. And you need to watch your back."

Jazzy hurried off, on a mission to find Avery, while Eden remained in her safe spot in the middle of the crowded room.

Helena patted Eden's shoulder. "*See*? This is what you needed. Tell people your story and watch your back. We're going to get rid of Roman and all his friends who think that killing others is the way to deal with problems."

Helena seemed confident that it would be easy, but Eden couldn't stop looking over her shoulder to see if Roman was coming after her. As soon as she stopped being careful, she knew that his fingers would be around her throat again.

Chapter 2

Xander settled into the black, cushioned chair. He was supposed to be comfortable, but as the bearded board member stared at him, Xander didn't think he would feel comfortable with whatever conversation the man was planning.

"You've had a chance to think over your decision," the man said.

Matt shifted in his chair next to Xander. "Sir, I think it would be easier for everyone if we just stayed here. I mean, the amount of resources necessary to send us back to the space station would be..." Matt spread his hands wide and made an incredulous sound with his mouth.

Xander placed a hand on Matt's arm. "We would still like the rest of the day to make our decision. I believe we were told we have until 9:00 a.m. tomorrow morning?" He didn't believe anything. He knew exactly what they had been told, but he was trying to be polite to this man who literally held his life in his hands.

The man assented. "You do have more time. I didn't think it would be a difficult decision however." He leaned forward and lowered his voice. "The board is cutting you some slack. You get the chance to live here even though you didn't earn medals."

"I *did*, actually," Xander said, feeling the need to remind this man that he would have been an official if Eden hadn't cheated. "However, I understand your point. I chose to be eliminated."

"Xander-" Matt tried to say, but Xander narrowed his eyes at his older brother.

"We will take the rest of our time to decide," he said forcefully, aiming the words more at Matt than at the board member. "I appreciate your patience."

The man nodded, and Xander took that as their cue to be excused. He rose and shuffled out of the conference room and into the bland hallway of the research center. Even though it wasn't far out of the large city of Sisimiut, it felt like it was on the edge of the world.

"Xander!" Matt started as soon as the door had closed behind him. "You know what we're going to choose. It's not even a choice. They're giving us a chance to *live* here, have jobs, have lives..." He laughed and shook his head as he reached for Xander's shoulders. "You're ridiculous for even pretending to think about it!"

"Eden is-"

"No," Matt cut Xander off. "I don't care about Eden. You saved her and everyone else on the space station. That was what we were supposed to do. Done, okay?" Matt's voice was rising.

Xander rolled his eyes as they stepped outside into the warm sunshine. He closed his eyes for a moment and just enjoyed the feel of it on his skin as Matt continued to explain why Xander was a complete idiot. Finally, his older brother seemed to have run out of steam.

"Okay, now that you're done talking, can we go to Sisimiut? I want to see Mom."

Finding more steam, Matt continued his list of reasons that Xander should stay on Earth. "See? You do care about her after all. Do you think she would hesitate for a moment with a decision like this? No, she would know the right thing to do."

"The selfish thing to do," Xander commented, turning toward the wide, dirt road that led to Sisimiut. If he had his bike, the journey would take maybe an hour or an hour and a half. On foot, it would take him a lot longer than that.

"Have you seen her already?" Xander asked, thinking about how Matt had disappeared the night before for a few hours. Matt had found some of his friends who had ended up being crucial in stopping the officials from interrupting Colt's missile launch, but he hadn't said much about his journey to find them.

The two guys fell into pace beside each other, and Matt finally answered. "No, I didn't want to go too far into Sisimiut, and I thought we should wait."

Xander glanced at Matt. Neither one of his excuses seemed exactly valid, but who was Xander to question him? Matt had been "dead" for three years. Maybe their mom should be prepared before he walked through the door.

"Well, I'm not going to wait anymore," Xander told Matt. He had already made his decision, the one the board member was hounding them for, but he wasn't sure how to tell Matt. Speaking it out loud would make it seem real.

Right now, he just wanted to see his mom.

"I'm trying to figure out what profession I would be better at," Matt said, rubbing his hands together as he thought. "I haven't kept up much with the physical, but I don't think it would take me long to get back in shape."

"Can you... stop?" Xander asked, trying not to give away his planned answer. "Think to yourself. I don't want to hear it."

Matt threw him a nasty look as they continued to walk in silence.

The sun that had felt warm and welcoming at first soon turned into a burning ball of torture. When Xander saw the familiar apartment building rising up among the others, though, he didn't care about the heat anymore.

He broke into a jog, sweat trickling down his back and making his gifted shirt cling to him. He didn't pay attention to whether Matt was right behind him or not and just let his feet lead the way up the stairs and to the door.

Stopping suddenly in front of the door, Xander debated if he should knock or not. He didn't have his key with him, but he tried the handle anyway.

The door didn't open, so Xander knocked, waiting impatiently on the balls of his feet. As he strained to hear the shuffling movement inside the apartment, Xander glanced down the stairs and saw Matt coming across the parking lot at a stroll.

The door swung open, and Xander saw his mother. He started to go in for a hug immediately, but stopped. She had withered away from a slightly plump woman to a bony one.

"M-mom?" Xander said, the familiar eyes in her face telling him exactly who she was.

"Xander!" His mom shouted, wrapping her arms around him.

Her lotion's fruity scent was so familiar that Xander felt a ball of emotions in his throat, threatening to choke him. He finally pulled back and pointed over her shoulder. "Let's go inside," he suggested.

As he glanced around once more for Matt, he saw him leaning against the railing at the bottom of the stairs. Xander motioned for him to wait a minute as he followed his mom inside to where she had been sitting on the couch with a blanket over her legs even though the a/c hadn't cooled it down nearly close enough to blanket level. A computer sat on the little table beside the couch, its screen open to a document.

"How are you here?" his mom asked once she had settled into her seat.

Xander sat on the other end of the couch, kicking his shoes off and falling into the old habit of leaning his back against the arm of a couch. Part of him was marveling at the very miracle of a couch. A couch! He hadn't seen one in what felt like forever. But the rest of him was trying to figure out how to answer his mom's question.

He took a deep breath and tried to explain what had happened. "You know I won a medal, but Eden, she...was eliminated."

His mom reached forward and laid one of her delicate hands on his leg. The movement was so familiar, something she had started doing when he had crossed that line from kid to teenager and didn't always want her hugs. But right now, he wanted his mom to wrap her arms around him like she had when he was a little kid. He wanted her to figure out how to fix everything.

Xander wavered in that moment, swallowing as he tried to find some sort of strength within himself. "I decided that I couldn't let her do it by herself. I had to be there for her. I knew you were sick, and..." he shook his head as he tried to make his reasoning make sense. In that moment, giving up his medal had been the only option that made sense. But he could tell by the way his mom was looking at him that she was having trouble believing him.

"I just couldn't see my life without her."

His mother smiled, but there was no strength behind it, like she was smiling to comfort him when she actually needed comforting. "I've always loved the relationship between the two of you. But if you were eliminated, that doesn't explain why you're still here?" A catch in her voice caused her last word to break, and Xander placed his larger hand on top of his mother's, patting it awkwardly to show that he loved her.

"We were shipped off with some of the eliminated, not all, to a space station. It rotates Earth, and it has some of the eliminated from years past." He paused. "Even Matt was there."

"Matt?" his mother whispered, tears filling her eyes.

Xander nodded and rose to his feet, rushing to spill out the rest of the story as he went to the door to find Matt. "We were in the space station, but an asteroid was heading toward us. Matt and I volunteered to veer the asteroid off course, and we ended up coming back to Earth. So, a missile was launched to hit the asteroid. And, now we're here."

He opened the door and peered outside. Matt was sitting on the bottom stair, gazing out across the sea of buildings below them. When Xander opened the door, Matt looked back at him. He didn't betray any emotion, but he slowly rose to his feet and began trudging up the stairs.

Xander's mother grabbed his arm and almost pushed her younger son to the side in an attempt to see out the doorway.

She stepped outside, the protruding veins on her bare feet lying about her age. "Matt," she whispered, staring at her older son as he reached the top step, towering almost a full foot over their mother. "Oh, you're...you're..."

Matt threw his arms around their mother, and Xander rubbed at his eyes to prevent anything like tears from forming. "Let's go inside," he suggested after a moment when no one said anything.

Xander held the door open as his mother and brother passed inside. His mother slumped into her place on the couch, her eyes turning back and forth from one to the other. "I have to...tell your father." She reached for her phone, then drew her hand back. "Do they...know you're here?" she lowered her voice like an official might be standing just outside the door.

Xander glanced at Matt. Matt answered, "They didn't know we were coming, but we're good to stay now. They said they'll find a place for us."

"Oh!" Xander's mother said, clasping her hands together. "Oh, my boys again." She leaned back into the pillow and closed her eyes for a moment. Matt's face remained serious, and Xander went to the kitchen, filling up a glass of water to bring to his mother. It had been less than three weeks since he had lived here, but it felt different than he had expected being back, like he was walking into a stranger's home that he had seen only in pictures before.

"Here," Xander said, setting the water down carefully on the table next to his mother's computer.

She opened her eyes, an ethereal smile gracing her face. "This is more than I could have imagined. God is good. He is truly good."

Xander didn't know what to tell her. Or, it was more that he didn't know *how* to tell her. He had had to see her, let her know what had truly happened, and he planned to stay here tonight. But...he wasn't going to stay longer than that. He wasn't going to settle into a cushy job as an official while Eden lived out her days on the space station. He was going to accept the board member's offer to send him back to the space station. It was his only choice.

Chapter 3

Nervously, Eden approached the medical center a little later than her usual shift. The medical competition was today, and even though she didn't like the idea of the Olympics, she couldn't just boycott them.

A group of people her age and up to seven years older stood in the hall. A few of them were talking in low tones.

Eden looked around for Helena, but didn't see her. She had said she would compete in the medical competition, but she only had a few more minutes left to arrive.

Suddenly, one of the girls waiting next to Eden leaned toward her. "Did you hear that Roman supposedly attacked some girl?"

Eden's mouth went dry, and all she could do was stare at the other girl. The other girl must have thought she hadn't heard, because she kept telling her more and more details. "Basically, some girl claims that Roman put his hands around her neck, and she was just barely saved by some other girl who smacked him in the back of the head with a frying pan."

A frying pan? Where had she gotten that?

"Obviously, it didn't really happen, but it makes you wonder, right?"

Eden found her voice and frowned at the girl. "It *did* happen. *I* was the one he strangled."

The girl froze, blinked her eyes a couple of moments, then shook her head. "No way. Why would he strangle *you*?"

"It was...he... I saw him hurting someone else, after that other guy was blamed for the stranglings. And so...when he saw me see him, then he came after me."

"So, if that's true, why are you still here?"

A couple of other people waiting had heard Eden answering, and they gathered around her like a posse of reporters.

Eden glanced behind her, sure that Roman would appear at any moment and put an end to this conversation, a real end to it. "It's complicated. It all happened so quickly, but I'm not lying about it."

Two girls started asking her questions at the same time so that Eden couldn't decipher what either one was saying. She held up her hands in the universal gesture of "stop."

"I can't hear both of you, and the truth is, I don't want to talk about it. It wasn't...an enjoyable experience. It happened, but he's still here because no one cares what he does." She groaned under her breath, then turned away from the girls and looked down the hall to the window in the medical center door.

The whispers stirred up around her, and Eden knew that she was the center of the conversation. But then she didn't have time to think about it anymore as the door to the medical center opened.

Roman stepped out, followed by one of the guys who seemed to follow him around like a bodyguard and a girl with glasses and a tight ponytail.

"We are ready to begin the medical competition. There are two volunteers in the medical center who will be your sample patients. We will give you a variety of scenarios, and you will need to go through the actions of providing medical care."

Ice crept up Eden's spine and around her heart as she saw Roman standing there, so casually leading like nothing had happened. Her eyes fell to his hands. He lifted them just then and crossed his arms. Her eyes followed them, feeling them around her neck again.

As Roman turned and ushered two of the participants inside the medical center, Eden felt herself choke. She wanted to pull away the thing grasping her throat, but there was no *thing* there.

The door shut behind Roman with a loud thwap, and some people immediately began complaining about the rules of this competition, as though the rest of this poor imitation of the Olympics had been fair in any way. Eden brought her chin down to her chest and closed her eyes, trying to hide within herself.

But her mind kept throwing crazy scenarios at her. What if she went into the medical center to compete, and everyone else who was supposed to be there left her alone with Roman? Maybe someone would need to go to the bathroom, and someone else would leave for a drink of water, and…

Eden hunched forward, realizing that she was on her knees before even feeling the floor.

"Are you okay?" someone asked her.

Eden didn't move, just breathed in and out. It was okay. Roman hadn't done anything since he had attacked her. He wouldn't do anything now. That was what Eden continued to tell herself, though it was hard to make herself believe it.

"Eden," the voice said, and Eden looked up, pushing herself to her feet when she saw that several people were staring. Helena was the only friendly face among them.

"Do you need a minute? Save our spot," Helena commanded the nearest person. She grabbed Eden's arm and marched her down the hall, away from the medical center. The more steps they took, the more Eden felt like she could breathe.

"Okay, I'm fine," she said when they were far enough down the hall. She took a few deep breaths and leaned against the wall.

"What's going on?" Helena asked.

"Just…about Roman. It doesn't matter. I'm fine. I don't know why I got freaked out."

"Did he try something?"

"No, he just gave the instructions, but I didn't realize that he was going to be judging the Olympics. I haven't been that close to him since it happened."

Helena nodded sympathetically. She slung an arm around Eden's shoulders and stayed there silently as they both breathed in and out. After a few minutes, Eden felt calm once again.

"I need to get back in line," Eden said. "I have to compete."

"We do, unfortunately." Helena made a face. "But we're both going to get easy medals. We actually work at the medical center. Everyone who works there is going to get a medal for sure."

"For sure?" Eden asked.

Helena shrugged like it was a "no duh" question. "We practice every day."

Eden wondered why Helena had felt the pressing need to study, then, if she was so sure they would all get medals. Maybe she was trying to throw Eden off so that she wouldn't win a medal? But no, out of everyone here, now at least, Helena was one of the people she trusted the most. "But I've only been here a short time, and because of everything with the asteroid…"

"Studying wouldn't have hurt, but don't get in your head about it."

The line moved forward slowly, too slowly.

Finally, after over an hour had passed, Eden was at the front of the line with Helena directly behind her. She could see through the tiny window, and every time she saw Roman's blonde hair flash by, her stomach dropped. But she wouldn't be alone with him. Besides, if she was…then at least when her body was discovered, there would be no doubt about who did it.

A sad-looking boy came out of the room, not making eye contact with anyone as he marched down the hallway. Eden pushed open the door to the medical center and stepped inside, taking deep, soothing breaths.

Roman and the ponytailed female were staring at her. The woman took the lead, pointing Eden to one of the beds. "This will be your patient. He'll tell you what he needs, and you'll do what you can to fix him up."

Eden licked her lips, wanting to ask a question. Something like, "do I actually stick him with a needle or just pretend?" But Roman's eyes were drilling into her, and she couldn't find her voice.

Nodding, Eden turned to the guy who was lying prone on the mattress. He clutched his arm, but when he met Eden's eyes, his lips curled up in a little smile, like he couldn't believe the ridiculous role he had to play.

"Owww!" he said in such a fake way that Eden's nerves fluttered to the outside of her consciousness.

"What's wrong?" she asked.

She heard a tapping noise and turned to see Roman and the girl marking something on little screens.

"My arrrrrrrm!" the guy cried.

"Tone it down," Roman said, unimpressed by the guy's performance.

"Okay, let me have a look at your arm," Eden said. The guy reluctantly let go of his arm, and Eden took his hand, starting to press the warm, clammy skin to see if he reacted. When she reached the place near his elbow, he yelped and tried to pull his arm away.

"Did something happen?" Eden asked, trying to pretend that this was a real patient. If she could focus on who was in front of her instead of who was staring a hole in the back of her head, then she would do better.

"I just fell off the treadmill," he said. "It hurts so baaaad!"

Roman's friend peered over the half-wall. "Keep it down, Simon. I can't pay attention to what's going on over here when you're doing that."

Simon grinned and lowered his moaning to just above a whisper. "Oh, oh, oh!"

Eden giggled, but immediately straightened her face. This wasn't funny. She had to focus on what to do to help Simon, or she wouldn't earn a medal in these stupid Olympics.

She had discovered that the guy's, Simon's, arm was hurt. But just how hurt, she wasn't sure, since all of this was imaginary anyway. She glanced at Roman and the ponytailed girl, but they were just staring at her, watching her like an extinct animal.

"Let's get some ice on it first of all," Eden suggested so that it looked like she knew what she was doing. "Then I'll evaluate it further."

They might not have pain medication, but ice was not in short supply. She got some out of the tiny freezer and wrapped it in one of the stained cloths. She pressed it up against Simon's arm, and he nodded his thanks.

"Now, just let me know on a scale of one to ten how bad it hurts," she said, continuing to probe his arm as she desperately tried to figure out something more medical to do than apply ice.

Simon started shouting out different numbers as she pressed his arm, but Eden didn't really pay attention to them. Maybe if she just pretended it were broken and treated it that way, then she would be fine.

"Looks like you've broken it," she said, refusing to look at the two judging her as she made the proclamation. "I'm going to set the arm, then wrap it up. You won't be able to move it for a few weeks."

Simon nodded, obediently silent after another nasty look from the man on the other side of the partition.

Eden went to the drawers, confident at last that she knew something as she took out the proper equipment for wrapping up his arm. They didn't have the materials for making a cast, but there were several wraps and slings. She grabbed one of each.

Then, she returned to Simon, grabbed his arm near his elbow and pretended to set the bone. She made quick work of wrapping it up and sliding the arm into the sling. She sat back, not sure what to do next.

When she finally dared a glance at Roman and the ponytailed girl, she saw them tapping away on their screens. She shifted back and forth, nervously glancing over the partition at the other person participating in the test.

"Next round," Roman proclaimed.

Simon whipped off the wrappings, tossed them on the end of the bed, and clutched his stomach. "Oh! Ooooh!" he groaned.

It happened so quickly that for a moment, Eden thought he had actually hurt himself. "Oh, what happened?" she asked.

"My stomach hurts. It won't stop hurting."

"Ummm," Eden stared at his stomach. "Maybe..." she didn't say anything else as she thought. The first thing her mom would ask was "what did you eat," but that wouldn't really apply here since they all ate the same food. It couldn't be food poisoning. The next thing her mom had always asked wasn't something she generally went around asking guys her age, but she had to play the part.

"When's the last time you pooped?" she asked, trying to phrase the question as delicately as she could.

Simon looked at her, eyes wide, then he laughed.

"Simon!" Roman reproached, and Simon tried to get himself together.

"I'm sorry, but I just didn't expect her to get it right away, and the way she asked that like she was talking about the weather..." He continued laughing, and Eden tried to keep her face a mask of seriousness.

"So, that's it?" she asked.

"It's been a couple of days," Simon said.

"Well, if you're constipated," Eden said, "I think I have something that can help." She went to the cabinets and rummaged around. Supplies were short on the space station, but there had to be something she could give him. After looking through all of the cabinets, she shook her head and got him a glass of water instead. It wasn't the fastest way to get his bowels moving again, but it would help.

"Drink this and keep drinking water," she recommended. "It should help things get moving again."

Simon took a sip of the water and glanced up at Roman.

"Last one," Roman said, moving his finger to indicate that they should go more quickly. Simon drained the last of the water, throwing his head back as he gulped it quickly, then flopped back onto the bed and squeezed his eyes shut.

Now that Eden had gotten used to the strange nature of this competition, she felt ready to figure out what was going on.

"I...I...I can't stand up," Simon said, dramatically trying to sit up and flopping onto the bed again.

"What's wrong? Are your feet hurting?" Eden asked, moving down to that end of him.

He shook his head and stared up at the ceiling like he was watching a sports game up there. Eden thought for a second, then moved up to his head and touched his forehead. Of course it wasn't hot, but she had to pretend. This felt ridiculous.

"Any other symptoms?" she asked.

He blinked his eyes and shook his head.

"Faintness?" she asked, deciding to go through a list so she sounded more professional.

"No, I'm not faint," Simon said. He promptly pivoted into a sitting position and tried to stand. He stumbled and almost fell, so Eden had to grab him under the arms and support him. He was much taller than she had thought now that she saw him standing.

Awkwardly pushing him back onto the bed, she said, "Please don't try to stand again. You're obviously very dizzy. Your...blood sugar could be low." She gripped onto something that sounded realistic. "Let me see what we've got for that." She went back to the cabinets, a picture in her mind of something she had seen in the back of a drawer. Was it a real memory or something she had conjured because the thought made her mouth water?

No, there they were, packets of sugar, the tiny packets like they used to have at restaurants, back when she and her parents would go out to eat occasionally.

"Here," she said, grabbing one.

"That's enough!" Roman said, holding out his hand. "No need to actually open it."

Eden pretended to give the packet to Simon, and he pretended to eat it. "Great, thanks!" he said.

Biting her bottom lip, Eden glanced at the ponytailed girl who nodded her head. "You can go," she said.

As Eden left the room, she realized that Helena was already elbows deep in the little space beside hers attempting to solve that person's issues. She silently wished her friend good luck and escaped the space.

As she walked down the hallway, trying to think of something to fill the day that stretched before her, she felt Roman's hard stare, the same one he had given her during the competition, boring into the back of her head. She glanced back once, but no one was looking at her.

Still, she felt his eyes on her as she tried to get as far away as possible from the medical unit. The space station wasn't big enough though, because once she had reached the far end, she still felt Roman hovering over her.

Chapter 4

Xander waited in the boardroom of the research center, his knee jiggling up and down. Matt stood at the back of the room, looking at a display of space station models.

"Now, this one would actually be better than the one we have up there. Look at all the space inside," he said, pointing to a model that had been cut open to reveal four distinct floors. "Even though it's not as much privacy, larger bunk rooms would give everyone more space outside of the rooms."

Xander shrugged. He didn't want to debate the positives and negatives of different space stations. He wanted to make his decision before he could change his mind. He had considered telling Matt what he was thinking, but he knew that Matt would never agree. It was better just to announce his decision and go through with it, forcing Matt to go along with him.

The board member finally hurried inside, a screen in his hand. He set it on the table and pushed the chair aside, clearly thinking this would be a quick meeting that didn't merit sitting.

"You've made your decision?" he asked, without any formalities.

Xander nodded, then announced as calmly as he could, "We're going back to the space station."

The board member froze in what he was doing and frowned at Xander.

Matt whirled around and approached Xander, laying a heavy hand on his shoulder. "What my brother meant to say was that we appreciate the option of letting us choose, but we're staying here." Matt spoke the last two words forcefully, more to Xander than to the board member.

The board member wrinkled his forehead and stared at them for a moment. "So...you're..."

"Going," Xander answered forcefully, hoping he wouldn't have to wrestle Matt to the floor right then. The man glanced back and forth at them for another moment, pushed himself back from the table, and carried his screen out of the room without another word.

"Man, are you crazy?" Matt exploded, pushing Xander roughly as soon as the board member was gone.

"No," Xander said, trying to calm the anger that started to flow through him when Matt had made contact. In his head, he couldn't accept that the three countries, or Greenland in particular, had enough extra materials to waste a ship on sending Matt and him back to the space station. Weren't they supposed to be reducing, reusing, and recycling, not destroying materials for two individuals who had been eliminated?

Matt continued to go on about how he wasn't getting on any ship and how if Xander wanted to get on, then he was throwing away his life. Xander tuned his brother out as he marched toward the doorway and looked out into the large room that served as an observatory. Scientists busily bustled around, grabbing things, calling to each other, then looking at screens filled with figures.

He didn't see Colt.

"Man, are you listening to me?" Matt asked, grabbing Xander's shoulder again.

Xander slapped his brother's hand away, tired of his space being invaded time and time again. "Yeah, I hear you. But *I'm* going back. I can't just start a life here, knowing that they're up there." He glanced in the direction of the sky, even though the only thing he could see was the ceiling of the room.

"Get over it. Eden thinks you died heroically to save her. Yay! Now move on." Matt continued to speak harshly, but Xander grabbed the handle of the door and yanked it open. He didn't want to get angry. He rarely did, but Matt knew how to trigger him.

Matt continued to follow him, listing all of the perfectly sensible reasons that he should stay. Once they had stepped outside of the research center, Xander finally whirled around.

He motioned for Matt to follow him, and they walked in silence for a few minutes until Xander was sure that no camera from the research center would be able to see them or pick up on their conversation.

"Since you won't shut up, I'll tell you. I have a plan. I'm not just going back up there to live happily ever after on a thousand square feet of space station. I'm going to get Eden home, and the others too. I don't know how yet, but it has to be possible."

For once, Matt didn't have anything to say for a few minutes. Then, he just shook his head slowly, like a disappointed father. "Xander, I know you think you like this girl, but I promise you that there are plenty of other ones here, with medals, who would agree to date you the moment you're suggesting it."

Matt turned back to the little village beside the research center. They could see a couple of people milling around. "Seriously, go ask one of them right now."

"No," Xander responded immediately. "It's not about finding someone to date. It's...okay, it's partly about Eden, but it's also...if they have enough resources to waste on sending you and me back to a space station because we're *supposed* to be there, then they have enough resources to keep these people alive. How many people do you think are on the space station?"

Matt rubbed his head and actually considered Xander's question. "I don't know. Four, five hundred?"

"It sounds like a lot, but not when you think about the thousands, tens of thousands of people that live, spread out across these continents." Xander was starting to get excited about his idea, but he knew that he couldn't let it stop him from thinking rationally. "I need to talk to Colt," Xander finally added. "He'll know. He'll be able to look at it from a different angle and see if it's really possible..."

He looked up and realized that Matt was still staring at him. "So, you're going to risk your life to save other people?"

Xander nodded slowly.

Matt shook his head, but at least he had stopped ranting. "Fine, risk yourself, but you're not going to risk my life. I'm not going." He took a step back from Xander, like that made it final.

Xander took a deep breath and shrugged. "You have to. They won't accept me being the only one to go back."

"I don't care. I'm not going back there." A wild look had entered Matt's eyes, and he glanced around like someone might grab him and shove him into a spaceship at any moment. "You're crazy, but I'm not."

"Let me just talk to Colt first," Xander said. "If I can get in contact with him and understand what materials he has access to, then I stand a chance."

Matt studied the research center from their distance. The large dome at the top had a circular telescope, one of the largest he'd ever seen, sticking out of the top of it. Other than that, the building looked pretty nondescript.

"I'm going to see Mom again," Matt said. "That's where we should be, not here."

Xander nodded, acknowledging that his brother was right. "Tell her I love her."

Matt snorted and acted like he was going to say something sarcastic, but for once, he shut up. "Bye," he said, offering Xander his hand.

Xander smacked it and pulled his brother toward him, then they set off in opposite directions, Xander to find Colt and Matt to find their mother. Xander moved forward slowly, almost feeling like the slower he moved, the slower the time moved. Doubts from Matt started to creep into his head, and it was hard to get rid of them.

Chapter 5

Eden stood next to the wall, crossing her arms and staring at the ugly, patterned carpet as she waited for her name to be called. All of the insecurity she had felt at her last Olympics came back and settled in her stomach again.

But Helena was right. There was no reason for her not to win a medal. After the competition, she and Helena had talked about what had happened. Apparently, her "sick person" had had her figure out the same problems. She had also easily figured out all three.

Roman announced each name, and the person had to push his or her way through the crowded room. Not everyone was there, but most people were, which meant there was standing room only, and even then, people had to suck in their guts so others could squeeze by.

Roman called Helena's name, and she began the procedure of squeezing through the crowd, leaving Eden against the wall. She should have tried to get closer to the table where Roman was calling names so she wouldn't have to push past so many people. But even while Eden was thinking this, Roman's voice stopped for longer than it had between each name.

A crowd of people stood to his right, holding the tiny metal badges that had been fashioned from the metal panels they had taken from the ship that had brought Eden. Roman stared out across the group of people. "Everyone else, you have one more opportunity to win a medal in the physical competition. Tomorrow at nine in this room if you want to compete."

Then, he hopped off the table, and people protested as he carelessly pushed his elbows into their sides, arms, and faces.

"He..." Eden said, looking down at her hands like she might notice that she had received a medal after all. She squeezed herself into as small a person as she could be as people aimed themselves toward the doors that led to the rest of the space station. The room began emptying out, and Eden soon felt a touch on her arm that felt different than the rough pushes of someone trying to get through.

"Eden?" Helena asked, and Eden just shrugged. She didn't know how else to explain what had just happened.

Suddenly, her silence turned into a flood of words. "I did everything right. I figured out the three illnesses, and I treated them the best way they *could* be treated. But Roman...he didn't want me to pass. *He's* the reason I didn't get a medal!"

Eden whipped her head around, but Roman had left the room long ago.

Helena bunched her lips into a knot, her eyes narrowing as she understood Eden's accusation. "Everyone else who works in the medical center got a medal," she said.

Eden reached up and ran her fingers through her brown hair, decidedly limper since she had arrived here. "He wants me gone. He wanted to make sure I was one of the ones kicked out. That's not...that's not fair."

"It *has* to be because of what you've said about him, about how he tried to kill you."

"But he did!"

"You don't have to tell me," Helena was bobbing her head. "I was there. I saw it all."

"But why did you get a medal then?"

"Roman wasn't judging mine, just that other guy."

Eden shook her head. No one believed her, or if they did, they just thought it was some interesting story, like a ghost story, something to be told while laughing. She felt lost now, knowing that she didn't have a chance of...well, anything.

Waves of fear lapped at the edges of her mind, threatening to drown her.

"Eden," Helena said softly after a moment. "It's not over yet. If you think a bunch of-"

"Hey!" a guy's voice said, interrupting Helena's quiet one.

Eden tried to paste a neutral look on her face. She didn't want anyone else to see how much she was struggling, how that competition had been her only chance to stay on this stupid space station.

It was the guy from the medical competition, the one who had pretended to have a broken arm and all the rest of the stuff.

"You okay?" he asked.

Eden opened her mouth to say something, but then just nodded. That was easier than trying to make conversation when she was dealing with such strong disappointment.

"I'm Simon," he said, holding out his hand to Eden. Eden paused, then finally reached out and shook it.

"I know Helena already, but I don't think we've met. You're from the new group, right?"

Eden nodded again, deciding that inserting her name into this conversation would make her look at least a little bit like she wasn't about to cry. "I'm Eden."

Simon nodded and stood there for another couple of seconds. He smiled at Helena, then at Eden. His eyes seemed to flick back and forth between the two of them, landing clearly on Helena's medal then not seeing one in Eden's hands.

"You...didn't win one? How?" He bent his head to the side like Eden might be hiding it from view.

"No," Eden said, her voice rising an octave as the despair took hold of her again.

"What? No way! You were one of the best people who did me. I mean, not, did. Well, worked on me...if that makes sense." He laughed, and Eden wanted to smile. She wanted to tell him that she was not judging his awkwardness, but it was difficult to be friendly or comforting when death loomed in front of her.

"So, what happened?" Simon asked after a moment.

Helena took the reins. "She didn't win because Roman doesn't want her on the space station anymore."

"What? No! Roman's a good guy."

The comfortable feeling that Eden had naturally been feeling around Simon disappeared immediately. If he thought that Roman was a "good guy," then Simon was either blind or stupid.

"No, he's not," Eden responded darkly. "He's responsible for all those people who died, and he tried to kill me too."

Simon stared at her, blinking almost comically for a moment.

Eden knew it was a risk talking to someone who seemed close to Roman, but she was going to get thrown off the space station anyway. "He came after me when I saw him with his hands around a girl's neck."

Simon's eyes dropped to Eden's neck as she touched her fingers just above her collarbone where the bruise still was. She winced as she fingered the delicate skin. "Helena saved me," Eden almost whispered, finishing her confession.

"No..." Simon said, his eyes darting back and forth. "Roman?" But he wasn't protesting like he had before. Now, he just sounded dumbstruck.

Eden nodded. Helena reached out and squeezed her shoulder, and Eden pushed the terrorizing thoughts away. None of them seemed to know what to say, and Eden didn't want to stand there any longer.

The sudden possibility that she hadn't won a medal because she simply wasn't good enough settled into her brain. *Helena* had been there when Roman had hurt her, and *she* had gotten a medal. Maybe Eden just wasn't worth her place in this community.

"Well, I should go now," she said, taking a step back.

"Wait," Simon said, reaching out to grab her arm and just missing. Eden tucked her arms safely behind her back so he wouldn't try to grab them again.

"What?"

"If Roman really did that..."

"He did!" Eden assured him.

"Then he can't be here any more."

If she had been talking to Xander, she would have congratulated him on his stunningly brilliant conclusion and patted him on the back, but she did neither of those things now. She just stared at Simon, a sudden pang for Xander welling within her.

Simon suddenly whirled around, marched in one direction, paused, then turned back and marched toward the long hallway that connected everything in the space station. Once he had left the room, Helena squeezed Eden's shoulder again, then dropped her hand back by her side. "Are you doing okay?" she asked.

Eden shrugged. She was done talking. All she knew was that nothing Simon did was going to change anything. He seemed nice enough, but he wasn't in charge. She glanced at Helena's medal, which Helena was busy stuffing into her pocket, and felt the annoying, ever-present tears start to prick at the corners of her eyes. Why did everything have to go so wrong?

Chapter 6

Colt placed the sandwich in front of Xander, and he had to force his hands to move slowly. Even though he had been in the land of plenty (at least compared to the space station) for three days, he still struggled not to wolf down every bite of food in sight.

"Would you like an apple?" Colt asked, holding up a juicy, red piece of fruit.

"Um..." Xander's eyes flicked to his sandwich. "Nah, I'm okay with this."

"Apples are a good choice because they protect your body's DNA from oxidative damage. I'm sure you've heard the saying an apple a day-"

"I'll take an apple," Xander said to avoid Colt's speech about how he needed to make healthy choices for his body.

Colt grinned, an awkward grin that showed his two crooked teeth on the right side, and passed one to Xander. "I knew you would once you understood how important the antioxidant effects of their phytochemicals and fiber are."

Xander wasn't sure if he understood the effects at all, except the effect of putting Colt into a good mood for what Xander was going to bring up. Xander had spent last night in his old bedroom. But tonight, he would spend as long as he needed talking things through with Colt so that he would understand exactly what his options might be.

The tiny home was just enough space for one person. Blending in perfectly with the larger townhomes, Colt's was just the top floor and had a tiny kitchen and living room with a couch against the half wall that separated the social space from the "bedroom."

"Are you going to be an official?" Colt asked after he had finished chewing. "I heard that the board has extended an invitation to Matt and you to stay and have jobs here."

"They have," Xander said, putting down his sandwich just as he was about to take a big bite. He kept a hand protectively on it as he talked. "However, I'm considering their other offer- the chance to go back to the space station."

Colt's eyes rounded, and he coughed on the bite of sandwich he was swallowing. He took a moment to compose himself before he put his sandwich down and clasped his hands together, studying Xander like a newly arrived project. "Why would you consider going?"

"The same reason I went in the first place- Eden."

Colt studied the wall, his eyes darting back and forth like he was computing numbers that were written there. And in *his* mind, he might see numbers there. "I understand your affection for her, but I can't imagine you would knowingly go back to the space station that has so many problems."

Xander had told Colt a little more specifically about the space shortage (sharing a bed with another guy was not a comfortable option) and the crappy food. He even described the bodies he had seen in stasis. "I'm not planning on staying," Xander said. He gazed longingly at his sandwich but then leaned forward to garner Colt's attention. "I need your help."

Colt reached for his apple and took a bite while maintaining eye contact. "I'm not going to do anything to risk my position." He touched his wrist delicately. "I was arrested for...finding out about the space station. And you..."

The fight that Xander had dragged Colt into just to get someone to care about the space station flashed through his mind. "It's not going to be like that," he said.

Colt once again studied the wall and seemed to be considering different aspects before looking back at Xander, who used the time to take two large bites of his sandwich. He was still chewing ravenously when Colt began speaking.

"What is it you are planning to do?"

"I'm not sure yet, but whatever they use to shoot me up there, I want to bring it back. I'm going to bring as many people as I can."

"Emily?" Colt asked, and Xander hurriedly agreed.

"I'll bring anyone you want. Emily, or...whoever else you can think of."

"Just Emily," Colt responded softly.

They were silent for a moment, and Xander bit into his apple, the crisp crunch of it filling his mouth with juice he hadn't tasted in a long time.

Xander explained further. "They told me that the ship they use every year to send the eliminated self-destructs a few hours after it gets to the space station. Can you disable that function?"

Colt blinked. "I understand the inner workings of basic space vehicles. However, I've only ever worked on a spaceship in theory. I've never actually been in one."

"You're a smart guy. You could figure it out."

Colt accepted the compliment with a short head nod. "If I participate in this perilous endeavor, I could risk my position and end up being sent on the spaceship with you to the colony of eliminated..." he trailed off as he considered this possibility.

Xander polished off his sandwich and nodded. He didn't want to hide anything about the situation. "You're right. It's a risk. You have to decide if it's worth it for you. Is it worth it to get Emily back here?" Xander knew that pulling on Colt's affection for his sister wasn't exactly a fair way to get him to agree, but at the same time, Xander was starting to care less and less for what was considered "fair."

Colt carefully pushed the tiny bread crumbs on his plate together, still thinking and muttering to himself. "You're right," he said even though Xander hadn't said anything for five or six minutes. "I'll do it." He moistened his lips carefully as he seemed to bring himself back to reality. "You want me to disable the self-destruct function?"

"Yessss," Xander said. Now that Colt had agreed, he needed to risk asking for something else. "Can you also help me make sure it's prepared for re-entry?" He closed his eyes for a moment and recalled how he and Matt had re-entered the atmosphere. "When Matt and I came, we didn't have the right materials. The ship burned up, and we had to jump out using those full-body suits to keep us cool. It would be nice to just, you know, zoom back in without worrying about dying."

Colt took off his glasses and scrubbed at a speck before replacing them. "I can see how that would be concerning. I'll see what I can do, but like I said before, I'm not exactly...an expert in this area." Holding his half-eaten apple like a computer mouse, he began muttering to himself so that Xander only caught a few words. "...trajectory... insulation... success."

Well, that hadn't taken as long as he had thought. Xander relaxed in his chair and worked on eating his apple as Colt grabbed a screen and started scrawling things out on it with a stylus.

When Xander had finished his apple, he stood up and paced to the window at the front of Colt's tiny apartment. He peered outside and saw a couple of groups of people standing around, enjoying the relatively cool evening. A peal of laughter reached him, and for the first time since he had come back, Xander felt sad. He was leaving this behind, risking never coming back. If something unplanned happened when he reached the space station, or any number of things while he was hurtling through space, then he would lose his chance at a life here.

Xander allowed himself a few more moments of self-reflection before turning to see how Colt was progressing.

"The problem is that I don't know what they'll use to send you," Colt said, setting down his rubber-tipped stick that he had been using to scrawl things across the screen's face. "They won't want to waste materials on sending you something with extra space."

"When they sent us there," Xander explained, thinking back on when he had woken up in the tiny, bare room with steaming walls, "we were in individual rooms along a long hallway. There were no girls there, so there must have been two hallways, one for each gender." He shrugged. "That's about it. I'm sure there was some sort of control booth or something, but I never saw it."

"Two long halls?" Colt asked, rising from his seat and getting closer to Xander than necessary.

Xander took a step back so that he had a little bit of breathing space. "Yeah, two long hallways. At least, that's what I think."

"I've been in one of those!" Colt said. "Right after I got here, they took us on a tour. We saw one of those ships, and they told us it was being readied for space exploration. I told our guide that the setup didn't make sense for long-term habitation, but he ignored my suggestions. If..."

Xander let Colt continue to prattle on.

"...which would result in not only a prodigious waste of resources but also..."

A siren began wailing in the distance, a creepy keening that rose in pitch before dropping and starting all over again. Colt's eyes widened behind his glasses, and he hurried to the window and peered outside.

"Is that an ambulance?" Xander asked, even though something about the noise didn't sound right.

"No," Colt said. "It's...no...they're coming." Then, Colt ran to his front door, flung it open, and ran down the stairs to the first floor, leaving his shoes behind. Xander hung halfway in and halfway out of the doorway, wondering who was coming and why it was making Colt frantic. Then, he saw everyone else.

Lines of people poured away from the research center. Others were carrying random belongings and hurrying to an unkempt building a bit away from the main structures.

Shouts that didn't form clearly into words rang through the night.

Xander saw a four-year-old child rushing by, holding a stuffed animal and crying. Then, the whole world lit up.

Chapter 7

Standing as a glassy-eyed spectator, Eden squeezed up next to the wall of the largest room in the space station. The last competition was taking place, though she was unable to report what had happened during the last hour. Thoughts circled through her head, but the one that overtook the rest was the fact that she only had a day or two left in this place. Roman hadn't yet announced when the unchosen would be thrown out, but she didn't think he would allow them to stick around for long.

"Eden," Helena's voice said as her delicate brown hand touched Eden's shoulder.

"Huh?" Eden said, startling out of her thoughts.

"I've been looking for you," she said.

"Why?"

Helena wiggled her way forward, then stood aside, and Eden realized Simon was right behind her friend. "Hey," she said, operating on auto-pilot as she started to turn back to the competition in front of them.

"Can I talk to you for a few minutes?" Simon asked.

Eden sighed. The thought of having to make conversation and act like a normal human being when her second elimination was the only thing on her mind felt impossible.

"Um, can't right now," she kind of mumbled.

Helena repeated her answer in a louder voice. "She said she can't talk right now." Without giving Simon a chance to respond, Helena leaned closer to Eden, her lips only an inch from her ear. "I think you should go. He told me that he knows about Roman."

"About..." Eden didn't finish her question. Roman was just on the other side of the room, and she had felt his gaze more than once. Even though she didn't like talking or thinking about him, she wanted to know what Simon had to say.

Reluctantly, Eden ducked and twisted her way out of the crowd and into the more open hallway. Simon strode ahead of them. Eden glanced back, relieved to see that Helena was jogging to catch up with them as well.

Simon turned down one of the side hallways, and Eden had a momentary lapse of confidence as she remembered the bodies she had seen, all in out-of-the-way hallways. But then, Helena caught up with her and started tugging on her elbow.

When Eden turned the corner, she saw Simon standing with his arms crossed in front of a group of five men. Eden stopped a few feet away, glancing at their faces to determine what was happening. She recognized the one to Simon's right immediately. He was always by Roman's side. He had helped clean up one of the bodies. Had he known when he was getting rid of the body that his best friend had been the one who killed the poor girl?

"We've done some investigating," Simon said, no longer the slap-happy guy who had allowed Eden to fix up his fake broken arm. "You're right."

It was stupid the impact those words had on her. She *was* right, and she had always *known* she was right, but to hear someone say it changed everything. Eden wrapped her arms around her stomach like she was holding herself together and swallowed furiously a few times in a row. She pressed her lips together to keep them from trembling.

"Th-" She stopped herself. She wasn't going to thank him for believing her. That was ridiculous! "I am," she finally said, proud of how strong her voice sounded.

"Roman has been abusing his power!" one of the guys said, stepping forward beside Simon. Eden didn't know this guy, though she thought she had seen his face around the space station, not surprising since it was such a confined space. "We're done with it. We're not going to allow him to take any more lives."

"What are you going to do?" Eden asked.

"We're going to throw him out of here. He says there isn't enough room for so many people. Well, he's one of the ones going," one of the guys explained.

Another guy cheered.

Simon shook his head. "No, that's not what we said. We're going to have a trial. We can't just start killing people. That would make us no better than him."

Eden's eyes flicked from face to face. She hadn't spoken to any of the guys gathered here before, and she wondered if she could trust them. Her mind immediately conjured potential scenarios where they were trying to trick her into...but Helena was here too.

"So what do we do?" she asked. Even though there were seven of them standing there, that wasn't much compared to the whole ship. She studied the face of the guy who was always with Roman, wondering if he was just going to report to Roman what they were saying.

"Jayce is cool," Simon said, punching the guy's shoulder like he could read Eden's mind. "We're going to accuse Roman of what you say he did and present evidence in front of everyone here. And then, ask questions, you know, like they do in court when someone is guilty of something."

"But you can't...he won't..." Eden tried to explain. No one could stop Roman. Even having this conversation made her think something bad was going to happen. She glanced back down the hallway, but no one was coming their way. Most of the non-necessary personnel were in the main room watching the competition.

"We're going to make it happen," Simon said. "As soon as we start it, you have to join in." He looked at Eden closely, but Eden was so confused.

"Join in what?" she asked.

Simon glanced at everyone else, his eyebrow raised like she had missed something that everyone else already understood. "The plan," he said, emphasizing the last word.

Eden frowned at Helena who explained in better detail than any of the guys had. "During the ceremony for handing out medals, we're going to spread throughout the crowd. When Roman gets up on the table and starts handing out the first one, we're going to start accusing him of what he's done...see what kind of reaction he has when everyone is watching him and he's presented with his crimes. If he tries to get out of the room, these guys are in charge of grabbing him."

A couple of the larger guys standing there nodded at the mention of their part of the plan.

"I don't think I can do that," Eden said, imagining herself standing alone in a crowd of people and beginning to accuse someone of murder. She shook her head. "No way."

Simon spoke, "You don't have to be the first one to shout. I'll do that." He shrugged like they were discussing what kind of topping they liked on their pizza. "You just keep up the cry once it starts. Everyone else will start joining in. Before we came here, I took a class in psychology," he said, pausing as he remembered what life had been like back on Earth in Greenland, or Alaska, or Russia, wherever he had lived. "All people need to join in is to make it seem like 'everyone else' is doing something."

Eden thought this was the wrong thing to do, but at least these people were willing to do *something*. They believed her and wanted to take Roman out. She had to go along with it. "Fine," she finally said. "I'll do it." Simon grinned at her and raised his hand like he was going to hit her. Eden flinched before realizing he was offering a high five. She slowly gave him one, embarrassed that she had misunderstood him.

"I've got a guy in there watching the competition. They are giving the medals as soon as it ends."

"As soon as it ends?" Helena asked.

"He's been waiting a few hours or a day. Why is it different now?" Eden also wondered.

Simon shrugged. "Maybe he feels the pressure to kick the rest of us out of the space station."

Rest of *us*? Eden glanced at Simon and realized he didn't have a medal. Helena's was clipped to the bottom of her shirt like Roman had suggested, and Eden took a step to the side to scan the other people in the group. Only one other had a medal. Their risk meant more than anyone else, because they could stand aside and do nothing and be just fine.

Running footsteps made Eden jump back, stumbling over Simon's foot. She took a couple of faltering steps backward as he grabbed her arm and righted her.

"You alright?" he asked, even as his eyes were already moving to the guy entering their group.

"Uh, yeah," Eden said, her eyes lingering on Simon's face for a second. He wasn't bad-looking, seeing him up close like this. He had these intelligent eyes that were usually hidden by his bushy eyebrows but that she could see now. She studied him a moment longer, taking in his stubbled jaw and ever-present smile.

Then, the guy who had arrived spoke in a rushed tone, and everyone around Eden was rushing forward.

"It's time," Helena said when Eden didn't move immediately.

She took a deep breath to prepare herself and followed the group to the end of the hall.

"You two go on in," Simon said, briefly touching Eden's back. "Spread out once you get in. We'll come in a sec."

Her heart beating so loud that she hardly registered the sounds around her, Eden followed Helena into the main room where everyone was waiting to see who would receive the final seventy-five medals.

Spreading out was difficult because the crowd was so thick. People were standing shoulder to shoulder, leaving a small empty area right next to the table that Roman was using as a stage.

Helena squeezed Eden's shoulder, then started roughly elbowing her way to the left. A couple of people protested, but she got through anyway. Eden rotated in her spot, trying to find an opening as everyone shifted.

"Excuse me," she finally said. "Sorry, can I get through here?"

The guy frowned at her. "You can't see any different from there."

Eden shrugged and smiled awkwardly, then pointed to the space on the other side of the guy. "Just trying to...meet up with my friend."

The guy finally managed to inch a bit backward, and Eden squeezed through the newly formed gap before it could close. After persuading a few more people to move, Eden decided that she had separated herself far enough from Helena. She was probably fine. She slowly rotated in place and realized that only one row of people separated her from the empty space around the table. Immediately panicked, she wanted to turn around and move further away, but as she turned, she realized that would be impossible.

Some movement near the doorway of the room reassured her that the rest of the people in on their plan were getting in place as well.

Suddenly, the talking died down, like someone had pulled the plug. Even though no one had been eager to make room for Eden as she came, everyone moved back for Roman. The guy beside her stepped on Eden's shoe, and she yanked it away, almost falling into the girl standing next to her. There was an awkward reshuffling as they tried to get comfortable while so close together.

Roman climbed onto the table, and Eden saw two guys standing in front of him like bodyguards. One of them was the guy who had been in Simon's group; she thought she remembered his name being Jayce.

Roman held his hands up and called for silence. "Thank you," he said after a moment even though they had already been silent and still. "I will now begin reading the names of those who have won a medal in the physical competition. Once you hear your name, please come up here and collect your medal."

"Harrison Roberts," he said, and the crowd shifted and grumbled as someone who was standing all the way in the back started to move forward. He collected his medal, and Eden craned her neck, trying to see Helena.

"David James," Roman said. Once again, everyone shifted, but they mostly remained quiet. No one was shouting anything.

Eden pressed her sweating hands together, intertwining her fingers as she glanced around for more of the people who had been with Simon.

After two more names, she spotted one of them on the other side of the room near the wall. She didn't know where Simon was.

Another two names were called, and Eden started to worry. What if no one said anything? Were they just going to let her and the others without a medal be thrown out of the space station?

Then, spoken at the same time as Roman read another name, a shout came from the back. Eden whipped her head around in the direction of the noise, her heart thumping rapidly. What had he said? She hadn't heard it clearly, and everyone around her looked more confused than inspired.

After a glare in the general direction of the noise, Roman called the name again, "Madelyn Stuart."

A girl started elbowing her way through, and everyone shifted the few inches of personal space they had to let her through. Then the shout sounded again, and this time, the words were clear. "Roman is a murderer!"

Eden clenched her hands into fists, her eyes darting to Roman. She hadn't said anything, but when she saw him, he was staring right back at her, his eyes narrow slits of anger.

Another voice, "He killed my friend! I saw it!"

Those around the shouters started talking, an angry buzz building.

Eden had to do something. She had to say something. "He tried to kill me too," she said, but not nearly loud enough. Licking her lips, she looked directly at Roman. "He tried to kill me too!" she shouted again, the words making her feel better as soon as she was free from their weight.

"She isn't-" Roman tried to say, but someone else shouted him down.

Eden couldn't focus on the words that were being said. They sounded like they were being spoken underwater, bubbles of noise that didn't make sense. A couple of other people shouted questions at Roman, and the two guys in front of him took a wider stance, hands bunched into fists like they were preparing for a fight.

Tugging at the neck of her shirt, Eden displayed the bruises, which had turned a nasty purple color. A couple of the people around her gasped, and Eden forced herself to speak. "He tried to kill me, and he wants to kill other people! He should be held responsible!"

Her last few words caught on, and someone else echoed her. "He should be held responsible!"

"Responsible!"

"Roman should die!"

"He killed Emily!" someone shouted.

Too many voices overlapped, and Eden saw Roman glaring at her, his eyes slicing into her almost as painfully as a pair of knives.

As the hubbub rose, Roman bent forward and whispered something to the two guys standing in front of him. They nodded and moved toward the front of the crowd, which had started edging forward into the little empty space that had been left around the table.

"Only those who participated in the physical challenge should remain!" one of the bodyguards yelled. "Everyone else should disperse before anyone gets hurt!"

The other bodyguard, the one Eden had seen next to Simon, didn't shout anything. Instead, he leaned close to a couple of the people on the front line and said something. It was too loud for Eden even to guess what he had said, but she hoped he hadn't tricked Simon. They had to be able to trust him.

Those people turned around and started passing the message along to the rest of the crowd. It was pretty simple. "Be quiet, and Roman will be tried for his crimes."

Once it had reached Eden, she did her duty and passed the message along behind her. A calm seemed to sweep over the room, even though not everyone followed the directions.

Roman smiled from the table like everyone was obeying *him*.

Simon, slightly taller than the average guy, suddenly appeared at the front of the room. Roman turned his attention to Simon.

"Move back," he said, loudly enough that the now mostly-quiet room could hear him.

Simon shook his head and folded his arms. "You have been accused of a crime, and we want to hear what you have to say about it." Simon stood only a foot away from Roman, though Roman had the table giving him a height advantage.

Roman smiled and made a scoffing noise like he thought Simon was joking. "I think that these Olympics haven't been easy, and *someone* didn't win a medal. That *someone* has decided to try to get revenge on me, though I'm certainly not the only one judging. How about we bring that *someone* up here?"

Roman turned and looked directly at Eden then. Everyone turned to look at her too.

Eden wanted to sink away from their stares, but she couldn't. If she didn't speak up now and tell what had happened, then she would just be allowing Roman to silence her. "Excuse me," Eden said in a small voice.

The people around her wiggled and moved so that she could squeeze through. "Thanks," she muttered.

Finally, she was at the front of the crowd. Only a couple of people remained in the space around Roman, who still stood above everyone like a king. Simon, Jayce, the other guard, and Eden stood in the area with enough room to move their arms freely.

Roman glared at Eden for a moment, and the crowd seemed to hold its breath, waiting to see what would happen.

"Well, you don't seem to have anything to say now," Roman said after a moment.

Simon held up his hand and took a step toward Eden. That one step was all he needed to move across the open space and reach Eden's side. He set a hand on Eden's shoulder. She didn't look at him, but she looked at the dark, dirty carpet instead. After a moment, she made eye contact with Roman.

"Nothing to say?" Roman mocked. "Or trying to think up a good story?"

A couple of people laughed, and Eden's stomach churned. She had to tell what Roman had done. She had to make these people believe.

"*You*," she said, her voice accusing even if her hands felt shaky, "you killed two people. I don't know if you're responsible for all the deaths. Maybe Derry, the one you threw out of the ship, really was responsible for some of them. But *you*, I *know* are responsible for two."

Roman shook his head and crossed his arms. "You know I'm responsible for them how? You saw me examining two dead bodies that someone had called me to examine. Lise!" he called.

A bony girl with thin, blonde hair slipped through the crowd and looked up at Roman.

"Tell them about what happened on this so-called day where *Eden* caught me 'killing someone.'" He even did air quotes with his fingers to show how ridiculous her accusation was.

"I called you to deal with it," the girl said, her voice quiet.

"Speak up!" Roman commanded, taking charge of his own trial.

"I called you to deal with it!" the girl said louder.

"There you go!" Roman said. "Someone alerted me of what had happened, and I went to check it out for myself. Of course, the first thing I'm going to do is check for a pulse, which requires me to touch the person's neck."

"No," Eden said, shaking her head.

"No? I suppose I could have touched the wrist, you're right. But I've always had trouble detecting it that way. Neck is easier." He sounded almost conversational now.

"I *saw* you killing them. I saw one of them struggling," Eden explained, her eyes on Roman now. She couldn't seem to take them off him. "And *then* you came after me and tried. To. Kill. Me." She emphasized each word. She turned toward everyone else and displayed her bruises again.

Roman waved them away. "I don't know how you injured yourself, but don't put that on me."

Eden wanted to scream. He was so frustrating, and he had an answer for everything! But no, she had to remain calm. She turned toward everyone else and spoke to them instead of to Roman.

"I've just come on this space station," she said. "My boyfriend was the one who sacrificed himself to hit the asteroid." She choked over those words but seemed to get them out okay and was able to keep going. "He sacrificed himself so that *all of you* could live. But Roman is killing us one by one, the ones who come after him. He doesn't like me because of what I saw. Helena?"

Eden paused as she searched the crowd for her friend. Helena pushed her way through and took Eden's hand, her brown fingers interweaving with Eden's white. "Eden called for help when Roman attacked her. I heard her. I helped her. I hit Roman on the head with a chair." Helena half-smiled when she said it. "He probably still has a lump to prove it."

Jayce turned toward Roman. He motioned for Roman to move closer to him, and Roman bent down. They talked quietly for a moment, then Jayce reached up and felt Roman's head, his hand roaming all around.

He turned to the crowd as Roman resumed his position above everyone else. "Helena has testified that she hit Roman. However, I have just felt his head, and there...*is* a lump."

Roman's smile disappeared. Clearly, that wasn't what he and Jayce had discussed.

"Helena, can you explain exactly where you hit Roman's head?" Jayce asked.

Helena touched her own head on the right side near the back.

Jayce nodded once. "That's where the lump is on Roman's head."

"No....no!" Roman disagreed. "My head is...it's always been shaped like that."

His answer sounded so ridiculous that Eden wanted to laugh, except she couldn't. This was their only chance to get rid of him, and everything he said might be believed.

"I believe we have one more test, if Eden will agree to it," Simon said, speaking loudly. "Roman strangled Eden. He tried to anyway. The bruises around her neck should match his hands. Eden, would you...?" He didn't finish the rest of his question. Or maybe he did, but Eden simply couldn't conceive what he was asking her to do.

Roman filled her nightmares, and now she had to get close enough for him to put his hands around her neck again?

She clenched her hands into fists and took a step toward Roman. He sighed and rolled his eyes with a comical smile on his face like he couldn't believe the lowly citizens of the spaceship were actually accusing him of murder.

Simon stood directly next to Eden, and she took comfort from him being right there. If Roman tried something, Simon could intervene.

"Roman, if you would," Simon said.

Roman refused with a shake of his head. "Everyone's hands are basically the same size. You want me to put my hands around someone's throat to prove what? No, I won't do that. I wouldn't do that to poor Eden, who has clearly had a tragic past. You've been here... how many days? Not quite two weeks? Bruises can last a month or two. It's quite possible you had those before you got here."

"But-" Eden tried to protest, but the truth didn't seem to matter to Roman.

The crowd started talking again, their voices rising in pitch.

"*Excellent* point," Simon said, as everyone looked at him again. "Except for one thing. When someone has been hurt, they want the right person punished." He looked over the people. "If someone hurt you, would you go after someone else and try to make them pay? No! You want the person who hurt you to pay! Eden is the same. Those of you who know her, and those who have never met her, ask yourselves, why would she accuse *Roman* of trying to kill her if he never did?"

"Did she win a medal?" a high-pitched voice from the crowd asked, and Eden clutched at her shirt's hem.

There was silence for a good couple of moments.

"Roman did it!" Another girl shouted.

Eden craned her neck to see who was talking, but it was impossible when she was shorter than at least half of the people in the room.

"He... hurt me too!" the girl said.

Eden squeezed Helena's hand accidentally, not realizing until Helena squeezed her back how hard she had been doing it. The crowd started talking as the girl squeezed through until Eden could see her face. She didn't recognize the girl, but she had dark skin and bright green eyes. She was small, maybe not even five feet, and she looked at the ground shamefully.

"He...showed me his room, the one he has all to himself, when I first came, and he, um, forced me to do some things," she said. Her voice wasn't very loud, so Simon shouted what she had said a lot louder, making her fold into herself even more.

Suddenly, Eden couldn't let her stand there by herself anymore. She stepped forward and put an arm around the girl's shoulders. She squeezed her to herself. To Eden's surprise, the girl turned and hugged Eden, a couple of tears on her face.

Roman took this opportunity to laugh. Laugh! "Alright, now we've just gone crazy. I have a girlfriend, and she does all the things I want her to. Why would I want some girl who still looks like a kid?" His laugh sounded like a strange barking sound, and Eden clenched her teeth.

Simon spoke, "Roman, we don't understand why you do these things, and it's not our responsibility to explain why. You're welcome to if you want to." He didn't really give Roman a chance to speak though. He turned back to the crowd. "You've heard what these girls have to say against him. You've heard all the evidence. We're going to vote, but there will be no closed eyes this time. I want everyone to see that their vote really counts."

The girl pulled back from Eden and rubbed at her face, avoiding eye contact with Eden. "Sorry," she mumbled.

"Hey, you don't need to apologize for Roman acting like a..." she said a word she had never said before, but it was the only one that seemed to fit the situation.

The girl kind of sob-laughed as Simon finished yelling instructions. "If you think Roman should pay the ultimate price for his crimes, raise your hand!" he said.

Excited energy ran through the room as hand after hand raised. When Eden dared to look past the first row of faces, she saw so many hands in the air that it looked like a strange forest with multi-colored trees.

"That's our answer then," Simon said. He turned to Roman, and Eden did as well. She saw panic cross Roman's face as he realized what was happening. He leaned toward his bodyguards and tried to say something, but Jayce grabbed him and flipped him into a hold before Roman realized what was happening. Simon and another guy moved in and started restraining Roman as he shouted obscenities.

Eden watched as the crowd parted, making more room than they had been able to make before.

Simon led the way, several of the guys surrounding Roman as people in the crowd started shouting what they really thought of him. Then, he disappeared out the side door. Suddenly, Eden had to follow. She had to see this through. She had to make sure...

Her feet carried her down the open pathway before it could close again and down the hallway with floor to ceiling windows, the hallway where she and Xander had shared several special moments.

There they were, at the end of the hallway, fidgeting with the door that led to the airlock.

Roman wouldn't shut up, but Eden barely registered the sounds as she watched him being shoved into the tiny room. The door shut behind him, and Jayce fidgeted with the buttons beside it. Roman continued yelling, and Jayce looked up at Simon.

Eden stood a couple of feet behind them, unnoticed, as Simon leaned forward and pushed a button.

Suddenly, there was a loud whooshing noise, and her ears rang with the echo of Roman's cursing. A thump as the door on the outer side of the airlock closed, and it was done. Roman had gone from running the spaceship to being thrown out of it in less than an hour.

Chapter 8

Emergency lights flashed on, lighting everything with a strange, red glow. Xander had no idea what was happening, but everyone else seemed to have a job to complete. Without Colt there to ask, Xander decided that his best bet was to follow the stream of people and hope they knew where they were going.

He scanned Colt's apartment, but didn't know what might be considered important. So, he grabbed the fruit basket sitting on the counter. It had three bananas and two oranges in it. Then, he grabbed the fresh loaf of bread from the breadbox and shoved it in the fruit basket and took off.

Just as Xander was reaching the bottom of the stairs, the emergency lights went off. He stumbled off the last step, dropping the basket. Footsteps pounded past outside the door, and a child's wail echoed through the night.

Unsure if what he was bringing was even important, Xander scrambled his hand across the floor, blindly feeling. He found the bananas and dropped them into the basket. An orange rolled to a stop by his knee, and he threw it in the basket too. The bread was easy to find, but the second orange had been lost forever.

Xander ran his hand down the door until he found the handle and emerged into the night. Even though no lights were on, it was easier to see because of the faint starlight. He could hear more than see what was going on as body after body hurried past him.

He turned right, away from the research center, and for the first time, thought of someone else. Where was Matt? Was he with their mom? Were things okay over there? And what had happened to Colt?

"Inside, inside," a voice whispered loudly.

Xander sped toward the voice which was in front of a shack, a building that looked no bigger than a ten by ten shed. How were so many people fitting inside the place?

As he reached the doorway, Xander tried to slow down, sure that he was going to run into the back of someone. The people behind him pushed him forward, however, and he tripped when the ground in front of him fell away.

Someone in front of him kept him from falling on his face.

The person grabbed his hand, giving him enough time to steady himself and realize he was on a set of stairs. Was this some sort of underground bunker?

In that moment, Xander understood exactly what was happening. Someone had launched a missile at Greenland. What better place to aim the missile than at the research center?

The seriousness of the situation set in as Xander took the steps one at a time, sure he was going to keep going down, down, down forever.

Finally, he saw a light in front of him, a small beam like the light from a phone's flashlight.

"Name and house number," the person asked, marking something as each person entered. Xander had only a few moments to think about what he was going to say. They weren't checking ID, but if he tried to explain his situation, they might throw him out. He had seen the heartlessness displayed by individuals here.

"Visiting from Sisimiut," he said. "Friend is Colt, House 81." He briefly remembered seeing the number on Colt's door as Colt had showed off his tiny apartment. The person paused, but after a moment of consideration, didn't argue.

"Left," the person said.

That was when Xander realized that the space spread out both ways. He went left, putting his free hand out to run along the wall and clutching the basket of food with the other. The wall felt surprisingly cool, and Xander embraced the cold feeling that crept up his fingers. He kept moving, pushed forward by the people behind him. There were no lights down here other than the first one, and Xander had the strange feeling of walking into a large animal's stomach.

Then, a loud shout from behind him warned Xander that something was about to happen. He bent forward, curving into a protective ball and waiting for something to happen. A slam, then nothing for five seconds, not even the sound of people complaining or whispering.

Then, the whole world shook, and Xander fell to his elbows on the floor. His ears rang, and Xander struggled to remember how to move his body parts. For some reason, the stupid basket of food seemed more important than his health. He reached for it and felt the contents to make sure they were all there.

The person behind him, Xander couldn't tell if it was a man or woman, nudged him with a foot. "Keep moving," the voice said in a whisper.

When Xander tried to climb to his feet though, the world seemed to shake. He shook his head to try to clear it and felt for the steady wall to his right. There, it was still there, strong and cold.

As the ringing faded, Xander's stomach turned over at the screams he heard. Someone pounded on the door they had come through, the metal door rattling.

"In, in!" the voice called. But no one opened the door for the wailing woman.

"A second one might be coming," a voice said, and others passed the message along the line. No one else seemed interested in continuing to move, and the person behind Xander had stopped urging him forward, so he sank down again.

The children who had been stunned at first by the shock of it all were now screaming. Xander leaned forward on his knees, the basket of food under his legs. He took a few deep breaths and tried to figure out what was happening.

Was Russia or Alaska trying to come after them? But why? Why destroy more of the planet when it was already dying?

A second blast hit them a few minutes later, but this one wasn't as hard. The whole place seemed to shake, but Xander focused on keeping himself as still as possible so that he wouldn't be injured.

A blast of heat seemed to pass down the tunnel, and the wall no longer felt like a cool block of ice.

"What's happening?" Xander asked the person on his left, even though he couldn't see who it was.

That person didn't answer, but the person on his other side spoke up, clearly a woman by the sound of her voice. "It's Alaska. They've been threatening for months now, but I didn't think they would actually do anything."

"Alaska. Alaska. Alaska." The word was whispered over and over again, up and down the line of waiting evacuees.

Xander listened carefully, wanting to learn more. No one had even whispered anything about war while he was still living in Sisimiut. Or maybe he had been too distracted by the upcoming Olympics to think about anything else. No, he would have noticed if something had been happening.

Xander considered the conversation he had overheard while he had been at the Olympics. Two girls from Alaska had been talking about something, something about their country wanting to take over, but Xander couldn't recall exactly what they had said.

"Now we will really know what a hard life is," someone said.

Some of the children had started to curb their wailing, but there were still lots of tears. Then, names started being passed up and down the row.

"Ask for Alyssa Carter," the person on his left said.

Xander turned to the right and repeated the name. He passed three more names to the right before one of them came back.

"Tell them Alyssa Carter is here with Davis Kensington."

Each time Xander heard a name passed back, he felt a sense of relief. Families might not be together, but they were finding each other. He thought about the woman who had been outside the bunker when the doors had been closed. Was her name one of the ones being passed down the line?

Finally, Xander decided to pass a name of his own. "I'm looking for Colt Gerbert," he said. He heard the name echo away from him and wondered if he should be asking for Matt instead. Matt had been insistent about staying in Sisimiut, though. There was no way he had been close to the research center.

Colt's name was never passed back to him, so Xander started it the other way, with the person on his left. After a while, the name passing slowed down, and Xander still hadn't had anyone say anything back about Colt. Xander hoped he was okay.

With no more attacks, Xander wondered what they were going to do now. They couldn't stay down here forever. But suddenly, someone must have sensed that it was time to act.

Slowly, a low hum started up far away. Xander saw some tiny lights along the bottom of the wall start popping on. A light just to his left popped on, and Xander blinked against the sudden brightness. After a couple of blinks, his eyes had adjusted, and he saw by the number of lights how long the hallway really was.

They weren't in a hallway but in a series of open rooms. He had assumed the wall on his left was a mere foot away, but it stretched out a good seven or eight feet to make a tiny chamber.

"Find a place to sleep," a commanding voice announced. "We won't be coming out of here for a while."

Xander wished he had grabbed a blanket or pillow instead of his basket of fruit, but he stumbled toward the furthest corner of the room and sat with his back in the corner, his head leaning against one of the walls. Now that the adrenaline had started to fade from his body, the sleepiness came in full force.

People began reorganizing, and the noise level rose as those who had heard a loved one's name tried to find that person now. Xander let his head fall forward, his chin pressing into his chest as he wondered if anyone up in the space station would be able to see what had happened. Was the destruction bad?

The thoughts started to swirl into nothingness though as the sleepiness took over. Xander didn't fight it as it drew him into oblivion.

When Xander awoke, his neck ached. He slowly lifted his head, wincing as he dealt with the pain he had inflicted on it. He slowly reached up a hand and massaged it. Now, instead of hurried footsteps and name calling, the place was almost completely silent except for a couple of people snoring.

He slowly moved his neck side to side and found that the cramp was resolving itself. He couldn't stay still though. He had to do something. Xander rose to his feet and used the small lights along the bottom of the wall to guide himself over the sleeping bodies, trying not to hurt anyone. There had to be someone in charge by the doors. He would find whoever it was and ask a few questions.

Chapter 9

Guilt. That's what it was.

Eden had gone straight to her room after Roman had been thrown out of the space station. There had been a tomb-like silence in the large room right afterward before a few people erupted in cheers and started some sort of chant. Eden had needed time to process what had happened, but now she had been shut up in her room for nearly three hours. She needed something to eat, but she wasn't ready to face people who cheered when a life was lost, even if it was Roman's.

Eden thought back to Derry and how he had begged for his life before being thrown out of the space station. Technically, he had been murdered because it turned out he hadn't strangled anyone. But then again...what he had done at the Olympics made him not exactly innocent.

She struggled with the guilt of being mostly responsible for both of the people thrown out of the space station. If she hadn't been here, then what would have happened?

The door to their room opened, and Avery slinked inside. The only light was from a bare bulb that hung from the ceiling, but Eden could see right away that something was wrong. A dark slash across Avery's forehead indicated she had injured herself.

"Do you want the bed?" Eden asked, sitting up and brushing her short, brown hair out of her face. With only two beds and four girls to the room, Eden and Avery had been sharing since Eden's arrival. Still, she could understand wanting the bed to herself for a little while.

Avery shrugged and sat on the end of the bed, staring at the blank wall opposite.

"What happened?" Eden asked.

"I miss Maya," Avery said. "Sometimes, I just feel alone."

Eden glanced up at the cut on Avery's forehead and saw that the blood was still bubbling up. Eden glanced around for something to hold to the cut to stop the bleeding, but there weren't a lot of extra things around.

"Sorry," Eden said after a moment. Then, she added, "I feel the same since Xander's been gone."

Avery nodded and continued to stare at the wall.

"Your...head?" Eden said, pointing. "Do you want something for it? I can go down to the medical center and get a bandage."

"No, you should stay here. It's safer."

"Safer?" Eden asked, glancing at the door that did not have a locking mechanism. What was so dangerous out there?

"Roman's gone," Avery said.

"Yeah, I...I know." Eden picked at her nails, wavering about how much she should tell Avery. Since Xander had left, she had felt like a piece of driftwood just floating aimlessly on the ocean. Nothing seemed to anchor her down and keep her in place like he had. For a moment, a deep sadness filled her, and she felt herself on the edge of tears as she remembered her loss. But no, she couldn't. Not right now. She had just spent the last three hours wallowing in her feelings. She wasn't going to start the tears again.

"Now everyone's crazy."

"What do you mean everyone's crazy?"

"Well, I was working my shift at the garden, and a bunch of people burst in. They told me to get out of the way, and they started ripping up the plants," Avery said. She reached up and reverently touched her wound. "I tried to stop them at first with a spade, but one of them grabbed it from me. It scraped me here." She dropped her hand, and Eden lifted hers, trying to decide if she should pat Avery on the back or not. She didn't know how to react to Avery, but she wanted her to know that she wasn't alone.

"They just took the vegetables?" Eden asked.

"All of them," Avery said, choking or sobbing, Eden was sure which.

She imagined the scene- a bunch of crazy people hungry after years of sludge seeing their opportunity to eat as much as they wanted.

"They just shoved the grapes into their mouths. The vines were empty in a few minutes. And...vines can grow more grapes, but they kind of knocked everything over when they were trying to get to the root vegetables. I don't know how much can be saved. The seeds…" She broke off, but Eden understood.

She stood up, wanting to go somewhere but not sure where to go. There was no one in charge who could listen to her complaint. Suddenly, she realized exactly what she and Simon and everyone else had done. They had left this place without a leader.

She needed to find Simon and help him figure something out.

"You should go to the medical center," Eden advised Avery as she opened the door to their room. The hall was mostly empty, which was pretty typical of mid-afternoon when a lot of people were either putting in their afternoon shifts or napping.

When she reached the stairs though, she could hear noise coming up from below. She descended the stairs one at a time, dread filling her with each one. Who would be in the bridge when she got there? For a second, she thought of Matt, Xander's older brother, but no. He had gone off with Xander to destroy the asteroid.

Biting her lip, Eden pushed open the door to the stairs, and it was immediately pushed closed by a group of people speeding past. Eden stumbled backward, almost falling on the stairs.

She tried again, this time darting out the door and leaning against it so she could get her bearings. A group of kids was carrying produce in their arms like farmers on their way to an open air market. They cheered and took huge bites of the tomatoes. Eden's mouth watered, and she couldn't tear her eyes away from them.

Another group behind them chanted something about "cucumbers for all and to all a good night." They were handing the vegetables out freely, and Eden wanted some. Her stomach moved her hand out, and a large cucumber was placed in her hand.

Clutching it to her chest like a treasure, she remembered her mission and scurried down the hall to the bridge.

She knocked on the door, then pressed herself against it as a group of five people hurried past, shouting something about the gardens. Once they had passed, Eden stepped back again and stared at the door to the bridge, waiting for it to open.

Still nothing.

She knocked again. Maybe the people passing had made too much noise, and no one inside had heard her.

"No one is allowed in!" a shout inside the door told her.

Still clutching her cucumber, Eden leaned forward and shouted back, "Is Simon in there? I need to talk to him!"

As she waited for a response, she looked down at the cucumber, warm from her hands, and her stomach grumbled. Should she eat it right now? If she didn't, someone might take it from her and say she had to share it.

She took a big chunk out of it. Though it didn't have much taste, the familiar motion of chewing made her close her eyes and really enjoy the moment. The door suddenly popped open, and Simon stepped out into the hall.

"Eden!" he said. Then, he glanced down at the cucumber in her hand. "What are you doing with that?"

"Someone shoved it in my hands," Eden said guiltily. "I heard that the garden was raided."

Simon hung his head and nodded. "Yeah, and everyone's expecting me to be a leader, but I'm not. I wanted to get rid of Roman because of...well, obviously, what he did. But that doesn't mean I want to be a leader."

"Someone has to," Eden said. She heard the sound of hurried footsteps and flinched toward the wall, but no one came past them. It must be someone in the main hall.

"Not me," Simon said. "We have to have an election or something." He ran a hand through his floppy hair, none of the good-natured fun and smiles present now.

"Yeah, that's a good idea," Eden agreed.

"Just not...right now," Simon motioned to the hallway where everyone was going crazy as they gathered and ate through the food supply.

Eden slowly moved her chomped-on cucumber so that it was behind her back, embarrassed that she had given in to temptation, yet still wanting another bite. In fact, if everything were being stolen anyway, maybe she could get one of those juicy tomatoes. Her mouth watered as she stared at the ground and tried to control her stomach.

"Thanks for your help with getting rid of Roman," Simon said after a moment, and Eden remembered that she was supposedly having a conversation with him. The eerie sound of Roman's protests followed by the whooshing sound as the air had ripped everything out of the container echoed through her mind.

"Uh, yeah," she said. "He...deserved it."

"Maybe you could help organize an election?" Simon lifted one of his shoulders, clearly unsure how to even do that.

"I don't know..." Eden replied, even though she really wanted to say no. She wasn't a leader! The only thing she had ever been responsible for was a science project in fifth grade. She had ended up doing everything herself, and even though the project had been excellent, she had gotten a bad grade because her teacher said the project was about "teamwork, not about cutting others out of the equation."

A bell rang. The dinner bell. Eden's mouth started watering, the way it always did when she heard the bell for meals. She was hungry, *so* hungry. She didn't say anything polite to Simon; she just turned and hurried in the direction of the dining hall, taking a huge bite of the cucumber as she went. Somehow, she didn't think anyone would appreciate her showing up to dinner with food already in her hand.

As she stood outside the door, people passed her, and she choked the cucumber down. It settled into her stomach, but she still had room for more food, much more.

Getting in line, Eden waited patiently for a minute, glancing around at the relatively calm people. Then, someone started yelling at the front of the line.

Eden craned her neck to see what was going on, worried as she did so that someone was going to start a fight. Then, another yell, one she could understand. It was something about the food mixed with a few unsavory words.

A few people groaned, and two guys hit the floor, rolling around and throwing punches as they went. Eden took a few steps back, wanting to stay out of the way, but she still heard the noises- grunts, groans, and the sickening thud of flesh on flesh.

As the two fought, the line waiting for food curved around them, and continued to collect their dinners. When Eden reached the front of the line, she saw...sludge.

"For dinner?" she asked, even as she obediently held out her bowl and watched the tasteless muck plop into her bowl.

"There's nothing else," the tired-looking server responded, not making eye contact.

Eden glanced at the two guys. One of them was wearing a cloth around his neck, one that had probably been covering his hair so it wouldn't get in the food. He was taking punches because of what they were serving? That was just wrong.

Quietly, she took her bowl of mush and spooned it into her mouth slowly, trying to make it last as long as possible.

A few people chatted cheerfully around the walls of the room, their half-empty bowls sitting in front of them. Clearly they weren't hungry, and Eden had a pretty good idea why. Others were hunched protectively over their bowls, not talking to anyone at all.

Once everyone had been served, and the two guys fighting had disappeared somewhere to lick their wounds, Simon and Jayce came in.

A girl a couple of people over from Eden pointed at Jayce and shouted. "He's Roman's best friend! He probably knew all about what he was doing! We should throw him out too!"

Jayce spoke up before anyone could latch onto this girl's idea. "I was close to Roman so I could know what he was doing, but now that he's gone, it's clear we need a leader."

"No way! Any leader is just going to start killing people!"

"No leader! No leader!" someone chanted, trying to get it going. No one picked up his chant though, and he fell quiet after a moment. Eden wanted a leader, someone to run things fairly. Today's chaos had ruined their food supply, and a little worry nagged the back of her brain that the cucumber might have been her last taste of real food ever.

"We need a leader!" Simon shouted. "No country in the history of the world has survived without one, but we think you should choose. We're going to have an election to pick four leaders. They'll work like a team."

There was silence as everyone absorbed the idea.

"I vote for Gracen!" someone shouted.

Eden didn't know who Gracen was, but a couple of people started shouting her name. "Is Gracen here?" Simon asked, looking around until a dark-haired, dark-skinned young woman stood up. She nodded and glided to the front of the room. Even Eden couldn't take her eyes off her. Eden had never seen her around the space station before.

Gracen nodded to everyone. "Okay, so, Gracen will be one of the people you can vote for," Simon said, seeming to get in the swing of things. "Anyone else want to nominate someone?"

"You!" someone shouted.

Simon glanced at Jayce and shook his head. "No, sorry, don't vote for me. I don't want to be a leader."

"Come on!" one of his friends called. "You need to do some work for once in your life."

Simon laughed. "I'm working right now. That's enough for me. Other nominations? Come on!" His laugh seemed to break the tension, and people started shouting out others' names. Soon, a line of nine people stood at the front of the room.

Eden only knew one of them. He was one of the people who worked in the medical center, and she had spoken to him briefly a couple of times. Everyone else was just a face to her.

Each person was given the chance to speak for a minute about why he or she would make a good leader. Gracen went first. "I was captain of the soccer team back home, so I know a little bit about organizing people and getting things done. We won all of our games in my last season. That's a lot different from leading up here, but I'm willing to give my best and learn as I go." She shrugged. "I want to make this place better."

Gracen looked at the next candidate in line, a dark-haired boy, and the campaign speeches continued.

When they were done, Jayce called out the candidates' names and pointed at them one at a time. "Think about who you want to vote for, then after breakfast tomorrow, you can vote."

Having something to do seemed to calm everyone down, and as soon as Jayce and Simon stepped back, the nine people were swarmed with constituents, though Eden stayed back watching them and wondering how she was supposed to vote for strangers.

She had already scraped her bowl of mush clean, but the number of people between her and the table with the dishpan of water kept her from trying to move yet. Besides, it wasn't like she had something else that she desperately had to do.

"What do you think?" Simon asked, suddenly in front of her.

"Of...what?"

"The leaders and voting," he explained with a shrug.

"Yeah, I mean, I don't know any of them. But I guess people who have been here longer do. So, yeah, it's better than a dictator."

Simon smiled. "Well, with a name like Roman, I guess you can only expect a Caesar Augustus to come in and implement the guillotine."

Eden frowned, only catching about half of what he said.

Simon explained. "You know...history...the Roman Empire and...okay, yeah, never mind."

Then, he still kept standing there. Eden didn't know where to look. It was strange to stare at someone when you didn't know what to say, so she examined her bowl a little more closely. Even though she had cleaned out the bowl well, she saw one clump of mush on the left side. She stared at it, wondering if it would be rude to just stick her finger in and dig it out now. However, the cucumber had done something to make her feel full. She refrained from scraping it out.

"So," Simon said again, and Eden looked over at him, sure now that he was going to actually say something. But he didn't continue for an awkward moment. "I guess you're going off to carefully think about your vote, huh?" he asked.

"I should," Eden responded, watching as the people running continued to talk to others like they were campaigning for the presidency of the entire world.

Another couple of moments passed.

Determined to get out of this awkward scenario, Eden said, "Well, I'm going now." Some people had cleared out enough that she finally had room to move. She started weaving her way through those still standing around and rinsed her bowl out in the dingy water before moving to the door.

When she glanced back, she saw that Simon was still standing there on the edge of the crowd, watching her. Pretending she hadn't looked back at all, Eden hurried to her room, her safe spot. Did Simon *like* her? It seemed strange to think that anyone could, not when Xander had been there, her best friend and boyfriend all in one. But he was gone. So maybe...

Chapter 10

No one was able or willing to answer Xander's questions. After asking at least four people if they knew who was in charge and what was happening, he approached the stairs. It was a little darker here. Either the tiny lights needed new bulbs or they had never actually been installed .

Xander reached out, expecting to meet empty space, but a pair of doors had been slid into place to block off the stairs from their hiding spot. After some slow patting, he found the handles and tried to pull the doors open. Nothing happened.

"Hey! What are you doing?" someone said, finally stepping forward and taking the position of leader.

"I want to see what's left," Xander explained.

"No one is allowed outside right now. It's too dangerous."

Xander leaned against the door and felt how strong it was. He thought about the woman's scream and wondered what they would find whenever they did open the door. "Is there going to be nuclear fallout?" Xander asked, trying to remember what he had read about nuclear bombs.

The person shook his head. "No, all the nuclear weapons were destroyed."

Xander snorted. Sure they had been. The fact that Colt had known about missiles somewhere in Greenland meant that there were probably more dangerous things too, only available to those with higher clearance.

"So, what hit us then?"

"Probably one, maybe two, of their missiles. No cell service, either." The man pulled out his phone and stared at the tiny, lit screen dejectedly.

Xander patted his pockets, missing his phone. It had been *so* long since he had had it. Before the Olympics, his phone had gone with him everywhere. He had communicated with everyone that way. But now, it seemed strange to see a glowing box like the one that had contained his life.

A thump on the outside of the door made him jump away from it. The door shuddered in its frame but didn't open.

"Open up, Dukes!" a man's voice shouted from the other side.

Someone who had been sitting against the wall leaped to his feet. The one person in his way automatically jumped to the side, and Xander watched as he pulled out a key and unlocked the door, then slid aside large bolts at the top and bottom of the door.

A hiss and pop sounded as the door slid open.

A large man stepped inside, his chest preceding him.

"Shut the door," he commanded as soon as he was inside.

The other man moved to the other side of it and started to shove it closed when something moved at the bottom. Xander glanced down and saw a foot sticking into the space.

"It's...watch out!" Xander said. But the man just kept pushing until the door bounced off the ankle with a crunch and back into the man's chest.

"What...?" he said. He came around, saw the foot, then glanced out at the steps above, steps that were also in darkness due to the tiny building built over them. He shook his head, grabbed the dead woman's ankle, and tossed her leg over her head. Then, he got back to shutting the door tightly and bolting it.

"We are going to need some extra power," the barrel-chested man announced. "Dukes, do you have anyone in here who could step up and act as an official?"

"Sir, these are all scientists and their families. I don't think any of them would be able to properly handle a weapon."

"They don't have to be able to do it properly. We just need it to look like we have too many for them to count. They wouldn't have to actually do anything, though we could use a few who at least competed in wrestling."

Having eavesdropped on the whole conversation so far, it was an easy thing for Xander to step in, even though he was still cringing over the woman lying just outside the door. "I won a medal in wrestling," he said.

They both looked at him, and the barrel-chested man shook his head. "No, you didn't. I know everyone, and I've never seen you before."

Well, he wasn't a modest guy then. Xander hated explaining his situation, but here he went again, trying to explain how everything had happened. "I won a medal but forfeited it to be eliminated with my girlfriend."

The barrel of a guy blinked at him for a second. "Then how are you here?"

"I came back because a bunch of the eliminated are on a space station floating around, and they were going to get obliterated by an asteroid. I got permission for a missile to destroy the asteroid."

Xander was once more met by a pair of disbelieving eyes. "You're the reason they shot off one of the missiles?"

Xander shrugged, then nodded.

"You idiot!" the guy said, shoving his bulk into Xander's personal space. "Why do you think Alaska attacked us? I've been mulling over the reason this would suddenly happen. You're why! We shot off a missile! They felt threatened, and..." He continued his shouting while including quite a few colorful words.

Finally, he seemed to calm down.

Xander argued, "If people in Alaska weren't idiots, then they would see that the missile was heading toward an asteroid, not them. Besides, why wouldn't someone here communicate with them and let them know what was happening? It's their kids up there too!"

"You're not the one to tell us how to run things!" Barrel went off again, and Xander stood by patiently. Normally, he wouldn't tolerate someone yelling at him, but this guy obviously had a lot on his shoulders, er, chest that he needed to unburden. All Xander wanted was more information about what was happening outside this hiding spot.

Finally, he ran out of steam. Several people had gathered around to see what was happening, though they had left a space between themselves and the commotion, either out of respect for Barrel or out of fear for what he might do if his anger continued to grow.

"Anyway," Xander said, when he finally got a chance to speak again, "I'm offering my services. I don't have any experience with weapons, but I'm good in hand to hand combat."

"I don't know," he said, studying Xander in the low light.

Someone stepped up behind Xander, and he realized it was someone wearing the uniform of an official. "He's good," the official said. "I faced him in the research center, and he knows his stuff."

Xander bent forward a little bit to see the official more clearly, but he was standing in front of the light, meaning that his face was in the shadow. Was he one of the ones whom Xander had fought? It was strange to think that they could have been sleeping almost next to each other, even though Xander had been throwing punches at him a couple of days ago.

"Fine, you can come with me. We just need bodies anyway," Barrel said. He turned back to Dukes. "I need forty to fifty more. Get them and send them to me at the other shelter."

He turned around, motioned for Xander to follow him, and pushed open the door with a quick shove. He marched outside, and Xander winced as Barrel stepped on the woman's hand like she was nothing.

Even though he knew it was impossible, Xander bent down next to the woman and checked for a pulse, Barrel's flashlight bouncing over her body and across the walls. As he got close to her face, though, he realized that her skull wasn't shaped correctly. It looked as though she had headbutted a truck. The stairs just under her were slick with blood, and Xander hurried up them to get away from her. The image of her smashed head continued to haunt him, though.

Once they had pushed through the door at the top of the stairs, Xander had to pause and take in the scene in front of him. What had been rows of townhouses close to a large research center with a bubble of glass that allowed researchers uninterrupted views of the sky had become piles of building materials.

Dust filled the air, and Xander bent his head down and buried his nose in his shirt so he could breathe easily.

All of the townhouses had been leveled. There were probably usable things that could be picked out of the rubble, but none of the people in the space below had homes to return to now.

The research center was also gone. It felt for a moment like Xander had been set down somewhere else. The world he had emerged into was not the one he had left the night before.

The barrel-chested man had already strode ahead, and Xander jogged to catch up, breathing in motes of dust. The man didn't seem bothered by the dust, but Xander coughed a couple of times as he hurried alongside the man.

What was the point of this destruction? If Greenland had been able to find a solution that would allow the Olympics to be abolished and the human race to flourish again, they would have shared it with both Russia and Alaska. That had been in the initial agreement, but now, Alaska had destroyed all of their research. Xander couldn't help being angry about it.

What if there hadn't been a warning?

There would be bones mixed in with the rubble of the homes.

Suddenly, the barrel-chested man stopped and got on his knees. He lifted up a metal trapdoor that was built into the ground next to a large rock and dropped inside. Wondering if he really wanted to be trapped in a small space with this large man, Xander dropped into the space next to him.

He found himself in a passageway that seemed only about six feet tall. He reached up and closed the door, his eyes blinking to adjust to the absolute darkness. He heard some scraping next to him as Barrel messed with the lock on the door.

"Follow me," he barked and moved down the passageway.

Xander wasn't six feet tall, but he still felt like his head was going to hit the ceiling with each step down the hallway. The noise of the man's footsteps changed, then something hit Xander hard in the face. He groaned and held a hand to his face, bending forward to protect himself as he tried to figure out who had attacked him. Breathing hard, Xander slowly stood up and moved his hands in front of him.

A wall.

That's what had hit him.

Laughing a little at himself now that the pain had subsided, Xander turned into a hallway that was dimly lit. He could see the large man's shape ahead, hunched forward to make it through the tunnel. He clearly didn't care that Xander had taken a moment to make amends with the wall.

Moving his lips and nose to make sure they weren't injured, he tried to hurry after the man. He had stopped, however, and now that Xander could see, he stopped too, just short of running into the brick of a man.

After some clanging, Xander heard a door squeak open. There was a moment of awkward squeezing as Xander managed to push past the large man who took up nearly the whole passage and insisted on standing with his hand on the door as Xander went through. Then, the man took his time locking up the door again before making the awkward squeeze again as he led Xander further down the hallway that was quickly lightening.

Suddenly, they were in a large chamber where a few officials leaned over a table and talked in quiet voices.

"I've brought a recruit. More are on the way. We'll be ready for Alaska when they come. You lowlifes aren't good for anything, even getting recruits."

The men who had been standing at the table leaped to attention when the large man spoke. "Yes, sir!" they chorused.

Then, the large man started marching toward another doorway. Xander glanced back and forth between him and the other men. Should he follow the large man?

One of the men who had stood at attention motioned for Xander to come over to him. "What can you do?" he asked.

Part of Xander wanted to break out in some crazy line dance he had learned with Eden back in high school, but he knew that wasn't what the man wanted to know.

"I won a medal in wrestling," he explained. "I'm good at hand to hand combat."

Without warning, the man dove at Xander. Taking only two seconds to understand that this was a test of his abilities, Xander folded forward to absorb the blow on his butt as he hit the ground. As soon as he touched, he rolled over so that he was on top of the other man.

He was halfway into putting the man in a decent hold, when he slithered out of Xander's grasp and got to his feet again. Xander had his hands at the ready, waiting for the other man to make a move. He didn't, though.

"Not bad. I thought I would have you down in under five seconds."

Xander shook his head. "I could probably use a little workout after having almost three weeks off, but I still remember everything."

"No time for that," the guy said. He held his hand out, and this time, Xander determined that he was offering to shake hands, not trying to attack him. "Russell," he said.

"Xander."

They shook hands, and Xander was allowed at the table where the men were looking over some sort of plan.

Xander leaned close to Russell who was rather lanky for being an official. "Can you tell me what's going on? I heard the alarms, but no one has really said what's happening."

"Alaska is attacking. We've known it's going to happen, but I guess some of us thought that they were just bluffing. Every country was left with a few missiles, sort of a way of saying we wouldn't mess with each other because we all have the same weapons. But they..." Russell shook his head, "...they actually used theirs."

"Can't we just shoot them back? Bam, we're even, no big deal?"

"No, because then Russia would be the only one with missiles. We can't let that happen."

Xander began to understand that this was more complex than just telling Alaska to play nice. "What are we going to do then? Why was the..." he had almost called him Barrel outside of his head, "that man asking for recruits then?"

"Alaska has a plane on the way here. It's not far off. We don't know who's on it or what will happen, but we need to be prepared."

Then, Russell shut his mouth and listened as the other men talked about different strategies. Xander finally understood the gravity of what was happening. When he had seen the fallen buildings, he hadn't been able to accept that everything was real. Now, though, he knew it was.

Chapter 11

The next day after lunch, everyone had four blank scraps of paper in their hands. They slowly filed forward for their chance at the pens. Eden scanned the faces of those who would be receiving their votes, their somber looks indicating just how important this vote was. Eden didn't know any of them, and she felt inadequate to even be voting. Jayce and Simon, though, had said everyone should vote.

Eden tapped Helena's shoulder, and Helena turned around. "Yes?" she asked.

"Who are you voting for?" Eden whispered, trying to keep their conversation quiet.

"I'm definitely voting for Latisha," Helena said. "I wish Simon was running. I would vote for him."

Eden nodded in agreement as a couple of guys walked down the line after voting. "Hey, you shouldn't be trying to force someone to vote your way," one of them said to Helena as he passed.

"And you shouldn't be telling me what to do," she shot back. "I don't remember your name being on the list of people we can vote for."

The guy kind of lunged at her but without any strength behind it, like he just wanted to make her flinch. Helena stared him down, her jaw set, not moving as he sauntered out of the room. After a moment of glaring at his back, Helena turned around and closed the space between her and the person in front of her.

Eden's stomach flipped over. She kept expecting someone to appear and discipline them. But there was no one currently in charge. She realized just how important this vote was.

When it was her turn, she bent her head close to the small slips of paper and wrote down "Latisha" followed by three other names that she remembered. Her votes wouldn't really matter anyway, not with so many other people voting. She stuffed her paper in the box and stepped away from the table.

People were already starting to count and separate the votes into piles, and Eden knew that the announcement of the winners would take place soon. She followed Helena to the edge of the room where she was closely watching those still voting.

"I hope we can trust the people counting," she said as Eden reached her.

Eden opened her mouth to assure Helena that of *course* they could, but then she realized that she didn't really know. Even though Eden had cheated in the Olympics, it had felt wrong every step of the way. Before that, she had had the faint idea that some people might break the rules but that it wasn't to be expected. Now, she was starting to question everything.

She remained by Helena's side, only because she had nothing else to do.

After standing there for ten or fifteen minutes, she realized that someone who had just voted wasn't heading out the doors of the large room or finding a place along one of the walls to watch. He was heading right toward them.

"You've already voted?" Simon asked, leaning against the wall next to Eden.

"Yeah," she responded, glancing at Helena who was still staring at the people counting votes. Helena didn't say anything, clearly assuming that the conversation wasn't meant for her.

Eden swallowed. "Am I allowed to ask who you voted for?"

Simon shrugged and glanced around. "I mean, I don't have any secrets. I voted for Latisha, Harry, Gracen, and Jameson. What about you?"

Embarrassed about how her selection process had gone, Eden sort of shrugged. After a moment, she said, "Gracen, Latisha, Brody, and Victoria."

Simon nodded. "A couple of people said they were going to vote for me even though I didn't want them to. I really hope they don't waste their votes on it."

"If you got enough votes but didn't want to be the leader, then what would you do?"

"I won't get enough votes," Simon said. He shrugged after another moment of silence. "I wouldn't mind being a leader of something smaller, like the entertainment department." He made a face. "Roman was right about one thing- there are too many people here. After they raided the gardens, we have...not much food left."

Eden had noticed her gruel that morning had been her fourth meal in a row of the stuff. "Something still has to be done," she concluded.

Simon nodded. Then, he put a hand on Eden's shoulder, like a friendly hand, not one of those stretch and put the arm around the girl's shoulders type of thing. But still, Eden didn't know how to take it. She bent down and pretended to adjust her shoe to escape the pressure of his hand. As she was down there fiddling with the shoestrings, she realized that Simon must like her. It wasn't a suspicion or just a possibility anymore. It seemed like a sure thing now.

It was a weird realization. She didn't think she was anything special, especially since most of her recent thoughts had been about survival. Roman still haunted her when she was trying to fall asleep at night.

Finally, she stood up, and Simon was still there. Eden didn't know what to say to him, so they just stood there, next to each other. He was nice enough, and funny when he wanted to be, but he wasn't Xander.

Finally, Eden said she was going to her room for a little while until the winners were announced. Simon's statement that there were still too many people on the space station followed her all the way to her room.

When she opened the door, she was surprised to see all three of her roommates sitting there- Jazzy, Avery, and Nicole.

"Oh hey!" Nicole greeted her cheerfully.

"Aren't you supposed to be working?" Eden asked, before realizing how rude she probably sounded.

"Afternoon off for voting, but I'm not even voting!" Nicole said. She laughed and snuggled up closer to the wall before patting the space on the bed before her. The mattress of the upper bunk had been dragged off and covered the remaining floor space. Avery sat with her legs extended in front of her and her back against the wall. Jazzy was curled into a little ball under a blanket at the other end of that mattress.

Eden carefully stepped over the floor mattress to the space at the end of Nicole's bed. She had been hoping for time alone, but it was hard to get that with so many people. Roman had wanted to cut the ship by half. She imagined two of her roommates disappearing. Sure, it would give them more space, but was it worth it?

"We are having a celebration!" Jazzy announced. From under her blanket, she produced something long and orange.

"What is-"

"Look, carrots wouldn't be the normal party food back on Earth, I know," Jazzy apologized. "But, it's not mush, and that's a good thing. I saved this one, well, half of this one, for you."

Eden was not proud of how quickly she grabbed the carrot, but once it was safely in her hand, she lifted it to her nose and took a deep sniff. It smelled of dirt, as though no one had bothered rinsing it off after plucking it from the greenhouse. But something about that dirt, about that familiar smell of the ground she had spent hours lying on as she stared up at the sky- it made her long for home in a way she hadn't since she had arrived. She had been so excited to still be alive that she hadn't really taken the time to let it settle in that she would never experience the sunshine on her freckles again.

"Are you going to eat it?" Jazzy asked, laughing.

Eden realized that her eyes were still closed, and she was sniffing at the carrot like some sort of suspicious rabbit. Grimacing, she shoved it into her mouth and took her first bite. It crunched loudly between her teeth, and even though it was warm, it reminded her of when her mother had tried to go through that healthy snack phase and only let Eden have cucumbers, carrots, or bell peppers after school.

The memory made Eden's eyes sting with tears.

"Are you okay?" Nicole asked, immediately wrapping her arm around Eden's shoulders.

"Yeah, uh huh," Eden said, around her crunchy carrot. She could feel the other three girls staring at her as she ate.

Finally, Jazzy started a conversation, and Eden felt less like a bug under a microscope. "I really want these leaders to work," she said. "But I just don't know if they're going to be any different."

"I don't care if they are good leaders as long as they don't go around killing people," Avery said, glancing at Eden's neck. She still had bruises that showed above the collar of her shirt, and Eden bent down so that her chin covered them. She took another crunchy bite of her carrot and sighed.

"Thanks, Jazzy. This is really good."

Jazzy laughed. "I know, right?! I'm tired of them giving us tiny little vegetable cubes and calling it a real dinner. There was so much food in the garden, and no one even stopped us from taking it."

Eden glanced at Avery who had reached up to touch her forehead wound. She didn't say anything, though, which was normal for her.

"You were with the group of people who raided the garden?" Eden asked, and Jazzy nodded excitedly.

"It was so cool! I mean, Roman was keeping all that food from us, and now, even though we have to hide it, it's like we can actually eat again." Jazzy reached under the lower bunk and pulled out her little stash of carrots. "All I could get were these, but it's kind of good because they don't go bad quickly. And I know exactly how many there are, so don't take any."

Eden saw Jazzy smile as she issued the warning, but Eden knew that Jazzy wasn't joking. She might not have the law on her side, but she was going to protect those carrots.

"What are the new leaders going to do now?" Avery asked, piping up from her spot in the corner.

Nicole sat up straight. "I already know. Someone told me."

"Told you what?"

"What they're going to do. There are still too many people on the space station, so they're going to get rid of the bodies in stasis and put some of us in there."

Eden gasped. Nicole knew about the bodies in stasis?

Avery covered her mouth and half coughed, half moaned. "No! They can't do that! Maya has to be there!"

Nicole now turned her attention to comforting Avery as moved to the mattress on the floor. "I'm sorry, Avery, but she won't know the difference. She's been asleep for all this time. She won't know what's happening."

"But I will!" Avery sobbed. "They can't just...I need to see her." Avery stood up, but didn't go anywhere. "That's cruel! They can't be that cruel!"

"They'll vote on it, I'm sure," Nicole said, not sounding as confident as she had when she announced the bodies would be dumped.

Avery hung her head and pulled her knees up to her chest, absorbing her grief. Eden tried to quietly snap off another piece of carrot, but it rang loudly in the quiet room. Jazzy laughed, then glanced at Avery and toned it down.

"I think they might just ask for volunteers to get thrown out. There's got to be some people who are done with life here and want to..." Jazzy didn't say the words, but Eden understood.

"Probably not that many, and why does it matter? I mean, yeah, sharing a bed with a stranger is weird, but..." Eden explained.

"We're not strangers anymore," Avery pointed out.

"Well, I mean, I've only known you, what, three weeks now? It hasn't been long. And what I'm saying is it's not that big a deal. I mean, yeah, it's crowded, but so what?"

"You tell them!" Jazzy cheered her on. "Tell them to stop making a big problem out of nothing."

Avery remained quiet, tucked in her corner and trying to accept the potential consequences of having so many people on the ship.

Suddenly, the alarm on the wall sounded once. It normally rang in the morning when it was time for the first shift to get to work, but it didn't usually ring in the middle of the afternoon.

The girls all looked at each other, and Nicole leaped to her feet, then jumped over the end of the mattress on the floor. "Everyone must be done voting. Let's go see what happened!"

Eden shoved the last, large piece of carrot into her mouth and chewed quickly. She didn't want anyone to see her eating as she entered the large dining hall. She was the last one out of their room and spent a moment closing the door slowly as she hurriedly chewed the rest of the carrot.

Finally, when she had swallowed the last of it, she turned around and walked quickly to catch up with her roommates. A small piece of carrot felt like it had lodged in her throat, and she swallowed multiple times trying to get rid of it with no luck.

When they entered the large dining space, Eden coughed, trying to get the piece of carrot out of her throat. The room was packed. The only space remaining for Eden was just outside the door. She couldn't see over other people's heads, but she could hear the person announcing the names.

"After all the votes have been counted," a male's voice announced, "we have found that four of the nine candidates had more votes than anyone else. Once the leaders have been announced, I'll show them to the meeting room where they can figure out how to control the rest of us crazies."

Eden half smiled, and there were a couple of laughs. A lot of people didn't think it was funny, though. Maybe everyone was worried that these leaders would turn out to be as bad as Roman had.

Wiping her nervous hands on her pants, Eden listened as the voice read the names out loud. "Jameson, Gracen, Brody, and Vince."

There were some boos and some cheers. Eden tried to match the names that had been called to the faces she knew, but she couldn't remember who Vince and Jameson were.

Everyone in front of Eden started moving, trying to make room, and the only way for her to move was backwards. She took a few steps back, and the crowd in the large room seemed to spit out the four chosen leaders.

She recognized Gracen and Brody right away. She had voted for both of them. Jameson she recognized as someone she had seen working with Jayce and Roman. She wondered why people had voted for him when he had been one of Roman's closest friends. She didn't trust anyone Roman had liked. Vince had a long, blonde mane that put Eden's short hair to shame.

People cheered as they left the room, and a few people followed them down the hall. Eden stood to the side, so that she wouldn't get trampled. Well, their leaders had been chosen. Would they make a difference in life on the space station?

When Eden turned around, she saw Simon waving to her as he squeezed out of the dining space. This time, she didn't feel awkward as he came toward her to start a conversation. She welcomed the distraction from her serious thoughts.

"Hey," she said, smiling.

Chapter 12

The men around the table weren't making enough room for Xander, so he wandered down one of the two hallways that led out of the room. As he did, he found that this bunker, if that was what it was actually called, was set up better than the other. He pushed open a door along the hallway and realized that he had stumbled into a room that was set up with a bed. Someone was in it, under the covers, and Xander hurried backwards, letting the door close.

Why was one evacuation area set up so well while the other one wasn't?

He glanced down the hallway and saw similar doors along it, assuming they led to other rooms with comfortable looking beds. Retreating to the room with the table, he started to head down the other hallway when someone called him back.

"What are you doing?" the guy asked.

Russell pulled himself away from the table and slapped his friend on the shoulder. "Xander's a good guy," he said.

"You met him five minutes ago. That doesn't mean anything," the guy said, and he threw Xander a nasty look before backing off.

Just then, the door to the room opened, and the room filled with noise as reinforcements, mostly men, entered. They were talking like they were on an adventure, not on the cusp of going into war.

"Listen," one of the men around the table said. The new arrivals circled him, paying close attention.

"A plane is on its way from Alaska. We have to be prepared for them to-" He didn't get to finish telling them how to prepare before he was interrupted by someone who didn't have the build of a soldier.

"Why wouldn't we just shoot them down? Easy. Then, we don't have to get our hands dirty."

"The problem is…" the man said, taking his time to answer. Xander immediately understood that he didn't have a good answer for the guy's question, which made Xander doubt his authority. "That's not the plan," he finally concluded. Having had a moment to think, he added. "If we shoot at them, they might have time to change course and avoid the missile."

"You want to do things your way," the questioner concluded.

"It has nothing to do with my way or your way. It has to do with not questioning authority," the man said darkly. Russell hunched down, and Xander could tell he wouldn't be the one to question anyone.

Just then, the barrel-chested man burst into the room. "Time!" he shouted. "Unit 1 after me. Unit 2 to the north."

The men who had been surrounding the table when Xander first entered grabbed up weapons from the table. Some shoved heavy-duty helmets on their heads. They started rushing from the room while the large man watched to make sure everyone was going where they should.

"Move! Move!" he shouted.

Only half the people in the room started moving.

"We don't know what unit we're supposed to be in," Xander said, glowering at the man. He had already dealt with derisive comments during his short time on the space station. Everyone in the kitchen had expected him to know what he needed to do when he had never had any training.

The man pointed an arm down the middle of the room and waved to the right. "Unit 1." He pointed to the left. "Unit 2. Get a weapon, and let's go." The man opened a closet just off the second hallway, and everyone hustled inside and grabbed a weapon.

Xander had never held a weapon before. They had been outlawed since before he had started his training. Why the man was trusting such dangerous implements to people who had never used them before was beyond Xander.

Still, there was something exciting about holding the weapon in his hands and feeling the heaviness of it. Xander noticed a few vests, maybe five in total, hanging on the wall by the door of the small room.

"Can I-"

"No, and put that weapon back," the man commanded. Then, he shouted loudly so that everyone could hear him. "Grab those against the left wall!"

Xander glanced at the ones on the left wall and the right. They looked identical, but he set his gun back against the wall and picked up one from the wall indicated.

"Faster!" he shouted, and Xander scurried out of the room, trying to remember everything he had ever seen or read about shooting a gun.

But everything was moving too quickly for him to think about it for long. He rushed down the hallway after everyone else feeling vastly unprepared. At least he had trained for hand-to-hand combat before the Olympics, but most of the people grabbing guns behind him had never done anything besides sit behind a desk.

They were being sent to their deaths.

"Unit 1," Xander heard from somewhere in front of him.

He peeled off with that group, and they were going down a different tunnel, the only light a pinprick ahead of them. Xander felt like he was stumbling blindly.

Suddenly, a loud screech, and the movement slowed.

No one spoke as the light grew closer. Then, Xander was pulling himself through a trapdoor and into the open air beyond. The air was still filled with debris, and Xander pulled up the neck of his shirt to cover his mouth and nose, making it easier to filter the oxygen.

The men in front of him moved with a certain franticness, and Xander fell easily into the game of follow the leader.

With no practice in armed combat, Xander ducked down behind a crumbled building and squat-ran in the direction of the research center, hoping he would instinctively know what to do when the time came. Suddenly, the air around him swirled, and the zooming of a motor made Xander realize that the plane was landing there, right there.

The leader sped forward, and Xander pushed himself to keep up, remembering every day he hadn't worked out since winning his medal in the Olympics. That shouldn't negate the years of training before that, but his head was in the wrong place.

As they sped forward, Xander with no clear plan, he wondered how Eden was doing on the space station. Then, his mind jumped to wondering if Greenland had been attacked in multiple places or just here. As the plane's engines deafened his ears, he heard a shout. He held his gun steadily, both hands grasped around the handle, his finger ready on the trigger.

The plane slowed and skidded to a halt, its wheels bumping crazily over the rocks that scattered the ground.

Those with Xander had taken refuge behind the shrubs, and he crouched, half-hidden behind a thorny bush.

He waited, each second feeling like an eternity as the plane continued to slow, the pilot taking his time as he steered it in a curve before he ran into a line of trees.

A crack behind Xander made him whip around, and his brain took only a second to understand what was happening. The unfamiliar clothing, the masked face. This wasn't someone from Greenland.

"Freeze or I shoot!" Xander said, realizing that the man was unarmed.

The man advanced toward him slowly, his eyes on the gun. The only part of his face showing was his eyes, and they darted nervously from the gun up to Xander's face. Did he know that Xander hadn't had much experience? Was his hold on the weapon that off?

"Freeze!" Xander shouted again, faintly aware that other things were happening around him but too focused on the person in front of him to fully process them. The man continued to move forward, one slow step at a time.

"Last warning!" Xander said.

The man continued to move, and Xander shifted his aim for the man's leg, his stomach twisting in guilt as he pulled the trigger. The gun lurched in his hand, and the crack made Xander take a step backward.

The man fell to the ground, and Xander rushed forward, wanting to help him even though he was the enemy. However, when Xander got there, the man was rolling onto his back. He grabbed Xander's legs and pulled him to the ground. Throwing the gun out of arm's reach, Xander pinned the man's arms and slithered out of his hold, doing what he did best.

As soon as Xander was free, the man pulled him down again, rolling on top of him. Breathing hard, Xander loosened the man's grip, then threw a punch. His knuckles throbbed as he pulled his fist back and punched again.

The man's grip loosened, and Xander rolled him onto his back and pinned him. He took a few deep breaths, the dust tickling his nose as he waited to see if the man would keep fighting.

Xander could feel the man's chest heaving under him, but he had stopped struggling. Taking a risk, Xander let go and rushed to pull off the man's face-mask. Now that he could see his full face, he realized that the man was barely a man. He had probably competed with Xander in the Olympics that had just finished.

"What are you trying to do?" Xander asked him.

The man studied Xander sideways, as Xander pressed one side of the guy's face into the dirt. "I don't know anything," he said. "I just did what they said."

"What'd they say?" Xander asked.

"We had to parachute off the airplane, and then…" He didn't keep going, but Xander understood anyway. The airplane was a distraction.

The sounds around him slowly came into focus again, and he heard gunfire, lots of gunfire. Xander didn't have anything to use to tie the guy up, but he didn't think he would run. Xander climbed off him, but kept him in a hold, wondering what he was supposed to do with his hostage.

"I thought I hit you with the bullet," he said. "Guess I have bad aim."

"You did," the guy said. "Left leg."

Xander didn't let go of him just in case it was some sort of ploy to get him in a bad position, but he didn't see any blood. He shook his head. "You would be bleeding if I had," he said.

"You hit me. I don't know what with, but it hurt like hell."

No. No, Xander didn't want to believe it, but his brain was telling him that the reason Big Guy had been so insistent on which weapons they took was because some of them were set up differently. He had been given a weapon with blanks, and if that's what he had, then that meant everyone else who had been gathered as a volunteer had the same thing.

He closed his eyes, his grip steady on his prisoner, and let out a long breath as the sounds of combat all around them continued. A few *pops* indicated that more guns were being fired, but if they would actually do anything was a completely different question.

Finally, Xander had gathered his thoughts, and he pulled the guy up. "You're coming with me," he said, knowing he couldn't take him right to their underground hiding spot. That would give the spot away, and Xander wasn't that dumb. He wanted to get away from potentially flying bullets, or blanks, and find someone who would actually give them direction on what to do.

So, bending forward, Xander ushered his captive forward, running in a crouch, a vise-like grip on the guy's wrists. They finally escaped the shrubbery and entered the world of destruction that the fallen buildings had created.

Xander led his captive to the far end of one of the rows of townhouses and indicated that he was to sit on the ground. The guy sat and pulled up his pant leg immediately to look at his leg. A small bruise was forming, about an inch across, but there was no blood. Seeing it confirmed Xander's suspicions about the ammunition in the guns, and he wanted to punch Barrel and show him what he thought of his willingness to send people to their deaths, thinking they had guns when they really didn't.

Xander stared at the guy, and the guy stared back at him. After a moment, the guy's eyes darted away, and a second later, he leaped up and tried to make a run for it. Already anticipating the move, Xander lunged in front of him, tripping him before he had fully climbed to his feet. Pulling one of his favorite moves, Xander twisted the guy's arm behind his back and held him there. He could pull the arm up further and really make the guy scream, but Xander wasn't trying to hurt him.

After a few wiggles and pushes, the guy finally gave up. Xander felt the fight flood out of the body underneath him. Just to make sure the guy wouldn't try anything again, he pulled the guy's arm up past the point of discomfort and held it for a few moments before letting go and pushing the guy to sit with his back against a pile of rubble. The guy cradled his arm and pouted.

"So," Xander said after a minute, watching someone run back in the direction of the hidden trapdoor. Based on the person's stance and build, Xander was guessing it was one of the untrained volunteers. To draw the guy's eyes back to him instead of what other people were doing, Xander started a conversation. "What's your name?" he asked.

"Hudson," he said.

"Hudson," Xander repeated, nodding. "Nice to meet you. Were you at this year's Olympics?"

"Yeah, and you won a medal in wrestling. I remember."

Xander nodded and raised his eyebrows, nodding back in the direction of their recent battle. "I'm assuming you did too? To be honest, I was too busy focusing on hearing my own name in that competition to pay attention to anyone else."

"No, I was in logic," Hudson said, "but they pulled in a lot of people for this...attack."

Xander pursed his lips and nodded. Seemed like Alaska had had a similar draft of unequipped individuals. "And what? Alaska wants to kill off more people than the Olympics do?"

Hudson shrugged again, either unwilling or unable to answer that question.

Suddenly, an explosion rocked the ground, and Xander lost his balance. He fell onto his arms, one of his elbows shooting pain up to his shoulder. He quickly rolled onto his back as the ground settled and his ears rang.

His lungs fought for clean oxygen as they remembered how to breathe, and Xander took his elbow in his other hand, expecting his skin to be hanging in shreds. Everything seemed to be in place, and he remembered Hudson.

But when he looked up, Hudson was running across the open space, heading toward where the plane had landed, closer to where the explosion was making it impossible to breathe.

Once again, Xander pulled up the front of his shirt to cover his nose and mouth, breathing the cleaner air underneath. His first instinct was to go after Hudson, but he didn't want to be responsible for something bad happening to him. What if Barrel decided that Hudson wasn't useful and wanted to off him? Xander wouldn't put it past the big guy.

As he stood there trying to make a decision, a stream of people came running out of the woods. Xander evaluated which side they were on in a quick moment and realized they were his. Some of them were running, but others were moving more slowly.

Xander ran toward them to help someone who was dragging his leg behind him. Xander stopped at the guy's bad side and wrapped his arm around his shoulder. They took a couple of awkward steps that way. Then, realizing that the lean build of the guy probably made him light, Xander scooped him up and followed the others. The guy grunted in acknowledgement as everyone gathered around the trap door, forced to slow down as they slid into the space one by one.

"You okay?" Xander asked, still holding the guy but now feeling a strain on his arms and a sharp pain in his elbow.

"I got shot," the guy said, closing his eyes and breathing through clenched teeth.

"We'll get you to someone who can fix you up."

But the guy was in so much pain that Xander wasn't sure if he even heard him.

Once everyone was in the tunnel, the trapdoor snapped shut behind Xander, causing the tunnel to go completely dark. He stepped forward slowly, trying not to hit the guy he was carrying.

"I got it," the guy said, struggling out of Xander's arms. He hopped forward, leaning on the wall, and Xander stayed right behind him just in case he got too weak.

Finally, they were in the large room again. A lot of people seemed to know exactly what to do, hurrying down the hallways on missions of their own. Xander, however, needed to talk to someone. And as much as he didn't like him, he thought Barrel might be the only one who could tell him what was going on.

Xander stood by the doorway, observing as someone began helping the guy who was shot and as others returned to the room, clearly having cleaned up already.

Finally, he spotted Barrel, half a head taller than the rest of the room. Xander pushed his way through the others toward the large man.

"You gave us blanks," he said, trying to keep his accusation calm even though he wanted to yell at the man who had nearly gotten them killed.

The man surveyed Xander, and there seemed to be a moment of recognition. "You're one of the new recruits."

Xander shrugged, not sure why it mattered.

Then, Barrel smiled. He *smiled*. Xander blinked, not quite believing that the man found some sort of humor in this situation.

"I can't give a bunch of real guns to people who would just kill themselves using them because they don't know where to point the barrel."

"I think any human on this planet knows which way to point a gun, but I appreciate the confidence. What were you expecting us to do? You-"

"I wanted you to look threatening, and guns with blanks do that. You did your job. The plane has exploded, and we've killed at least thirty of their guys. I've got some guys out there now still searching for any who escaped."

Xander took a deep breath to absorb the news of these deaths. They probably hadn't been anyone that Xander knew, but the casual way he mentioned the death of fellow humans made Xander feel sick.

"Look, I'm happy to help my country, to help Earth as a whole, but you sending us out there like that, with no real plan, with no-"

"Plan?" Barrel interrupted again. "There was a plan. You didn't need to know it. You did what you were supposed to do."

"I'm not going out there to help you or anyone else again. You have no respect for human life which means I have no respect for you."

Xander turned and headed for the long hallway that led to the escape hatch. The man shouted something after him about how he had no choice, but they weren't quite at the point yet where everyone had lost all of their freedoms. Xander hoped they never reached it.

He marched down the long, dark hallway. When he reached the end, he reached up to open the hatch but hesitated. If he walked away now, where would he go? He needed to be prepared to run into someone more skilled than Hudson had been, someone who might kill him on sight. He could just stay...

That would be the easy answer for now, but Xander had never been one to take the easy road. He reached up and unscrewed the latch.

Chapter 13

There had been so many emergency meetings recently that Eden had barely gone in to work her shifts at the medical center. No surgeries had been performed since the news had gotten out that there was no kind of anesthesia. Between the Olympics imitation and the voting, Eden had been busy rushing back and forth to the large room at the far end of the space station.

Today, she was headed there yet again to listen to what the new leaders had to say. There wasn't a lot to do on the space station, so even if they just wasted her time by saying they were honored to be their leaders and looked forward to doing it, blah, blah, blah, then at least they would have given Eden something to do.

However, when she pushed her way into the edge of the room, there was a somber silence that told her today might be more serious. A few people were whispering to each other, but a lot of them were staring at the front of the room, waiting.

Eden pushed herself up onto her toes to try to see the leaders gathered at the front of the room, but there were still too many broad shoulders and long-haired heads blocking her way. She sighed and went back down to her normal height, wishing there was some rule about the short people getting to go in the front.

"We will give everyone a couple more minutes," a male's voice said. Eden thought it was Jameson's, but it was impossible to tell from her view. She stumbled forward as someone pushed through behind her.

"Sorry, sorry," she apologized, backing off the pair of heels in front of her. The guy turned around and smiled.

"Hey!" Simon said. "I was wondering when you would get here."

"Oh, hey," Eden said.

"Here, move up this way." Simon turned to the side, creating just enough space for Eden to slide past him. She kept her eyes down as she slid past him, trying not to recognize how close they were. Then, she was in front of him, and the moment had passed.

She turned half around so that Simon would be able to hear her without her having to shout. "What do you think they want to tell us?" Even though Simon wasn't one of the leaders, he seemed to have the inside track on what was happening.

"It has something to do with the overcrowding," Simon said. "I think they've come up with something."

"What?" Eden asked.

Simon shrugged, looking genuinely puzzled. "I don't know, but if they use the 'O' word, I'm marching out of here. I'm not talking about orangutans either."

Eden half-smiled, knowing that the Olympics were much worse than any announcement of orangutans. "You won't get very far. This place is only so big."

"Thanks for the reminder," Simon said, irritation in his voice. Eden thought the irritation was at their situation, not at her, but she couldn't be sure. So, she just kept her mouth shut and turned back to the front. There were still quite a few people in front of her, but at least she had a peek at the front of the room now.

One of the guys stood on the table like Roman always had. Eden was pretty sure it was Brody. Someone reached a hand up, and he lifted Gracen onto the table. Then, the table squealed, and they both hopped down, laughing, making jokes about how the table had already done too much for them.

"I'm just going to shout. Let me know if you can't hear me!" Brody said.

Eden smiled just a little bit at his attempt at a joke.

"Great, look, we've spent the last twenty-four hours talking about how many people there are and looking at the food supply and our ability to replenish it. It's not good. I'm not going to pretend that everything's okay. It isn't."

Jameson cut in then. "Brody is being nice. We're looking at two or three months of food before we use more than we are producing and run out of stores. That means, two to three months until people start dying of starvation."

Eden pressed a hand to her stomach. Sometimes, she already felt like she was starving to death. It was hard to imagine feeling even worse.

Gracen spoke up, her voice an octave higher than the other leaders'. "If we are able to cut the population some, we should be able to get the garden up and running again, and that would supplement what we have right now. Depending on how much we cut the population, we would be able to extend that time indefinitely."

"Who are you going to kill?" someone shouted out from the gathered crowd.

"Yeah!" someone agreed, anger in his voice. "Who are you going to throw out?"

There was silence for a moment, and Eden could tell that everyone was probably thinking the same thing she was. *Please don't let it be me.*

"We want volunteers," Gracen finally said. "Some of you who are done living on the space station. Maybe you don't want another few years here. Maybe you are tired of what life has to offer. I've been in that place before myself."

The room remained surprisingly quiet. "Volunteers to be pushed out the hatch?" someone finally asked.

Vince finally spoke for the first time. "We have actually been looking through the controls in the bridge. There is a way to shut off oxygen to part of the station, a few rooms at a time. Volunteers would go in those rooms, get comfortable, and we would shut off the oxygen."

No one spoke. Eden felt a curl of terror wrapping itself around her. They said "volunteers," but who would volunteer for that? What if they picked her out and forced her to go into that room? She wasn't ready yet.

"It would feel like going to sleep," Vince continued. "Without oxygen, your brain would slowly cease to function, shutting down its awareness first. You wouldn't feel any pain."

Eden hunched forward just a little. The people around her didn't allow any more room for her to move, but she felt like she was going to be sick. This was wrong, so wrong. Someone at the front of the room continued to speak in a low rumble about where to go if someone wanted to participate.

His use of words like "appreciate," "participate," and "easy" made her stomach feel even worse.

Suddenly, there was a hand on her shoulder. She turned. It was Simon's hand.

"Are you okay?" he asked.

"Yeah, um, just...yeah, nothing."

He smiled a little. "I don't know if I can diagnose you as good as you diagnosed me, but I can try."

Eden shook her head. She appreciated that Simon was trying to make her feel better, but she didn't think anything could at this point. She tried to listen to whatever one of the leaders at the front of the room was saying.

"We're not going to force anyone to make the sacrifice at this time, but *something* has to be done if we're going to be able to keep spreading the resources. Please, think about it. We'll do it in twenty-four hours. And if enough people volunteer, then we won't need to do anything else."

Gracen stepped back, and Eden let those last few words echo through her brain like a threat. *Then we won't need to do anything else.* What else were they going to do? *Force* people to commit suicide? Maybe the leaders didn't elaborate for a reason.

People started to move around, and their voices now rose loudly as they discussed this newest development. Eden listened to snatches of conversation around her.

"No way am I gonna do that. It's not a bad idea, but I don't want to choke to death. I mean, it would be like drowning, just without the water around you."

"They said it would be painless."

"Well, yeah, but who would volunteer if they said you would suffer? No one. They have to say that."

Eden turned slowly, the thought briefly flickering through her head that maybe it would be an easy out. She didn't have her family or Xander anymore. All she did was work in the medical center, then go to her room and let her thoughts drown her. Maybe...but no. As soon as she thought of asking Xander his opinion, she knew what he would say.

"Just because I gave up my medal to be eliminated with you doesn't mean you should give up now. You are so talented." Eden smiled ironically at the idea. She hadn't danced at all since she had arrived here. She just hadn't had the inspiration, the excitement, the desire, or the space to create a new piece.

"You're not thinking about doing it, are you?" Simon asked, turning away from the conversation he had been having with the person on his other side.

"No, I don't think I could do it."

"Me either. I mean, I'm not ready to die yet."

"What will happen if no one volunteers?" Eden asked tentatively.

"Someone will," Simon responded confidently. But one person or two or three won't make a difference at all. Only a mass sacrifice would.

"I need some space," Eden mumbled, only halfway directing her words to Simon.

"Yeah, take your time to think."

Eden paused in the middle of wiggling her way through the crowd. She turned toward Simon. "Thanks," she said. Then, she turned and hurried away as quickly as she could while ducking, squeezing, and pushing herself through the crowd of people and into the still crowded hallway.

After climbing up to the second floor, Eden hurried to her friend's room. She hoped that Helena would be there. If she weren't, then Eden would wait until she returned. Out of all the people in this space station, Eden trusted Helena's opinion, even though she was only a couple of years older.

She knocked on the door, but no one answered. Knowing it would be impossible for someone to be in the tiny room and not be able to hear her, she knocked again, just in case the person inside didn't realize how urgent it was.

"Eden," she heard her name.

Eden turned around and saw Helena striding toward her, her long braids dancing all around her. Her face was serious, and as she got closer, Eden saw that her eyes were red.

"I wanted to talk to you," Eden said, stepping aside to let Helena lead the way into her own room.

"Let's talk in here," Helena said, settling onto the lower mattress. It was strange for a room of four people to be unoccupied, but then again, a lot of people were still in the dining hall discussing the decision they now faced.

Not having so many people around her listening helped Eden feel calmer about the subject. Still, when Helena looked at her and nodded for her to begin talking, Eden's throat felt suddenly dry.

"I don't know what they're going to do when no one volunteers," she said.

"I guess that means you're *not* volunteering? Good," Helena reached over and squeezed Eden's shoulder. They weren't *best* friends. They had barely known each other two weeks, but that show of support made Eden feel suddenly emotional. She stared at the ground and swallowed a couple of times until the emotions started to dissipate.

"What about you?" she asked.

"No way. Yeah, I'm bored sometimes. So what? At least I'm alive." Helena ran her fingers over her braids.

"But what if..."

"They won't throw people off the ship," Helena said right away, reading Eden's mind. "They're good. I trust them on this."

Eden used to believe that people were either good or bad, but now, she wasn't sure. It seemed like they could be some of both. She thought about eating the stolen vegetables and how that act made her just a little bit of the problem too.

"But what are they going to do?"

"They'll focus their efforts on the garden or on producing food some other way."

"*What* other way?" Eden asked, desperate for answers.

"I don't *know*!" Helena finally admitted, "but they'll figure something out. Don't worry about it."

But Eden couldn't just stop thinking. What if only two people volunteered? Their sacrifice would mean nothing. What would two people giving up their sleeping spaces and meals really mean in the long run?

"Just think about something else," Helena suggested. She reached under the bottom bunk and pulled out a pack of cards. She smiled as she shuffled them. "I borrowed these from the game room, and I've been playing solitaire for hours at a time."

Eden watched as Helena gave the cards one last shuffle, then laid them out on the ground and began flipping them over so quickly that Eden wasn't sure how she could see all the cards before deciding she couldn't use them.

Watching in silence, Eden started to feel a little calmer. She barely glanced at a card before Helena was moving it to a new place.

But then, as Helena moved a stack of cards to the top of her space, successfully restacking them backwards, the fear hit Eden again. She just had to get through these next twenty-four hours. Then, she would know if she needed to keep worrying.

Chapter 14

Outside of the underground hideaway, Xander blinked against the light. There was still a film in the air, some sort of residue from the recent explosions, and Xander's skin felt grimy as he walked into it. His only plan right now was to find Colt. He hadn't been in either one of the hideouts, at least as far as Xander knew. He wondered where else he could have gone after he had run out of the townhome last night.

Had it really been less than a day ago?

Barrel had insisted that the weapons weren't nuclear, but Xander wondered if they were. When would he start to see the effects? Would he just fall over and be in pain? Or would his hair start coming out in clumps?

He turned toward the rubble of the research center, wanting to see it up close.

In the distance, he heard a few shouts. He thought the person might be trying to communicate something, but he couldn't understand any words from it. Then, a gunshot rang out, and Xander froze. He remembered what one of the officials had said about others still out here trying to track down the remaining Alaskans. He had to be careful if he didn't want a bullet through his head.

Bending forward, he ran awkwardly to the ruins of the research center. When he reached them, he saw that concrete was mixed with glass and brick. On one side, he could see an expensive-looking microscope peeking out untouched by the building crumbling around it.

Xander reached for it, a large piece of concrete scraping his arm, and started trying to extract it, not for any reason other than he couldn't believe that it was still intact after everything. He wanted to examine it more closely. But then, he realized that there was a crater right in the middle of the building. He could see something peeking out of a hole driven deep into the earth that had definitely not been there before. If Colt had been inside the research center, then he wouldn't have survived.

As Xander walked the perimeter of where the building used to stand, he sensed some movement toward his left and turned, crouching and ready for whatever might come out at him.

A rabbit streaked across the rubble, completely crazed by everything that was happening, its white tail held high as it looked for cover. Xander took a deep breath and continued his walk around the building, alternating his gaze between the rubble and the rest of the world. He wasn't exactly hoping to find a body part sticking out of the building's remains, but he expected it. Even though there had been an alarm, someone could have missed it- a researcher tucked into a corner room with music turned up in his headphones.

Xander had reached the side of the building that hugged the road. Large cracks ran across the pavement in places, but other places were completely undamaged. Looking around, Xander didn't see anything in either direction.

As he looked left, toward the main area of Sisimiut, he remembered his mother. He wanted to start walking down that road, running maybe, and see if that area had been attacked. What would he do if a missile had been aimed right for his apartment building? There was no sort of efficient warning system or underground hiding place like they had here. At least not that he knew about. Was the plan for the researchers to save themselves and their families and let everyone else die?

Still, Xander stood on the road looking in that direction for a long time. Suddenly, a person appeared over the edge of the ground further down the road.

The person's appearance was so sudden that Xander froze for a second. Should he run forward or away?

In that split second, the person, a guy if Xander could judge from this distance, started running in the opposite direction. That made Xander's decision for him. He took off after the guy, putting all of his effort into catching up with him. He slowly closed the space.

Then, the guy looked back to check on Xander's progress. Xander definitely didn't recognize his face, though that didn't mean anything since he hardly knew anyone in this research village. Then, the guy tripped on a piece of broken pavement.

Xander winced as he watched the guy fall forward, his hands stopping the fall. However, as soon as he hit the ground, he rolled onto his back and got up, even though Xander could see blood dripping from his hands. Having lost that time, the guy must have realized that he wasn't going to be able to outrun Xander.

He turned around and faced him, hands balled into fists as the blood spilled down them, drip, drip, dripping onto the ground.

Xander stopped six or seven feet away, breathing heavily from the run. He took the guy in- his tattered clothing, his dark hair, and his wild eyes. "You're from Alaska?" Xander asked.

The guy glanced to his right. There was nothing for him to be looking at other than trees, but they were too sparse to hide someone else. Still, Xander took a step or two backward and kept his eyes on those trees, just in case someone was waiting for him.

The guy didn't respond, but Xander stayed busy scanning him in case he had a weapon. He would think he would have pulled it already by now, but he didn't want to do anything stupid that would get himself killed.

"You from Alaska?" Xander asked again when the guy didn't answer.

The guy glanced to his left, but there were only the cliffs over there. Xander realized that they were approximately in the area where he and Matt had landed. He remembered climbing out of the water and up those very rocks to stretch out in the sun, the glorious sun. He must just be looking for an escape.

Should Xander wrestle him into submission and take him back as a captive? For what? So Barrel could have someone to torture? No way.

"I'm not here for you," Xander said, but that didn't take away the wild look of the guy.

Xander took two cautious steps toward him, and the guy took one backwards. "Hey, I'm not helping the Greenlanders," he said.

There, something finally got through the guy's thick skull. He slowly unbunched his fists and took the chance to glance at the flayed skin on them, evaluating the damage. Xander winced when he saw a couple of strips of skin hanging off the guy's hand.

"Who are you?" the guy finally asked in a husky voice.

"I'm just..." Xander fumbled over what to say. Who was he really? He was supposed to have been an official for Greenland, but he had thrown that opportunity away. Now, he was here when he wasn't supposed to be. He decided only part of the truth would help him align with this guy, and for some reason, he wanted the guy on his side.

"I was eliminated," Xander said, "but I escaped."

The guy stared at him, open surprise on his face. "You- how have you been staying alive? Eating?"

Xander shrugged and looked around for an answer, still keeping a close eye on the guy but trying to look casual. "I've found some food, taken some. Somebody offered me some." He shrugged again like staying alive in a world that didn't want you was no big deal.

"I can't go home," the guy explained, clearing his throat. He then started coughing and hawked up an impressive-sized loogie. "The plane's been destroyed. I have no way to contact home, and they're hunting us down."

Xander noted that the guy had referred to Greenlanders as "they" not "you," so he had done the right thing not aligning himself with them.

"They shot my friend," the guy said, shaking his head and staring at the ground for a few minutes. "I'm going to die too."

Xander understood the feeling of despair. He tried to think of something to tell the guy, but he had nothing comforting to offer. They both just stood there, and Xander listened to the guy's raspy breathing. His curiosity got the better of him. Still not completely relaxed, he started asking questions.

"What's it like living in Alaska?" he asked.

The guy lifted one shoulder, then dropped it. "I don't know. Normal, I guess. Go to school, then train, then the Olympics. Now, just training, preparing for *this*."

"Don't they know that if somebody figures out a solution to heal the planet that it'll help everyone? Why would they destroy the research center?"

But Xander didn't get to hear an answer. Instead, someone yelped over by the rocks, and he immediately ran over. The guy also ran, and Xander kept his moving form in the corner of his eye, wary of the guy's potential motives.

The last thing he needed was a sneak attack from behind.

Xander peered over the edge of the cliff and saw someone lying at the bottom. He felt sick to his stomach as he scanned the body and realized that the person was still alive. Someone was bending over him, but Xander couldn't tell if the other person was hurting or helping.

"Hey!" Xander yelled, and the man kneeling whipped his head up to look at Xander. In that moment, Xander was able to see a few things. First of all, the man bending over the body had a gun. Secondly, the person lying on the ground was Colt. Xander could see his glasses smashed and several feet away from him. Third, Xander realized that the gun was up and pointed at him.

"Freeze!" the man shouted, his gun's aim steady on Xander before whipping around to face Xander's new acquaintance. "You too! If you move, I shoot!"

Xander took a deep breath, thoughts chasing themselves through his head as he tried to figure out the best course of action. Based on the guy's equipment, he looked like one of the officials, one of the real officials, not one who had been pulled into fighting because Barrel wanted more manpower. That meant his gun was probably equipped with real bullets.

"I'm a Greenlander!" Xander called out.

The guy next to him moved his head in Xander's direction, like he couldn't believe Xander had just called that out after their conversation.

Speaking quietly and trying not to move his lips, Xander said, "Say you are too."

The guy next to him didn't do anything as the one below continued to aim his gun steadily. "Prove it!" he shouted back.

"How?" Xander asked. Should he shout out the location of the underground hiding places? That didn't seem like the brightest idea.

Colt groaned and started to sit up, but the guy with the gun motioned for him to stay down. "I've got this," he said, loudly enough for Xander to hear him.

"Colt!" Xander called, hoping that his friend wasn't too hurt to identify him. "Tell him who I am!"

Colt groaned again and tried to sit up, this time succeeding. He dragged himself backward a couple of inches and looked up into the sky. Xander waved down at Colt, but that only made the guy next to Colt swing his gun around, so he stopped moving at all.

"Xander?" Colt said. His voice sounded weak, but it was clear enough.

Xander wanted to laugh. "See? He knows me!"

"That doesn't prove anything," the guy said, staring menacingly at Xander. "He could have just called you any name. I've never seen you before, so I don't know what you're doing here at the research center."

The menacing tone in the guy's voice made Xander start evaluating his escape options. How many steps backward would he have to take before the cliff would block him from view? And how long would it take that guy to climb the cliff and shoot Xander without any further questions?

"Uh, I know that Colt works in the office on the first floor, down the left hallway, at the end and in the corner."

The guy with the gun paused, then bent forward a little and kept his voice low as he said something to Colt. The two talked for a minute, and the guy finally started to lower his gun. "He says he knows you." The guy with the gun glanced at the guy next to Xander, then bent down and asked Colt something else.

Xander slowly lowered his hands from where he had been keeping them in plain sight. He glanced at the guy too.

"They're going to kill me," he muttered, and Xander heard the fear in his voice.

"No, they aren't," Xander said. "Colt's a good guy. He's hurt. Let's go help him. Once you've helped, they can't do anything."

"Shows what you know," the guy said.

"I'm coming down!" Xander called. "I'll help you get Colt up the cliff and to someone who can help!"

The guy with the gun seemed to approve of the plan, and he watched as Xander carefully turned his back and began to climb down. The whole climb, Xander wondered if the guy might just lift his gun and shoot him before he reached them.

When Xander reached the ground though, he didn't have any bullet holes in his back, which he counted a good thing. He craned his neck up and saw that his new friend was halfway down, taking the time to carefully pick his footholds.

"Xander," Colt moaned, and Xander immediately moved toward his friend, forgetting for a moment that the person next to Colt had recently been pointing a gun at him. He glanced at the guy as he reached Colt, but the guy was watching Xander's companion.

"What happened?" Xander asked as he evaluated Colt's situation.

"I fell," Colt said.

Xander whipped his head up to the top of the cliff then back down. "From up there?" He couldn't believe Colt was still alive.

"No, I was climbing down. The missile was coming, and they wouldn't open the door. I had to get away. And when I started climbing down, it hit and shook everything. I fell part of the way."

Colt reached toward his legs and started trying to roll up the pant leg on one of them. "I don't want to look, but I know I have to face the truth."

"Don't," Xander said, stopping Colt from exposing both of them to whatever was happening with his legs. Colt groaned and looked relieved as he shifted positions. "We have to figure out how to get you up there." Xander studied the cliff face again with a new goal in mind, before shaking his head and glancing down the strip of rocky coast to see if there were any easier places to get Colt up. He spotted one where part of the cliff face was more like a steep climb than a straight up and down wall.

"We can take him up there," Xander said pointing. "One of us at the top, two at his knees. Looks like his injury is in his lower leg."

"No," the guy with the gun said, and Xander whirled around to see the gun once again pointed in his direction. "We'll do this my way. You two will carry him, and I'll walk behind to make sure you don't try anything."

Xander sighed, but didn't start complaining. He just wanted to carefully get Colt back to the bunker where he hoped someone would be able to help him. If he was able to do that without getting shot, he would consider it a win.

"I'll take his legs," he said, still unsure about this new guy's loyalty. The guy glanced at him, then at the gun, then moved to lift Colt behind his head, curling his arms around Colt's shoulders.

"My glasses!" Colt called as Xander lifted him with a grunt.

"They're broken," Xander said, taking one stumbling footstep forward as he found his footing. Colt groaned as Xander started to move, so he shifted his position and focused on holding Colt's upper thighs rather than his lower legs. Colt immediately stopped making as many pained noises.

"Hold up," Xander said as they reached the section of the climb that had seemed the most promising. He studied it again, and Colt yelped behind him. "Set him down for a second," Xander commanded, and they both set Colt gently on the ground.

"I'm going to lose my leg!" Colt said. "They're going to amputate it!"

Xander tried to shut out Colt's pitiful cries as he studied the climb they needed to make. Colt wasn't a big guy, but they had to be careful with his leg. It seemed like it was his right leg that was bothering him the most.

"Alright," Xander said. "I'm ready. You go first with his upper body." They turned Colt around, and Xander's new acquaintance began making the climb with Colt in between them. Xander clearly felt the presence of the gun behind them. However, he didn't think the guy would shoot him if it would mean that he would drop Colt and injure him further.

The air was silent except for puffs of heavy breathing and groans from Colt.

As soon as they topped the ridge, the guy with the gun waved it around, scanning the area near them. "Set him down," Xander managed, carefully laying Colt's legs on the ground. He looked up at the sky and took a few deep breaths, trying to figure out if he should let his new acquaintance, clearly an Alaskan, in on the secret of the underground hiding spot or do something to get rid of him first and at least give him a chance to live here on his own.

When Xander glanced at him, the guy was looking right back. The wild look had returned, and Xander had the distinct feeling that he was going to bolt if Xander didn't give him something to do right away.

"I'm ready," Xander said. "Let's pick him up again. I'll lead this time." If the guy with the gun found out that this guy was an Alaskan, then Xander had a feeling there would be more than one body to lug back.

As they got closer to the research center and the entrance to the underground space, the haze in the air made Xander cough. He shuddered as he coughed and almost dropped Colt. He wasn't the only one though. The guy with the gun started coughing too, his gun waving wildly back and forth.

"Hey, be careful with that," Xander said. "I don't need my head shot off."

"Be careful what you say," the guy said, recovering. "I'm the one with the gun."

"Yeah, they gave me a gun too, but it was full of blanks. Hope yours isn't the same thing."

"Want to find out?" the guy asked, pointing it at Xander again.

"Just get me there!" Colt shouted out. Someone rushed toward them, also carrying a gun, and the attention was diverted from Xander temporarily, until the official recognized the other guy. Breathing a sigh of relief that they weren't about to die, Xander handed over his half of Colt to the new official. He rolled his shoulders in their sockets and massaged them gently as they approached the door in the ground.

He glanced at the Alaskan. This was his last chance to leave, but the guy just looked back at Xander, begging him for something, Xander couldn't quite tell what.

"Let's go inside," the official said, lifting the door and allowing Colt and his entourage to pass through first.

Chapter 15

Eden slowly approached the rooms on the third floor that had been des-ignated for the sacrifice. She couldn't think of it in any other terms.

Even though she wasn't offering herself up, she wanted to see who was. As she slowed her pace, she realized that a lot of people had had the same idea as she had The hallway was crowded, but people seemed to be pressing themselves up against the walls, leaving a clear pathway down the middle for anyone who wanted to, dared to, enter the rooms.

Eden swallowed and waited nervously, wondering how much time was left and if anyone would end up taking the pathway through everyone else.

But then, a girl with blonde hair trudged through the lines of people. Eden covered her mouth as she tried to imagine what must be going through the girl's mind, her thoughts and feelings. Gracen stood at the doorway of the room and pulled the girl into a hug, whispering something before allowing her to pass through. The door remained open, and Gracen looked out hope-fully over the rest of them.

Eden shrank back against the wall and continued to stare at the ground. Would the newly appointed leaders start grabbing people nearby?

When she heard the shuffling of feet, Eden looked up again and saw three people one after the other walking forward slowly. The girl held her head high, nodding to others as she passed by. The two guys had their hands shoved in their pockets and their heads down, like they didn't want anyone to know what they were doing.

Inappropriate thoughts started passing through her head. What were the leaders going to do with their clothes after they were dead? Would they be stripped off the bodies, washed, and passed around to give those still living more options? As Eden watched the back of the girl's purple T-shirt disappear into the room, she swore never to wear any of their clothes.

There was another moment of silence. Eden looked back down the hallway and saw a few more people marching down the path in the middle of the onlookers. A lot of them displayed the same look of disparagement, but a couple of them smiled broadly, like they were about to do something exciting.

Then, the person behind Eden who had been clinging to the wall broke out of line and grabbed someone. "No! You can't do it!" she shouted into the girl's ear. "You promised me you wouldn't!"

Eden looked away, trying not to stare, but she couldn't help hearing what was happening.

"I have to do it. It's the only way. If some people don't do it, then they will start choosing. I don't want you to be chosen."

"But you're my *best* friend," the other girl cried.

A couple of people brushed past them and entered the room. She had been keeping a running tally, and they were now up to eleven people in the room, plus one who was being waylaid while she tried to get there.

Twelve people wouldn't be enough to save the rest of the ship. It wouldn't change rations that much. Panic was already setting in when Eden heard more footsteps. A group of people passed by, determined to reach the room without making eye contact with anyone waiting in the hall. Eden counted under her breath, reaching twenty-seven before the group reached the door. Once the last person had entered, Gracen peeked in. Then, she stepped inside and closed the door. Was she sacrificing herself as well?

Jameson appeared. "Alright everyone. That's our third room full. We need just one more roomful. If all of you would consider what doing this would mean for the rest of us, see if you can find it in yourself to make the sacrifice."

Everyone remained silent, and Eden studied the floor once more as Jameson opened another door and shifted back and forth in front of the group. Maybe her calculations were off. Two rooms had already been filled before she had arrived. Maybe that had a chance after all.

There were a few long moments of uncomfortable silence. Then, someone stepped forward. Eden glanced up and recognized him as one of the medics that worked in the clinic with her. He had never spoken to Eden, because he had always been in charge of something, too busy doing to have conversations with the new girl.

Eden didn't know much about him at all other than his name- Arthur. Yet, she felt some sense of loss when he stepped forward and silently entered the fourth room. Gracen emerged from the third room and conferred quietly with Jameson. Jameson nodded a couple of times, then Gracen pushed her way down the thin passageway between the clumps of people and disappeared.

"We need more volunteers!" Jameson called out piteously, and Eden felt the desperation in his voice. For a second there, a part of her wanted to volunteer just to prevent something worse from happening. But she couldn't.

She thought about Xander's sacrifice. He had given up his life so she could have one. If she sacrificed herself now, then his sacrifice would have been for nothing.

A couple more people appeared at the end of the hallway and dutifully plodded down the hallway to the empty room, speaking with Jameson first.

Jayce appeared and walked slowly down the hallway, speaking with people on each side as he went. A couple of people detached themselves and followed him. When he reached Eden, she didn't want to make eye contact as he spoke to her and the people closest to her.

"We need a few more volunteers. Is there anyone else willing to help give the rest of the people on this space station a fighting chance?"

Eden swallowed, and all she could picture was Xander climbing into the tiny spaceship and setting off. What had he been thinking when he crashed into the asteroid? Had he cried? Screamed? Prayed?

She bit her bottom lip and closed her eyes, swallowing hard, then again, as she felt the tears pressing into the back of her eyelids and forming a ball in her throat.

"We only need about fifty more people. But if everyone says 'someone else will do it,' then no one else will. Think about it. Could *you* be one of those fifty? Could *you* bring everyone else that much closer to their chance at life?"

One of the people next to Eden started nodding, crying as she did so. "I'll do it. I don't need to be here any longer. At least this way, I can know I'm actually doing something with my life." She moved away from Eden as Jayce continued down the hall.

Finally, he had reached the end of the lines of people, and he had maybe twelve individuals behind him. Jameson slapped Jayce on the shoulder and led the others into the room, staying with them for a few moments.

Eden closed her eyes, her mind scrambling for an option that didn't require a sacrifice. But she knew that the food situation was serious. She had barely had five bites of mush that morning, and she knew it would get worse and worse. Soon, she was sure they would move to only two small meals a day. And dying of starvation would be worse than going quickly like this.

She thought about Xander again, unable to shake him from this moment as she wrestled with her indecision. Sure, he had given her a chance at life, but if he had made his own decision to sacrifice himself, couldn't she make that same decision?

Still, the space between her and where Jameson had just emerged stretched before her interminably. She wouldn't be able to walk from here to there with everyone staring at her. But then, the person just across the aisle from Eden broke free and started shuffling, then jogging down the aisle.

Her body moved forward. She took a step out into the aisle, her feet feeling like blocks of concrete as she struggled after the other person.

"Eden," a low voice said, and she stopped immediately in response to her name. She wanted it to be Xander, but she knew it wasn't. Still, she turned around.

Simon had appeared, and he stood there watching her, his face solemn. "You just got here. You can't volunteer."

Eden quickly agreed with him. What had she been thinking? But she felt everyone's eyes on her, begging her to go through with what she had started. "I...they need..." she tried, but she wasn't able to explain.

"They need people. *We* do, but..." Simon dropped his voice. "You just got here."

Eden wasn't sure what he was trying to say, but all she knew was that he was offering her an out. She swallowed hard and looked around at the people just at her elbows. Then, someone else moved forward, someone she hadn't seen before. She studied the girl as she hurried down the aisle, head down, and Eden slid back to the side, hoping no one would remember her moment of weakness, wanting to volunteer but accepting the first excuse when it came.

Simon slid in beside her and placed a hand on her opposite shoulder so that his arm was around her. She realized immediately how tall he really was. Then, he leaned down and whispered. "Good, I thought I was going to have to be all gallant and offer to sacrifice myself *with* you."

Eden laughed hoarsely. Simon didn't know about Xander and how he had given up his medal to be eliminated with her. Eden hadn't wanted to talk about Xander at all after he had left with Matt, and she hadn't met Simon until then. Something about Simon's comment which was intended to be funny made her stomach twist.

This time, she stepped out into the aisle and ran in the opposite direction, right to the bathrooms. She let the door slam closed behind her, and she leaned on the side of the sink. The bathroom was empty. No one wanted to miss the action of who was volunteering.

She took several deep breaths and gripped the edge of the counter until her knuckles turned white. Xander was gone. He was gone. She knew this, but it still hit her hard. Letting go of the egotistical worry that someone might come in and see her, Eden let the tears fall.

Silent tears poured down her cheeks as her nose started running too.

The door swung open behind her, and Eden swiped her snot and tears on her arm as she stared at the counter instead of the mirror.

"Ohmygod, are you okay?" the girl asked.

Eden glanced up for a second, but she didn't know the other girl. She wished Helena were there. Eden just shrugged and nodded in the direction of the rooms where the sacrifice was taking place.

The girl pursed her lips and nodded. "It's hard. I understand."

But she didn't, so Eden stopped meeting her eyes in the mirror and turned on the faucet, splashing cold water on her face before the automatic feature shut off the flow. She took a few deep breaths and used the bottom of her shirt to dry her face.

Then, she marched out of the bathroom, planning to go to her room and curl up in a ball until everything was over. She wondered how the space station would feel with so many fewer people, but her stomach secretly rejoiced at the thought of more food.

As soon as she stepped out of the bathroom, Simon detached himself from the wall next to it. "Are you okay?" he asked.

Eden swallowed again, the lump already rising at the sight of Simon.

"Just dealing with a lot," she managed.

"With everyone...um, volunteering?" Simon said.

Eden knew he was trying to phrase delicately what was happening. But there was nothing delicate about any of it- it was a sacrifice.

"Yeah." She thought for a second, but she wanted someone to know, and Simon had been kind to her. He seemed like he could listen. "You know the two guys who took the spaceship to smash the asteroid?"

"Uh huh."

"Well, Xander, he was one of them, and he and I were...close friends for a long time. It's hard because sometimes I miss him."

"Ooooh," Simon said, drawing out the word. "I get it now. Sorry."

Eden shrugged, because it wasn't like Simon had pushed her boyfriend to go. Xander had volunteered with Matt. He hadn't asked her about it first either. "It's just, yeah, not easy. I mean, I don't think I've missed my mom as much as I've missed him. Does that make me a terrible person?" She kind of laughed as she asked it, because at the thought of her mom, she wanted to cry again. But maybe if she tricked her body into laughing, then she could control herself.

"I get it," Simon said again. "And yes, it makes you terrible, but I think part of becoming an adult is not wanting to hang out with our parents all the time."

"We never became adults," Eden said. "We didn't win medals."

Simon shrugged. "Who cares about those? We're still here, and we're older than all those kids thinking about the upcoming Olympics next May."

Eden swallowed and thought about what he had said. "But the adulting kit that you win," she protested.

Simon shook his head. "My brother got his. He was one year older than me, and he showed me everything in it even though it's supposed to be a secret."

"What was in it?"

"There was a manual with information on basic processes like how to apply for an apartment, how to apply for a job and change jobs," Simon continued to think. "It talked about changing a tire on your car if you happen to have one and caring for a space and fixing some basic things around the apartment like the toilet, vents, things like that."

Eden wrinkled her nose. It all sounded incredibly boring.

"Then, there were some tools in there for basic repairs, some first aid kit type stuff, and a celebratory drink that my brother shared with me even though he wasn't supposed to."

"I thought it would be something...I don't know, more interesting."

Simon shrugged. "I guess what they're really saying is that being an adult isn't interesting. You have to work five days a week and take care of the place where you're living." He shrugged. "I would have gone on being a kid for a while except for my parents having a ridiculous curfew."

It had been so long since Eden had thought about regular problems like having to be home at a certain time that she laughed at what he said. "Yeah, the problems we used to think were problems..."

Simon reached over and squeezed her arm near her wrist for a second.

Eden didn't know what to say, then he pulled his hand back.

Soon, a bunch of people rushed toward them, and Eden pressed herself against the wall. She wanted to ask what was happening, but she remained quiet and just watched instead.

A few moments later, Jameson and Gracen came from the area as well. They hung their heads as some sort of pressurized door closed across the end of the hallway. It moved slowly, like it was giving those who had volunteered one last chance to leap out of the way.

Jameson glanced at his watch, and Brody appeared, squeezing through the crowd to talk quietly with the two of them for a minute. After they had conferred, Brody squeezed back through the crowd and disappeared.

Then, in complete silence, strange for a crowd so large, they waited. Eden held her hands clasped together and pressed under her chin, her stomach turning over and over as she imagined what everyone in there must be going through right now. Were they feeling any pain? Was it like they were drowning as they desperately searched for oxygen?

Eden held her breath and listened for sounds of distress, but she didn't hear anything. After a few moments, she continued breathing normally, trying to see Gracen's and Jameson's faces, but they were turned away, faces down.

"We should pray for them!" someone shouted.

No one said anything, so the person prayed in a loud voice, asking for a blessing to the selfless people who had sacrificed themselves and that they wouldn't feel any pain. Eden echoed a small "amen" when he finished, hoping it had done some good.

A beep sounded, but the large door remained unmoved. She counted the seconds in her head. When she had reached five minutes, the large door started to recede into the wall where it had been before.

Clenching her hands into fists now, Eden dared to peer up. Nothing was different.

As a couple of people started to surge forward, Jameson turned around and held up his hands. "Please keep a respectful distance. Remain behind this line, please."

Gracen moved forward, and Eden trained her eyes on her, wondering what would happen if it had worked and what would happen if it hadn't worked. Would someone start yelling for help?

Everyone watched as Gracen cracked open the first door. She stood in the doorway, not entering. It was too far to see her face clearly, but Eden thought she saw a shudder pass down Gracen's back.

Finally, Gracen took a deep breath and stepped backward. She opened the door to the other room, looking for less time, before checking the two rooms that had been filled before Eden arrived. "It's done," she said, Eden barely catching the words. Jameson nodded and moved forward too. A couple of people tried to follow him, but he turned around.

"Please, give them space. We will have to dispose of the bodies, and we don't want everyone else to have to see them. Please go on and...do whatever you would normally be doing right now."

A couple of people turned and headed back down the hallway, but Eden couldn't bring herself to move her feet. They felt heavy, and she wouldn't believe they were dead until she had actually seen them for herself.

Vince, the fourth and final leader, appeared suddenly and entered one of the rooms with Gracen while Jameson remained outside, partway down the hall as a sort of bodyguard.

"We should go," Simon whispered, and Eden looked up, realizing that about half of the crowd had left. "You know, to remember them how they were before, not how they are now."

Slowly, feeling like each step was a difficult task, Eden turned her back on the slaughter that had just taken place and retreated down the hallway. Let their new life on the space station begin!

Chapter 16

Xander resolved to keep his eye on his new Alaskan acquaintance since no one else knew that he wasn't supposed to be in there. He didn't want him stealing some guns or hurting anyone especially since Xander had protected him.

"Medical is over here," the guy with the gun directed as they walked silently down the long, dark hallway, Colt in between them.

Colt groaned when Xander shifted his weight. When they reached the door, Xander spoke, "Let's set him down for a second. I need to give my shoulders a rest."

They placed Colt carefully on the ground in a sitting position, and Xander rolled his arms back, the tips of his fingers brushing the roof of the tunnel.

Finally, the door was unlocked and open, light flooding into the tunnel. Xander and his Alaskan acquaintance lifted Colt again and followed the official's directions to the room with medical supplies. They set Colt on the table, and Xander saw that Colt was sweating all over, even though he hadn't been the one carrying someone.

"You feeling okay?" Xander asked.

Colt shook his head, his eyes remaining closed.

"You!" the official said, pointing at Xander. "Go get the medic!"

"I don't know where he is," Xander said, relieved that Colt would at least get real medical care, not like what they offered at the space station.

The official narrowed his eyes and studied them. Finally, he turned and went himself, but Xander thought he heard a lock sliding into place in the door. His Alaskan acquaintance confirmed it.

"We're locked in," he said, turning the handle fruitlessly.

"He'll be back," Xander said, his attention mainly focused on Colt. He needed Colt to get better. If Colt couldn't help him, then there was no way he would be able to get back to Eden.

"What if..." the other guy started to ask, but Xander leaned closer to Colt. He took off his own shirt and used it to wipe at the sweat on Colt's forehead, unsure what a sudden sweat meant. Did he have a fever or something else?

"Colt," Xander said, and Colt's eyes snapped open.

"I feel kind of sick," he said. He pushed himself into a sitting position, wincing. Xander stepped closer to hand Colt the shirt. He could wipe his face, but before he could hand it over, Colt leaned forward and vomited everywhere. Xander leaped out of the way, but it still splattered over his shoes and pants, technically Colt's shoes since he had actually given Xander the pair.

The other guy started making retching noises, and Xander wrinkled his nose at the acrid smell. "Uh, let me see if there's..." he muttered as he opened the heavy-duty cabinets in the room. He found a few bottles of water and cracked one open to hand it to Colt, then found an empty, reusable cup.

"I hope this is clean," Xander said as he handed it to Colt and Colt rinsed his mouth. Then, Xander looked around for something to at least cover the mess and contain the smell, but he couldn't find anything that would work. The only thing available was his shirt, which Colt had laid on the bed beside him. Xander didn't have a wardrobe of extra clothes waiting for him, so he was reluctant to give up his shirt that easily. Instead, he just looked away from the mess and pretended it wasn't there.

The guy from Alaska pounded on the locked door. "They have to let us out of here!" he complained, his shirt covering his nose and mouth. He looked more panicked than worried.

"He'll be back," Xander responded confidently, but he wondered how sure he should be of that. Maybe the other guy would conveniently forget to tell anyone where they were, and they would be forced to accept this tiny room as their coffin. But no, he would send someone for Colt. He seemed to care about what happened to him.

He had no way of keeping time, but Xander thought it must have been at least twenty minutes before anyone came. The door opened with a click as the lock slid back into the door, and a man with thick glasses entered.

"Colt!" he said, immediately sidestepping the pile of vomit and leaning over his patient like it was normal for him to find a room so mistreated. The door was left open, and Xander knew immediately that he had to act.

"We will be back in a few minutes," he said to both Colt and the doctor. Then, he stepped out before his Alaskan acquaintance could make the move first. Once they were out in the hallway, Xander glanced around to orient himself. He had been more focused on Colt than where they were going when they had entered.

"What are you going to do?" Xander asked in a low voice.

The other guy kept his eyes on the space around him instead of looking directly at Xander. "I don't know. I don't feel safe here. Someone is going to figure out who I am if I don't produce some sort of identification, and..."

Xander nodded. He didn't need it explained to him. This guy was playing dangerously.

"I can get you out of here," Xander said. "But then you're on your own."

Someone passed them at a jog, and Xander slid closer to the wall to give the person space. He looked at the other guy again, waiting for some sort of answer. The guy slowly nodded.

"Yeah, get me out of here. I feel like someone is going to figure out who I am any second."

Xander nodded his head in the direction he intended to take, then started walking with a purpose toward the exit. He hoped he wasn't doing anything that was going to make them vulnerable, but he had to think about this guy as well. He seemed like a good guy, the way he had silently helped carry Colt here even though he didn't know him.

They reached the front room without incident, and Xander headed toward the front door. He had slipped out of there earlier unnoticed. That was how he had come across Colt in the first place. But now, the handle wouldn't turn when he tried it. He gritted his teeth and tried again. Still nothing.

"Hey, what are you trying to do?" someone shouted across the room at him, hurrying toward them.

Xander scrambled to think of a plausible excuse that they would need to leave, especially since he would be coming right back. "Uh, Colt, the guy we just carried in here, I don't know if you were in here when we passed through," he was overexplaining to give himself a reason. "He accidentally left his glasses where he got hurt."

The guy shook his head. "You both going out there to grab a pair of glasses that are probably broken?"

"He's...won't shut up about it," Xander finished and shrugged. "I can't help him feel better, so I figured why not get his glasses if he'll calm down."

The guy turned to Xander's Alaskan acquaintance and peered at him more closely. "How come I've never seen either one of you before?" he asked.

Xander once more took the lead. "We were visiting Colt here when everything happened. We actually live in Sisimiut."

The guy looked back and forth. "Just one of you should go to get them," he said, reaching into his pocket for a key. He jiggled the key in the lock, and Xander's Alaskan acquaintance patted him on the shoulder, a silent thank you for getting him out of this prison.

"I'll walk you down the hallway," the official offered, and Xander stayed behind as the two disappeared into the darkness that led to the trapdoor. Xander had done everything he could. He hoped that this guy was truly a good one and that he hadn't just been fooling Xander.

With no other specific errands to run, he meandered back to Colt's room, wondering how long the doctor would take with him. However, before he reached the door, he heard a buzzing throughout the underground space. It must have been some sort of alarm as everyone burst into action around him.

A couple of people rushed past Xander, then a couple more. Colt could wait a few minutes. Xander needed to figure out what was happening, his first thought being that someone had figured out that the guy was from Alaska.

When Xander reached the front room, it was already packed with officials who were slithering into some pre-decided order. He stood at the edge of the room and watched, carefully picking up potential clues.

Barrel made a reappearance, apparently undamaged from his encounter with the Alaskans. Everyone saluted, and his eyes scanned them before nodding and allowing them to relax their stance.

"Alaska has made an attempt to attack us, and we won't allow that to stand. We've already been communicating with Russia, and they plan to back us up in our attack on Alaska."

Xander clenched his jaw. They didn't need another world war.

"We must act now, before Alaska has time to launch another attack and think that they can do whatever they want to us. I will hand out orders shortly for who will go and who will stay here and protect our home. Do not leave this area. If you are able to get communication through to your family, do not tell them what we are planning. Do you understand?" he barked the last sentence with more than a little venom.

Everyone chorused, "Yes, sir!"

"Unit 4, remain here. Everyone else is dismissed." There was a rush as people hurried back down the hallways. Xander pressed himself against the wall and let them pass, watching as Barrel met with some higher-up officials. They kept their conversation low, and Xander fidgeted, trying to decide if it was worth it to try talking to Barrel. He seemed more like an annoying commander than someone who would really listen.

Finally, Xander pushed himself off the wall as the leaders dispersed, talking about what they had just decided. Before Barrel could command Unit 4 to come forward, Xander marched toward him.

Barrel turned and made eye contact with Xander, his eyes fixed firmly on Xander's face. "Xander Coxon," he boomed, his voice sounding like he spoke at permanent megaphone volume.

Xander's head jerked back, surprised that someone had called him by his name.

"I looked you up. Why are you not one of my officials?"

"I was…" Xander stopped himself from using the "e" word. It appeared that despite the fact that he knew he was eliminated, the system still hadn't been fixed to reflect the change. "Thinking about it," he finished lamely. Hadn't he already told Barrel anyway?

"Stop thinking and do. You'll be part of Unit 4."

Xander shook his head, stopping Barrel before he could continue his booming instructions. "I'm not an official," he said.

"You are now. We need everyone who can fight, and from what I read, you can."

"No," Xander said, his heart speeding up as he realized that he was countering a powerful man. "I'm actually going back to the space station."

"Space station?" someone in Unit 4 echoed the words in wonder before Barrel shot him a scathing look.

"You're going where I tell you," Barrel barked. "You don't get to escape this place while we're fighting to keep it liveable." Without waiting for Xander to agree, he turned to the unit and started laying out instructions for how the attack was going to work. At least he seemed to have a better plan now than he had with the Alaskan plane landing. Xander stayed to hear the plan, but he wasn't going to get in any transportation taking him to Alaska. He was going back to the space station and Eden. He just had to figure out how. Now, talking with Colt was more important than ever.

Chapter 17

Eden sat in her room avoiding people as much as possible. Since Avery and Jazzy had been moved to a now-empty room, Nicole was often over there, and Eden mostly had this space to herself. It felt like an unexpected sanctuary after always being around someone before.

There was very little paper available in the space station, or if there was some, she wasn't privileged enough to know where. So, Eden had taken one of the books from the library and torn out the last page. It was blank on one side and had an author bio on the other. No one would miss this sheet of paper. Using a pen she had found in the medical center, she began writing a letter to Xander. She couldn't tell everyone else what was happening to her, and something about pretending he was going to know made her feel a little calmer.

Dear Xander,

Things here have been terrible, worse than terrible. Some days, I feel hopeless. Yesterday, a bunch of people sacrificed themselves to fix the crowding and food issue. No one screamed when they were dying, so I guess it didn't hurt that much. But it still felt wrong.

I wish you were here. I don't have anyone else to talk to that understands me like you do. I know that if you just wrapped your arms around me and let me cry, I would feel better. I did meet

Eden stopped writing and took a deep breath. It felt wrong to write about Simon to Xander, even though Xander would never actually read the letter. Still, she scribbled over the last three words. She wanted to keep her memories of Xander pure and untainted by Simon and whatever sort of friendship she might feel for him.

> *I'm glad I'm alive, but sometimes, I wonder if all of it was worth it. You sacrificed your medal for me, then you sacrificed your life. I've given up my family, and I don't have you. It's hard to feel happy.*
>
> *I miss you.*

Eden didn't sign her name at the bottom of the letter because the last three words made her choke up. She wasn't going to cry again; she couldn't let herself, so she pinched her skin and focused on the prick of pain.

The dinner bell was going to ring soon, and just the thought of it made her mouth start to water. So far, she hadn't noticed much of a difference in the food, except there were a couple more spoonfuls of mush each meal. Dinner, though, was supposed to be the meal with real food, something from the garden or some sort of grain, whatever they could create to make it look more edible.

Even before the bell rang to signal the meal, Eden folded up the letter and tucked it under the mattress that she no longer had to share with anyone. It wasn't the best hiding place, but she didn't think Nicole would start looking for Eden's secrets.

When Eden reached the dining hall, a few people were already gathered there, and the smell of dinner instantly made her mouth water. A savory smell that reminded Eden of cookouts back home had her looking around for the grill.

"What are they serving us?" she asked someone, but that person didn't know. A lot of excited chatter ran through the room as everyone lined up, eager to be the first to taste whatever they had been saving up for this night.

Finally, someone wearing a cloth wrapped around her head came out with a big platter. Another person with a similar cloth brought another large serving tray. They stayed and began scooping things out of the trays onto plates as people filed by.

Eden tried to see past the people in front of her, but they weren't making it easy as they all craned their necks to see past the people in front of *them.*

At last, Eden had moved toward the front of the line. The first person was serving rice, something Eden had had a couple of times already on the space station. The only seasoning they used was salt, and usually not very much of that, so it wasn't one of her favorite dishes. It did make her feel full, though. Eden nodded her thanks and slid down to the second tray where someone was pulling out a piece of steak about as big as her hand and plopping it onto her plate.

Eden stared at it for a moment, not believing that she was finally going to taste meat again. She closed her eyes and appreciated the smell, wanting to hug her plate to her chest.

"Move," the person behind her rudely commanded, and Eden remembered that there were others still waiting behind her in line. She opened her eyes and looked around for a spot. As she continued scanning faces, she realized that she was looking for Simon. She didn't see him. He wouldn't miss a meal, would he?

It didn't matter. If she didn't start eating in the next five and a half seconds, her stomach was going to eat itself. She settled in against a small portion of wall that was unoccupied, and glanced at the group of people sitting in a circle and eating on her left. They were all staring at their plates like they had been served octopus and whispering in low tones.

Eden frowned. Why weren't they diving into the meal? It wasn't like they had meat every day.

Suddenly, everything clicked into place, and Eden felt incredibly stupid. Cows hadn't just popped up on the space station overnight. The meat had to come from somewhere, and now, the insistence on having everyone die onboard suddenly made sense. Maybe it hadn't been about comfort after all.

Taking a shuddering breath of revulsion, Eden looked around to see what other people were doing. The group beside her had finally stopped whispering, and someone was putting the fork, loaded with a juicy bit of meat, up to his mouth.

Eden's mouth watered even as she told herself what kind of meat it was. Watching his reaction like she had just spotted an extinct polar bear, Eden waited as he sank his teeth into it. A quick glance around told her that she wasn't the only one watching.

She turned her eyes back to the guy as he chewed the meat, then swallowed. She could almost see it going down his throat. And then he...did nothing. He blinked a couple of times and looked around at his friends.

"It...isn't bad," he said. He took another bite, eagerly chewing and ignoring what everyone thought of him.

Eden stared down at the slab of meat on her plate. She had to eat it, right? Her stomach chorused a loud agreement, and she slowly cut a piece of the meat.

Suddenly, she heard her name and dropped the fork and knife like she had been touching one of the outlawed guns. A few people away from her was Helena, waving and smiling.

Eden motioned with her head for Helena to come on over. There was plenty of space close to her. As Helena weaved her way over, Eden scanned the room, realizing that there really was more space.

"Can you believe it?" Helena asked, holding up the plate. "They cut those people up and cooked them like beef."

Well, apparently Eden had been the only person who hadn't realized immediately what was on her plate. "Are you going to eat it?" Eden asked.

Helena grimaced down at her plate. "I have to."

"Why?"

Helena shook her head and didn't answer. She just sawed through the meat using her fork and hand. She picked up the chunk and scrutinized it for a moment before dropping it into her mouth. Eden watched as Helena chewed, then quickly looked back at her plate when Helena glanced up.

"Are you okay?" Helena asked.

"It just seems wrong. I mean, they agreed to die so we could have more food, but not like this."

"How do you know? Maybe the leaders told them something once they had volunteered. Either way, it's not like not eating it brings them back to life. Yeah, part of me knows it's wrong, but I have to survive somehow."

Gripping the side of her plate hard, Eden stared at the bite-sized piece she had cut off, almost expecting it to jump off the plate and protest her morals. Her stomach grumbled again, and Eden closed her eyes. If she didn't eat in the next five seconds, she might die, and it didn't feel like it was an exaggeration to say so.

Gingerly, Eden picked up the piece of meat and placed it in her mouth like she was carefully setting down a piece of dynamite. The flavor immediately soaked into her tongue, and she started chewing before she could really decide what to do. By the time she had finished the bite, her hands were already grabbing the slab of meat, not bothering with a knife or fork. She bit down, and the juiciness sank into her mouth, with only a tiny nudging of guilt in the back of her brain.

Helena said something, and Eden had to focus to acknowledge something other than the meat in her hands. The slab was already mostly gone, and for the first time in two weeks, she was starting to feel full instead of just not hungry.

"I asked how you think it tastes," Helena asked.

Eden looked down at the mostly-gone meat mournfully, and her compassion returned in full force. She was eating...another person. Suddenly, her stomach turned over, and she wanted to spit out everything she had just eaten. She dropped the piece that was left back on her plate and focused on eating the rice, hoping it would soothe her stomach. "It's fine," Eden said, finally answering Helena. But it wasn't. Nothing was fine. This was how far she had sunk.

Chapter 18

By the time Xander had been able to break away from the group and find Colt's room, Colt looked a lot better. He was sitting up, and his leg was in a boot. "The doctor said I just twisted my ankle. I don't need the boot, but it makes me feel more comfortable about letting it heal." Colt held up his arm and displayed a bandage. "He also addressed this wound."

"You fell down that cliff and just twisted your ankle?" Xander asked, closing the door to the room and leaning against the wall.

"I slipped on one of the lower rocks," he explained. "I was almost to the bottom when the vibrations caused me to misplace my foot."

Xander half-smiled at the idea of Colt not being able to find his foot, but he tamped down his amusement at the way Colt communicated. "Look," he said, taking a deep breath and trying to think how to phrase things so that Colt would agree to his new plan. "I don't know his name, but the guy in charge out there-"

"Sergeant Flynn," Colt supplied.

Xander blinked and tried to match the name to Barrel's large build and hairy face. "Yes, he said that they're going to attack Alaska and show their strength while keeping some officials back here to protect Greenland. The point is that I no longer have the option to go back to the space station."

Colt frowned, reaching for his glasses before realizing that they weren't there. His fingers closed around empty air, and he dropped his hands to his lap as he considered what Xander was trying to tell him.

"So, they want you to fight with them. *Then* you can go back to the space station? To enact your plan for rescuing the eliminated."

"Yes, all I need is you to give me access to a spaceship and..."

Colt's eyebrows shot up. "That would involve larceny, and such a crime could result in my own elimination. Before, you only petitioned my assistance to improve the vessel."

"What about the spaceship you said you toured? You know where it is, and we could steal it easily."

Colt's wrinkled forehead belied his worries. "I conceded only to make upgrades to the vessel, not to poach it."

Xander had known that talking Colt into breaking the law wouldn't be easy, but he had hoped it would be possible. He went back to his original technique. "I'll take the blame if anyone gets upset. I need to get to the people up in the space station and give them the chance to come back to Earth. Emily would be thrilled to see you, I'm sure." Xander knew no such thing. Emily hadn't even mentioned Colt in her time up there, but then again, they had only worked together in the kitchen a couple of times. Xander would pull on the heartstrings if it were necessary to get back to Eden.

Colt nodded, just the slightest movement of his head. Xander knew that they needed to get moving on the plan before he had to convince Colt yet *again*.

Colt gingerly hopped down to the floor- someone had cleaned it while Xander had been gone- and shuffled slowly to the doorway. He was walking like an eighty-year-old man, but Xander curbed the desire to push him faster. He needed Colt, and he had to take him just the way he was. A few seconds or minutes shouldn't make a difference.

Colt turned right once they were out in the hallway, and Xander shuffled along beside him. After passing only one other doorway, Colt stopped and fumbled with the handle of a door. He opened it to a completely dark room.

Once Colt had flicked on the light, which caused a gentle hum to run through the space, Xander could see that it was a lab of sorts, but the smallest lab he had ever seen. The room couldn't be bigger than a eight by eight space, and it was stuffed with machines so that there was barely room for Colt to squeeze through and sit down in front of the computer. Xander remained by the door, the only other space for him to stand.

"I don't know if this will be considered a waste of the generator's energy," Colt muttered. "Someone may confront us about the misuse of its power."

Xander didn't respond as Colt turned the computer on, his fingers flying across the keyboard only a few moments later. He leaned close to the screen and squinted, his nose only a few inches away from it.

After a while, he turned and stared directly at Xander, acknowledging his presence for the first time since they had entered the room. "I would like to assist you; however, with this adjustment to the plan, we have a thirty-eight percent chance of being stopped by the officials, and on top of that, I have no idea if we'll be able to find the materials we would need or if the spaceship has since been relocated. I couldn't even begin to calculate-"

Xander cut in, "Colt, either you want to help me or you want everyone in the space station to stay trapped up there forever. Is everyone going to like what we're doing? No, but I'll protect you as much as I can. I'll take the blame. All I need is...access to a spaceship and instructions on how to use it. It would need to be outfitted to re-enter the atmosphere," Xander added, remembering the dangerous move he had made by jumping out of the ship when he had arrived with Matt. He tried to make it sound simple even though he knew it would involve a lot.

"Will Matt be going with you?" Colt asked.

Xander took a deep breath and slowly let it out. "I don't know where he is right now, and I'm assuming communication between here and Sisimiut is not happening?"

Colt shook his head. "Most places there won't have generators for back-up energy."

"Okay, well, I guess it's just me then. I hope you can teach me how to steer a spaceship."

Colt looked unimpressed. "You set its course. You don't have a steering wheel."

"Yeah, I knew that," Xander responded, remembering the tiny coffin of a spaceship in which he and Matt had arrived. "I'm just saying. If the course isn't calculated correctly, I won't know how to change that."

"I'll calculate the course correctly," Colt said. He turned back to the computer and typed in a few more things before powering it off. The hum in the room grew quieter now that not as much energy was being used.

Colt stood, extending one thin finger in between his boot and his leg to scratch. "I suppose I'm going to officially be a miscreant now."

"What do we need to do first?" Xander asked, less interested in Colt's self-reflection and more interested in getting a move on before he was forcibly pushed onto a plane heading for Alaska.

"We need to find a spaceship."

"How hard will that be?"

Colt clenched his teeth and shook his head doubtfully. "I know where the one was they showed us on my tour, but I don't know if it's still there. If not, then we may have to build one from scratch."

Xander smiled at Colt's joke, but Colt remained serious. That was when Xander realized he had never heard Colt joke. This probably wasn't a joke either. They had better hope they could find a spaceship.

GETTING OUT OF THE bunker was proving to be a problem. The door was locked, and neither one of them was privileged enough to carry a key. After attempting to sweet talk someone into giving them one, Xander had decided that they needed to steal one.

"I'm not sure if I'm ready to commit this act of larceny," Colt said. "Perhaps we can find another way."

Xander threw his head back, his frustration leaking through him. Colt was intelligent, no one would doubt that, but sometimes, Xander wanted to shake him. "We've spent the last two hours looking for another way. There isn't one, and it's going to be dark soon." Xander hadn't actually seen a clock recently, but he had to assume that the day was almost over. He had been awake for a long time.

"Are you feeling frustrated with the situation?" Colt asked, reaching for his glasses, his fingers closing on empty air.

Xander wanted to shoot back that he was feeling frustrated with *Colt*, but he kept his mouth closed and searched for patience within himself. "How about you just wait here, and I'll take care of getting the key? Just be ready to move once I get it."

Colt frowned but finally gave his nod of approval.

With that, Xander scurried off to an official he had been eyeing earlier. The official seemed to be head of Unit 2, and he had to have a key to get out. Colt had explained the setup of the place, so Xander hurried to the area where the higher-ups bunked in their own tiny rooms. Xander knocked on the official's door and tried to get rid of the nervousness.

A few moments later, the door was answered by an official who only had on an undershirt and his official pants. His feet were bare. He had clearly been relaxing.

The official frowned at him, and Xander held out his hand. "Xander Coxon, medal in wrestling." It wouldn't matter if people knew who he was. Once he stole a spaceship and left Earth, everyone would know what he had done. Stealing a key was nothing in comparison to that.

The official nodded, still looking confused. After a moment, he took Xander's hand and shook it. "How can I help you?"

"I need to talk to you about something," Xander said, glancing behind the officer to indicate that he needed privacy.

The officer took a step or two back into his room, and Xander followed him inside, letting the door shut behind him on its own. "You're not in my unit, are you?" the officer asked, looking Xander up and down.

"No, I'm Unit 4."

"You should probably speak to Official Gerty then," this official told him.

"I just think you would have better advice," Xander said, his eyes scanning the room. A basic bed sat with a tiny chest of drawers beside it, like a prison cell almost, except the official could walk into the hall whenever he wanted. There, the keys were lying on the chest of drawers behind a bottle of water. The room was so bare that Xander was sure the official would notice if he took the whole set. Xander would have to somehow only take one, and it would have to be the right one. He counted five keys from where he was.

"About what?" the officer asked.

Xander took another step into the room, his back against the wall and the official's against his bed. The room didn't offer much space. "A situation has happened with one of the other officials," Xander said, spinning the story he had made up, "I don't want to say his name, just get some advice."

The higher up official held his chin in one hand and stared at Xander hard. "It was like this," Xander said, reaching forward and grabbing the keys in a rush. He detached two keys, noticing the make and model on the two as being the same as the lock on the front door was.

"He was here," Xander said, pretending that one of the keys was a person. The official's body had lurched when Xander touched the keys, but now, he remained poised and watched carefully. "He started talking about how he didn't care what anyone told him, he wasn't leaving Greenland soil."

The official frowned, his large eyebrows curving down and half covering his eyes. "Who was this?" he asked.

"I'll tell you when I finish explaining. I don't want his name to make you change your opinion," Xander said. Humans are naturally curious. Xander knew that, and he wanted to keep the official guessing. Did he know who the key represented? Would he be able to guess it with a few more clues?

"So, he was here talking about all of that. Then *another* official, not me- I was just watching all of this- told him that he would do whatever he was told to do."

The official listening nodded his head, like that was the answer he had expected.

"So the first official," Xander wiggled the key, "started telling him that anyone who left for Alaska was going to die. They'd better say goodbye to their family right away, and he wished them luck. He was standing here. I guess that made the other guy mad, because he came over," Xander moved the key in a hopping motion.

"Then, out of nowhere, he grabbed the first guy's shoulders." Xander pushed the keys together so that they looked like one key. "And started shaking him telling him that he should respect authority and do as he was told. I thought he was going to punch him, but he didn't. So, I stepped in and said we should all cool down, and we would see what Sergeant Flynn decided."

Xander shrugged his shoulders to indicate that was the end of the story.

He made a big show of slipping the key back onto the ring and setting it on the side table with a clatter, pocketing the other one. The official crossed his arms, the confusion clear on his face. "What do you want me to do about this?"

Now that Xander had a key, he was eager to leave. "I wanted to know if I did the right thing, or if I should report the man who was complaining to his head official."

The official in front of Xander still looked a little confused. He finally shrugged. "If you can't make decisions like this on your own, I worry about the type of decisions you'll be able to make in the heat of conflict. Figure it out yourselves, and don't bother us unless something serious happens."

Xander nodded and took two steps backward so that he was at the door. "Yeah, okay, I'll remember that." He whipped the door open and hurried down the hall, not running but not quite walking either. He kept his hand in his pocket so that the key wouldn't fall out. When he reached the front door, Colt was sitting close to it, examining his boot.

"I can't walk quickly," he said as soon as he saw Xander. "I need to take care with my ankle."

"Let's get out of here, then we can worry about the speed we move at," Xander told him. But when he scanned the room, there were too many people. No one was guarding the door per se, but there was no way they would be able to sneak unnoticed out of the door. He leaned down next to Colt. "Is there any time when this place would be completely empty?"

Colt shrugged. "How would I know? You've been down here longer than I have."

"You go rest," Xander commanded as Colt started to chatter about the probability of something. "I'll find you when we have a chance to get out."

"I've been assigned to room 32A," he said. Xander nodded and watched as Colt hobbled out of the large room. Xander slumped down to the wall and watched as a few of the higher up officials conferred quietly in the opposite corner. His stomach grumbled loudly, and someone looked over at him.

"You know where the food is, right?" he asked after the loud grumble.

Xander's eyes lit up, and he shook his head. It had probably been almost twenty-four hours since he had eaten, and he had long ago lost track of the basket of food that he had saved from Colt's apartment.

The official pointed down one of the hallways, and Xander hurried away. He hadn't wanted to stick out by asking before, but now, he couldn't seem to move fast enough. He peered into a couple of spaces that had their doors open before he found the right place. All of the food was freeze-dried or canned, but Xander didn't care. An official stood in the corner of the space. "One can or bag," he said. "What's your name and number?"

Xander's hand stopped a few inches away from a can of peaches. "Xander Coxon. I don't have a number," he said. "I was visiting a friend when everything happened. I'm not an official."

"Then you shouldn't be in here. Everyone not fighting is supposed to go to the other bunker."

"I was pulled in to help," Xander explained. The guy frowned and reached for a radio on his hip. Xander rolled his eyes. "Ask Sergeant Flynn," he said. "He's the one who picked me and brought me here. I'm hungry, and I'm not going to wait another five seconds." With that, he popped the top on the can and fished inside for a peach slice.

The official wrote something on a screen, glowering at Xander. "Spell your name," he commanded like he was barely holding back his anger.

Xander spelled it out for him, then took the can of peaches down the hall, forcing himself to go slowly to make them last. What a way to feed the people protecting their country! Canned fruits and veggies!

As Xander walked back to the large room where the exit door was located, he found a clock that told him it was eight at night. It would be impossible for everyone to go to sleep at the same time, but he hoped that the room would at least empty out some. Fewer potential witnesses meant that even if someone saw him going out with Colt, he would have a chance of convincing that person that he and Colt were on an official mission.

The opportunity came two hours later.

Xander retrieved Colt, finding and waking him with no problem. He whispered the plan to Colt as they trooped back down the hallway. Colt reached up for his glasses and once again found them gone, rubbing his fingers on his shirt instead.

"I'm not sure if I'll be able to intentionally deceive anyone," he admitted.

"I'll do all the deceiving. You just nod your head to anything I say."

When they reached the front room, Xander was shocked to find it completely empty. No deception would be necessary.

He grabbed Colt's arm and pulled him at an even faster pace over to the front door, jerking the key from his pocket and fitting it into the lock. It slid in easily, but then it wouldn't turn.

Xander jiggled the key and tried turning it gently. Then, he took it out and slid it in again, wondering if he had pushed it in too far.

"Hurry up," Colt muttered, glancing around.

Xander gripped the key so tightly that it began cutting into his skin, but no matter how he tried to move it inside the keyhole, he couldn't get the door to unlock. With picture perfect clarity, Xander saw the other key with the same name brand that he had handled in the official's room. He had thought, wrongly obviously, that they had been two copies of the same key. But no, this was not the right key.

Shaking his head, Xander shoved the key at Colt. "It's not the right one," he said.

Colt examined the key, then slid it into the hole. A tiny sliver of hope rose up in Xander that maybe this genius could figure out how to unlock the door even if the key wasn't right, but Colt just shook his head, turning as a couple of officials came into the room.

"You're right," he said. "It doesn't fit."

Xander nodded and reached behind his back to extract the key from the knob without turning to look at it. One of the officials turned and looked directly at them. "What are you two doing in here?" Xander froze in his mission to jiggle the key back out of the lock and took a step forward.

"Just talking to my friend here about our orders to head to Alaska."

The official frowned, looked back and forth between the two of them, then turned back to his own conversation. Xander jerked the useless key out of the hole and motioned for Colt to follow him. Now, he had exposed himself by stealing a key from one of the officials, and they still hadn't gotten away.

Colt muttered to himself as they headed back down the hallway. "I have thought of an alternate way," Colt finally said. "But I can't be sure it will work until I've had a chance to look at the computers."

Wishing Colt had thought of this option *before* Xander had stolen a key, Xander followed Colt back down the hallway to the lab. Tiredness crept in at the edges of his mind, reminding him that running himself into the ground would do nothing for his brainpower.

Chapter 19

Even though her stomach continued to spin, twist, and knot itself, Eden had to be responsible and report for her medical shift the next morning. Helena was there as well, a brilliant smile on her face when she greeted Eden.

"Good morning!" she said brightly.

Eden nodded and swallowed, feeling like the meat was crawling up on little fingers, back up her throat. She swallowed again, hoping this one would shake the feeling.

"Today, we are back on track with the vasectomies," Helena informed Eden. "We should have two guys coming in twenty minutes or so."

Eden glanced around. "Where are the others?" She wanted to add "the real doctors," but she didn't because technically none of them had had the training that doctors back on Earth received before practicing on patients.

Helena frowned and glanced at the clock. "They should be here already. Henry is usually reliable. I'll go check on them," Helena muttered something else that Eden didn't quite hear, but she was already pulling her smock over her long braids and pushing out the door.

Eden remained in the medical center alone as the clock ticked to the official beginning of their shift. Nothing was out of order that she could busy herself rearranging, so she paced back and forth.

No more than five minutes later, the door to the medical center swung open, and Eden's head snapped up as she anticipated Helena's return. It wasn't Helena. It was Simon.

"Good morning," he said, smiling just as brightly as Helena had.

"Oh, hey," Eden replied.

Simon looked around. "Looks like your job as a medic isn't as exciting as the medical competition was."

Eden smiled a little when she thought back to how they had met. "Actually, during my shifts, I don't usually have a lot to do." Eden thought back to the time when someone had rushed in and told her that a girl needed help. That girl had ended up being dead, not much Eden could do to remedy that.

"Ah, so you get an easy job," Simon said. He frowned. "Who else is supposed to be in here? Shouldn't just be you unless you're so brilliant that you don't need any help."

Eden ignored his attempt at a compliment and answered his question. "Helena is in here, and some other people too, but I don't know their names."

"I guess I'll just have to stay here and keep you company so your shift doesn't get too boring," Simon said, settling comfortably onto the middle of one of the stark hospital beds.

Eden ducked her head as she realized that Simon was flirting with her. "I wouldn't mind that," she said, the words escaping softly.

Simon grinned back at her, and there was a moment of acknowledgment between the two of them. Eden couldn't put words on what it was or what it meant, but when Simon started speaking again, Eden realized that the sick feeling in her stomach had disappeared.

"Did you want to be a doctor back on Earth?" Simon asked with serious interest.

"No," Eden answered automatically. "I honestly didn't even like science class that much. But when I started seriously focusing on the Olympics…" she paused at the word, her mind flashing back to all the stress and competitions she had gone through.

"When you started focusing," Simon repeated slowly, trying to get her back on track.

Eden nodded. "I guess I realized it was my only chance even though I didn't want to go into any of the fields that require a science medal."

Simon's gaze was intense, and Eden felt like she couldn't make eye contact. She stared at the floor, Xander popping up in her mind. Instead of reveling in his memory as she normally did, she pushed it away. He was gone. She needed to move on with her life, and Simon…he seemed like a good guy.

"So, forget about the medals for a second," Simon said, "what would you have done with your life if the world was like it was before where you could learn anything you want and get any job you want?"

Eden took a deep breath and thought about his question, really thought about it. When she glanced up at him again, he was looking at her with that intense look again. Maybe if she were sitting beside him, it would be easier to avoid his gaze. She took one long step to the bed and turned, pulling herself up on it and plopping down on the crackly cushion with a soft plunk.

"I wanted to be a dancer," she admitted. No one else knew that. Xander had, of course, and her parents had probably suspected. But for the most part, she had kept her secret desires to herself.

"A dancer," Simon repeated.

"Yeah," Eden felt obligated to explain. "Like, how they used to have theaters and dancers would perform in live shows. Or maybe own a dance studio and teach little girls how to dance." She shrugged. "I don't know. I didn't think about that a lot, because I knew it wouldn't happen."

"Can I see something?"

Eden frowned. "What do you mean?"

Simon shrugged, and Eden felt the movement next to her more than saw it. "Your dancing."

Eden shook her head, her short, brown hair hitting her chin. "No way. I don't dance in front of just anybody."

"Ah, so I'm an 'anybody' now," Simon said. "I thought I might be at least a friend."

Eden glanced at him out of the corner of her eyes, feeling a warm excitement at this new friendship or whatever it might be. "No, it's just...I don't know. It's like the dances that I've created are really personal. They all mean something special to me. Besides, I don't even have music."

Suddenly, Simon was on his feet beside the bed. He stuck his arms into the air at crazy angles and gazed off into the corner of a room, like he was trying to imitate a tree. Then, he started doing a crazy dance, wiggling his hips, shaking his arms, and tapping his feet.

Eden laughed as Simon moved like he was being electrocuted. She couldn't help it. By the time he finished, he was laughing too. He walked back over to the bed and stood in front of Eden as they tried to recover. As soon as their eyes met, they started laughing again, and Eden clutched at her stomach. The muscles were starting to burn from laughing.

"Okay," she gasped, "Okay, we have to stop. Don't. Just don't."

Simon had thrown his hands up in the air like he might be off again, but he just grinned at her. "So, now that you've seen my specially-created dance, can I see yours?" he asked, dropping his arms back down by his sides.

Eden took a deep breath, then shook her head. "Maybe I'll create a piece that doesn't need music, but the ones I've created, they've all been for someone specific, my parents or..." She didn't say Xander's name, but the feeling of him being close by hung in the air.

"Okay," Simon finally accepted her answer. "You let me know when you're ready." He still stood in front of her, and his voice gently wrapped itself around her, letting her know that he could be a safe space if she gave him the chance.

Looking up at him, their eyes caught, and this time, she didn't dissolve into rounds of giggles. She just stared back at him, wishing she could tell him everything, wishing he would accept her for who she was, despite how different she might be from the person she presented herself as.

Then, she wasn't quite sure how it happened, but he kissed her. He bent over her, his hands on either side of her legs, pressed against her hips and on the crinkly hospital bed as he pressed his warm, mush-smelling lips to hers.

A squeak made them both pull back, and Eden turned to the doorway to see an unfamiliar guy stepping through. He glanced at them and seemed to figure out what they had been doing, but looked more confused than anything else.

"I'm supposed to be having a surgery?" he asked. "Where are the doctors?"

Eden pushed Simon's arm out of the way and leaped to her feet, smoothing her scrubs down. "I can get you ready," she said. "The doctor just stepped out for a second."

The guy didn't seem convinced, but Eden pointed to the other bed and asked him to sit down. When she glanced back at Simon, he was grinning at her, and she seemed to glow. Maybe he didn't know everything about her yet, but there was time for that. Their kiss seemed to seal the fact that they would have a chance, lots of chances to get to know each other better.

Chapter 20

"Yes," Colt confirmed, his nose only a couple of inches from the screen. He sat back and gazed at Xander.

"You can do everything from the computer," Xander summarized. "You don't even have to leave this space."

Colt nodded, his head moving up and down at two times the speed of a normal nod. It probably didn't help that Colt had been drinking coffee like he had just found water in the middle of the Sahara Desert. "I'll buzz you out, give you two hours to get there, then set it off."

"But what if I don't get there in time?" Xander asked.

"Three?" Colt asked.

Xander stared at the piece of paper that was acting like a map. Colt had drawn a rough estimate (though he had still used a ruler) of how to get to the spot where the spaceship was hiding. He wasn't actually sure it was there, but Xander was sure they would find out once Colt remotely set it off. Luckily, he had been smart enough to hack past the firewalls and access information he wasn't supposed to have.

"I wish I could give you some sort of signal," Xander muttered, "to let you know I'm there."

Colt shook his head. He started to reach for his glasses but then remembered they weren't there, his hand hanging in the air. "You have my timepiece. I'll give you three, but I can't be in here any longer than that or someone will start to wonder what I've done. If they weren't so preoccupied with Alaska, I would be more worried about them detecting I'm in here sooner."

"Okay, then," Xander said, standing up. He reached out for Colt's hand, and they shook. "Thank you for everything. And I'm going to bring Emily back down here."

Colt licked his lips, one of his eyebrows twitching. "I'm not sure how they will be received. What will we do if..."

"What are they going to do? Waste another spaceship sending us back? We'll take care of it. We'll be fine."

Colt didn't seem so sure, but Xander had to believe in what he was saying. The other alternative was that they would be shot on sight, either because someone thought they were from Alaska or because they had to prove a point.

"I hope I see you again soon," Xander told Colt. Then, he turned and marched down the hallway to the main room at the front.

Once there, he checked his watch and realized he had exactly four minutes until Colt would unlock the door. It was nearly six in the morning. The two had only taken a short rest between their efforts the night before and their current effort to escape. Glad that he wouldn't have to tug along a limping Colt, Xander positioned himself one long step away from the doorway.

Then, he bent down and fidgeted with his shoe, while he took another glance at his watch. It was surprisingly difficult to look busy with his shoe for a full minute. But then, he heard a low buzz, stood up, and pulled the door open, disappearing through it more quickly than he had thought possible.

As the door clicked into place behind him, Xander turned his head back and forth, trying to see through the complete darkness. It literally felt like he was swimming through black water.

Stretching out his right hand, he found the wall and began walking along the passageway, hoping for some sort of indication that the end of it was near.

His fingers brushed into the corner a moment before his toe found it, and Xander pulled back exaggeratedly, bracing himself for an impact that didn't come.

He reached up, found the lock, and turned it, squinting at the faint sunlight that was starting to light up the world. Suddenly, he heard footsteps behind him. It sounded like multiple people.

Xander grabbed the edges of the doorway to the outside world and pulled himself out, letting it shut behind him. It clanged down louder than he had intended, and he gave himself only the quickest of scans to see if there was any potential danger. However, he had listened in to a couple of conversations the night before, and he knew that all of the officials out looking for Alaskans had been pulled in to prepare for their new mission.

Wondering where Matt was and if he were safe, Xander set off at a run across the open space, hoping to get to the rubble that used to be the research center before anyone else emerged from the passageway. Once he slid behind a number of concrete stones that still stood in a fairly unbroken wall, Xander took the opportunity to breathe and check his watch. Only seven minutes had passed since Colt had buzzed open the door. It had felt much longer.

Just when Xander was about to push off the wall and find a steady pace to reach the spaceship's potential hiding spot, he heard voices behind him. He squatted down and listened.

An official's voice shouted something, but Xander couldn't quite understand it. The matching, measured steps told him that a unit of officials were heading somewhere, and if Xander had to bet, it would be to take off on their mission to teach Alaska a lesson.

Xander dared a peek out from his hiding spot and saw them headed east of where he had been planning to go. Indecision gripped him. Wouldn't the airplanes be stored in the same place as the spaceships? Should he just follow them? What if the spaceships had been destroyed?

But no, Colt had explained their location and assured him that they were far enough away to be safe from the recent attack.

Xander watched the officials hurry onward, heading toward a wall of stone that seemed impenetrable. Xander took a deep breath and pushed it out again slowly. No, he would trust Colt. Colt had never been wrong, and if the spaceships and elimination were both such well kept secrets, then they probably weren't stored with the airplanes.

Once Xander felt confident that none of the retreating officials would be able to see him, he darted out from his hiding spot and hurried in a northwestern direction. He couldn't go too far west or he would end up in the ocean, but Colt suspected that the entrance was along the lonely, dirt road that hugged the coast. Xander followed Colt's advice and kept close to the rocky outcroppings in case someone happened to be driving along the road.

After moving along at a brisk jog for a while, Xander checked his watch. Nearly an hour had passed. Colt had estimated it was three miles away, so

Xander should have passed it now. He hadn't spotted any of the landmarks Colt had mentioned, though.

Discouraged, Xander scanned the patch of road he had just come from, only seeing groups of gray rocks as the waves broke on them. The distance between the road and the ocean had lessened, so that he was maybe only six feet above the rocks where the water was hitting. Should he climb down on the rocks and try to see if he had missed something along the cliff face?

Xander watched the water coat the rocks and saw a green film on their sides. They would be slippery. Trying to walk on those rocks would be like signing his own death certificate.

"Go on or go back and look more closely?" Xander muttered. He had wasted ten minutes standing there, and he had just decided to go on when the water receded back, the undercurrent sucking it out from between the rocks, and Xander spotted something green along one of the rocks, a lighter green than the algae. It looked out of place, and he decided to take the risk and climb down.

Gripping the side of the road tightly, Xander lowered his body to the sharp rocks and found a foothold just as the ocean threw itself against him, soaking him from the knees down with cold spray. He winced but continued to climb sideways, closer to the green mark.

When he was a foot away, he confirmed that the mark was manmade. However, as he looked around trying to figure out what it indicated, he didn't see anything out of place. The ocean continued to soak him, and his foot slipped, squeaking along the side of the rock as he grabbed something high and dry again.

Breathing out slowly, Xander pulled himself back onto the road. The bottom of his pants were soaked through. Not ideal, but he didn't care about them so much as the fact that the time was slipping away. He now had just over an hour.

Turning his attention away from the lower rocks, Xander craned his neck up to see the larger rocks above him. Just as he did so, a loud roaring sound shook the air. Xander ducked before realizing it was an airplane. He watched as it flew off toward the west, toward Alaska.

Had anyone seen him? Not that it mattered at this point.

Then, Xander spotted an opening in the rocks above. He wondered if it were real or if he were imagining it out of desperation. His eyes trailed back down the rocks from the hole to the ground, and he didn't see a clear path. After checking his watch one more time, Xander darted across the road and grabbed a promising-looking rock to pull himself up.

Once on top of it, he shook his head as he looked at the options for another handhold. This cliff was not meant to be climbed, which meant that the hole he had spotted was probably nothing. Should he turn back or keep on this path? If he were going to make it to the hole in time, he would have to really focus on climbing. He couldn't turn back, waste more time searching, then come up here and still make it to the hole.

Xander craned his neck back, but he couldn't see the hole from here. He closed his eyes and tried to calm his thoughts, so he could make the best decision. Finally, he shook his head. He was where Colt had told him he thought the spaceship would be hiding. He just wasn't seeing the opening by the base of the road that Colt had described. He would climb, and keep climbing.

Now that the decision had been firmly made, Xander repeated the process of finding a rock and pulling himself up, over and over again, without pausing to check his progress. He knew he wasn't going to have much time when he reached the hole. Then, suddenly, it was in front of him.

He had pulled himself up on the edge of the hole, and now, he gripped the sides tightly as he leaned in and tried to see inside. Near where his hands held on for balance, he saw that the rock had been cut, chipped away at, and he didn't think it had been done by any animal.

As he peered into the depths of the hole, he saw a tiny pinprick of light close to the bottom. It looked manmade, but he couldn't be sure. His mind scrambled, trying to think of potential explanations that would clarify what the light was and why it was at the bottom of a deep, black hole.

As Xander leaned out into the blackness, his stomach swerving at his boldness, he saw another light, exactly like the first. Suddenly, he was sure that he was in the right place. Those lights had to be manmade, but how was he supposed to reach any sort of rocket from here? He and Eden had been drugged when they were put in the space ship. How would someone have been able to feasibly carry them up here and shove them into a ship?

The answer was that it wasn't possible. There had to be another opening, but-

Xander's thoughts stopped as he watched the whole cavern suddenly light up. Tiny bulbs along the walls flooded the space with light, and Xander's grip tightened as he realized exactly how high up he was, teetering on the edge. Well, he had definitely arrived in the right spot. There, below him and pointed upward was a spaceship, something much bigger than what he and Matt had used to come back to Earth. This had to be a replica of the one that had taken him to the space station in the first place.

His question was...how would he be able to get there from here? A distance of probably twenty feet stretched between where he was standing and the spaceship. No amount of long distance jumping would take him there now.

Then, Xander saw that a ladder ran up the inside of the rock wall directly to where he was standing. The spaceship seemed to come to life, and the rocks around it rumbled and started to move. Xander spent only a moment looking around in awe before he realized what it meant.

The spaceship was going to take off soon.

Swinging his body around more quickly than was safe, Xander found the first couple of ladder rungs with his feet and scrambled down, his hands slipping on a few of the rungs and causing his heart to leap into his throat.

Finally, he reached the ground and studied the sky above him. The rocks had now shuddered aside enough that there was an opening, like the top of a volcano. The spaceship made an angry sound, and Xander knew the engines were getting ready.

"Go, go, go," he urged himself, darting across the open floor to a thin ladder that led up to the side of the spaceship. His ankle turned as he climbed, but he forced himself to put pressure on it again and again until he reached the door. He fumbled with the handle for a moment, relieved when he discovered it had the same turn and jerk mechanism that the tiny spaceship had had.

Once inside, Xander slammed the door after himself and looked around the small hall. He needed to find a control room. The whole machine rumbled underneath him, and as Xander took one step inside before reaching a rectangular hole in the floor that seemed to stretch forward, he realized that the spaceship was turned sideways. He would need-

Just then, a crackly announcement sounded over the speakers. "I have achieved our goal! The ship won't self-destruct!"

Xander barely had time to process Colt's scratchy speaker voice before the spaceship's sounds burst from a low rumble to a roar. Xander fell back onto the floor as gravity smashed into his chest, making it hard to breathe. He was *not* prepared for this journey by himself.

Chapter 21

Eden giggled as Nicole sat across from her, her legs curled up under her on the mattress she had pulled off the top bunk and spread across the floor. It felt like a long time since she had giggled like this what with starving, competing in two sets of Olympics, and losing Xander.

But now, she couldn't stop smiling.

"No way!" Nicole said, eyes widening as she shook her head. "*Simon?*"

Eden shrugged and giggled again. "Look, I still don't know a whole lot about him, but I like him from what I do know, and... he's fun."

"I always thought he would go for someone, I don't know, less serious," Nicole said.

"I'm not *that* serious," Eden said. "I mean, considering everything that's happened in the last few weeks."

"True," Nicole nodded. "It's not normally... this crazy here. Honestly, sometimes it's kind of boring. But anyway, tell me how you know he likes you. Did he say something?"

Eden thought back on their kiss, the one that had been interrupted. It had only been a day ago, but she already felt like the details around the edges were fading. She didn't want to forget any of them, so even though she didn't say *everything* out loud to Nicole, she smiled as she remembered the smell of his freshly-washed hair and the smoothness of his cheek under her fingers.

"Well, we kissed and stuff, so yeah, but before that, he just kept wanting to talk to me. And yeah, he's different from..." she skipped saying his name, "well, before, but I like it. He's...nice."

"Oh, come on, nice? That's the best you can do?"

Eden could think of other adjectives to describe Simon, but she hadn't been the one to start this conversation. Nicole must have suspected something, because she had asked, and it had sort of come spilling out.

"I don't know if I want to talk about him yet," Eden said, wiggling a little further away so that her back was against the wall.

"Well, I want to hear about him. Come on! Just tell me at least if he's a good kisser."

Eden looked up at the bunk bed above her trying to hide her smile, but Nicole saw it anyway.

"He *is*! Oh my god, you don't even have to say anything. I already know it. You know, he was dating Georgia last year- do you know her?" Nicole barely paused to give Eden a chance to tell her that she didn't want to know Simon's dating history.

"But she was so *boring*. He was always joking around, and she would just give him this look like he was a child. She was *way* too serious for him, but too boring to interest anyone else. I think he finally broke it off. I don't know. You should ask."

Eden was definitely not planning on asking that. She lay back against the mattress. "I think I'm going to rest now. We had a *lot* of injuries on my shift this morning," she said, thinking back over the array of smashed thumbs, cuts, and a potential concussion.

"Fine, fine," Nicole stood up and stretched, easily lifting her thin mattress back onto the top bunk bed. "But I'll be back in a while, and I want to hear the details eventually."

"Eventually" sounded like a long way off, so Eden nodded her head. Nicole shut the light off as she left, and Eden lay in the darkness for a few moments, trying to get her thoughts to slow down. Her brain danced a picture of Simon in front of her, and she thought about what she knew about him. She didn't know much about his life before. Most of the time they had spent together included the here and now. She would have to change that if she wanted-

Knock, knock.

Eden sat up on her elbows, wondering who was knocking at her door. Nicole usually just flounced in. Maybe it was Avery or Jazzy looking for Nicole.

"Come in," Eden called, just loud enough for whoever it was to hear. The door squeaked open, and Eden turned her head to see that the head poking through the door was Simon.

"Oh, hi!" Eden said, sitting up immediately and running a hand through her hair.

"I just got off my shift," Simon said. "Thought I would come see what you're doing."

"Oh, just resting," Eden said. "Come in."

Simon moved to shut the door behind himself, and Eden realized that in preparation for her nap, the light had been off. "Can you hit the switch?" she asked. She didn't want them to both sit in the dark, though the idea of that sent a strange kind of thrill through her.

Simon smashed the switch on the wall, and the bulb flared to life, though it still did a terrible job of really lighting the room. Shadows lingered in the corners, and Eden felt them more with Simon here.

He stood just inside the doorway for a moment. "So, are you going to invite me to sit or should I just stand here?" he asked, rubbing his shoulder against the wall like he was trying to make himself a more comfortable spot.

"You can sit," Eden said. She reached above her head and grabbed the mattress off the top bunk to start pulling. The angle of her arm made it difficult to do, so she stood to finish pulling the mattress off the frame and plop it onto the floor.

"I see," Simon said, kicking his shoes off and sitting with his legs crossed. Because the mattress on the floor was a little lower than Eden's, his head was just a few inches below hers. He looked up at her, and they kind of watched each other for a moment. Eden felt growing embarrassment with each moment.

She swallowed and looked away, picking at the blanket that was crumpled on her bed. She wanted to fill the silence, and her lips jerked against the tight restraint she had put on them to avoid saying something dumb. No, she had to think of something worth saying, not just fill the space with a bunch of "so's."

"What are you planning to do tonight?" Simon asked.

Eden smiled and tried to relax herself and not think about how she looked or sounded so much. "I don't really have anything planned. I usually read a little while, but…" She didn't finish because she wanted Simon to invite her to do something.

Simon nodded, the corners of his mouth turning down to form an upside down smile as he approved of her answer. "I always think I should read more, but I never do. I seem to get to the end of the day without reading, then I think maybe I should have made time for it."

"I'm reading this book right now!" Eden said, pulling her current read out from the back corner of the mattress. She held it out to him. "It's interesting all about these robots that look like humans. You can't even tell the difference. Makes you wonder."

"Wonder what? If some people on here might…be…robots," Simon moved his body jerkily as his head flopped forward like he was running out of juice.

Eden shoved him with her sock foot, and he flipped back to life.

"No, I never wonder that," she said. "But thanks for sticking a new worry in my head."

Suddenly, the alarm on the wall flared to life. Instead of its usual dim yellow glow that shut off when she pressed it, it was a bright red. Eden frowned at it for a moment as a siren blared; then she tried to press it with her foot. It didn't turn off.

"What's going on?" she asked, raising her voice to be heard over the siren.

Simon stood and stared at it for a moment before he shook his head. "I've never seen this happen before, but it's got to be some sort of emergency. Put on your shoes, and let's see what's happening."

Eden followed his instructions, slipping her feet into her tennis shoes, then pulling up the backs. Simon held open the door, and Eden didn't even think about shutting off the room's light as they entered the hall.

People were streaming down the corridor, all heading in the direction of the stairs. Eden frowned and looked to Simon for guidance. He pointed to the stairs, and Eden agreed. Following everyone else was probably a wise decision.

Simon reached for Eden's hand, and she didn't hesitate before taking it. She didn't feel any sort of spark, but she took comfort in knowing that she wasn't facing whatever this emergency might be alone.

For the number of people hurrying down the hallways, there was almost no conversation. Eden glanced at the faces behind her as they rounded the curve in the stairs, and everyone remained solemn.

Finally, it became clear that their destination was the large room where meals were served and important meetings were held. As she and Simon found a place in the room, she realized that it wasn't nearly as crowded as it had been before. It used to be impossible for everyone to fit inside, but now, everyone had found a spot, and there was a little bit of wiggle room.

Eden slowly registered that she and Simon were still holding hands, and she was suddenly aware of her hand getting a little sweaty. She wanted to yank it away and wipe it on her pants, but she didn't want Simon to think she was yanking it away because she didn't like him. So, Eden stared at the far wall where an alarm blared.

Jameson, one of the newly elected leaders, rushed through the room, and everyone moved to give him the space he needed. Even though a couple of people asked him questions, he didn't stop to answer. He just ran toward the far end and disappeared down the hallway where Eden had first realized she was in space.

"What do you think's happening?" Eden asked.

Simon squeezed her hand, then let go, and Eden felt disappointed. Why was he letting go? "Maybe I should see if they need some help."

"Doing what?" she asked, trying to stall him so he wouldn't leave her facing this alone. She stood on her tiptoes and managed to see over a few shoulders, but her view didn't extend far. She did see Helena surrounded by some other people and staring expectantly in the direction where Jameson had just disappeared.

Vincent stepped up on the room's one table and waved his arms. He tried to say something, but Eden couldn't hear anything over the blaring alarm. Vincent finally yelled something to the side, and someone disappeared down the hallway.

A few minutes later, blessed silence fell on the room as the echo of the alarm faded away.

"I need everyone to remain calm," Vincent said. "If you were part of the last recovery crew, I need you to make your way down that hallway. Everyone else, please wait here."

"What's the recovery crew?" Eden asked immediately as Vincent led maybe twelve individuals down the hallway.

Simon frowned and shook his head. "That's the group that gathers supplies from arriving spaceships, but a ship has never arrived except in May, after the Olympics."

"There's a ship arriving?" Eden asked.

Her question and variations of it were being repeated throughout the room.

"I don't know," Simon said. He elbowed the guy next to him, and they started talking quickly back and forth.

Then, a hush fell starting at the side of the room where the door to the hallway lay. The hush quickly turned to crazed chatter, but Eden still couldn't see anything. She bounced on the tips of her toes.

"What's happening?" she asked Simon.

Then, she heard her name. The person in front of her said it, then the person beside him.

"Are you talking to me?" she asked.

The guy turned around. "Are you Eden?"

"Yeah?" she answered, not quite sure of herself. Why was Vincent calling for her? She didn't know anything about being a part of the recovery crew.

"Go up there," the guy said, stepping aside so she could squeeze through.

Eden glanced back uncertainly at Simon. "Why do they want me to go up there?" she asked.

Being much taller, Simon stared over a few heads seriously. He didn't speak for a minute, so Eden grabbed his hand and started to pull him through with her. If she were going to be given a task all of a sudden, then she wanted someone doing it with her.

"Excuse me," she said.

The guy who had identified her shouted over her head. "Eden's coming through!" he shouted.

Simon tried to pull his hand out of hers, but Eden held on tightly.

Finally, the last person in front of her moved, and Eden breathed a sigh of relief that she could move more freely,

"Come o-" she stopped when she saw the people standing in front of her. Next to Vincent was...no, it wasn't possible.

Eden stared at Xander, her hand automatically releasing Simon's as she took step after step after slow step.

"You..." she tried, but she couldn't think when she was staring at the face of someone she had been sure was dead. His chin had a little hair on it, and his hair grew from his head like a bush instead of neatly combed back like it used to always be.

"Eden," Xander said, and his voice was just right. It was exactly how she had remembered it whenever she missed him most.

"How are you alive?" Eden asked, blinking a time or two, thinking he might disappear just after each blink.

Xander glanced around as she felt his familiar, rough fingers curling around hers. "Can we go talk somewhere?" he asked, and she realized that everyone was watching them like they were zoo animals.

"We need a report first," Vincent said, inserting himself between the two of them. "I'll gather the other three, and we can sit you down and hear about what happened."

"I want to talk to Eden first," Xander said. "And who are you?"

Finally, there was a question that Eden could answer. "We voted for new leaders after Roman..." She trailed off as she realized how much Xander had missed.

"What?" Xander looked around, his grip on her hand tightening as he studied the nearby faces staring at him. Eden squeezed his hand gently.

"Let's go talk," she suggested in a quiet voice.

"Fine, but we'll meet you in the bridge in thirty minutes," Vincent said. "I'll prep the others. Don't be late." He sounded like a domineering parent, but he probably just had all the same questions Eden did.

Freed at last, Xander tugged Eden down the aisle that had formed between them and the doors. "Should we go to your room?" Xander asked, and Eden agreed.

It would be the most private place. Surely, Nicole would think to give them some privacy for a few minutes. "I just can't believe you're...alive," Eden said, glancing at Xander on every other stair to make sure he was still beside her.

She reached out and ran her hand up his arm, her finger going to the scar just above his elbow from a classmate's stapler in middle school. There were the two little holes, just as they had been for the last six years.

"You're...but the asteroid was destroyed, and Roman said..."

"Where is he?"

"He was thrown out."

"Out?" Xander jerked his head sideways toward the big room.

"Yeah," Eden nodded, trying not to think about how it had been when he had suddenly left the place. "A lot's happened since you've been gone."

Their words were almost overlapping in their eagerness to be shared. "Here," Eden said as Xander almost took her past her room. She pushed open the door, and the little bulb glinted from the ceiling, lit since she and Simon had been talking. Eden closed the door behind them as Xander settled onto the mattress on the floor. Eden settled next to him and experimentally laid her head on his shoulder.

"I've missed you," she said after a moment or two of silence.

"I've missed you too," Xander replied. He took her hand and promptly laced his fingers through hers. "I didn't know if I'd ever get back here."

"But tell me what happened. I'm so confused. I mean, I thought your ship was destroyed by the asteroid. And even if it weren't, it would have taken you a day max to get back here. So...how did you do it?"

Xander laughed. "Magic," he teased. "No, it was honestly...a miracle. Do you remember Colt?"

Eden frowned, scrunching her eyebrows down. The name sounded familiar. "I know you've told me about him before. He's not one of your wrestling buddies, is he?"

Xander laughed at that, and Eden eyed him.

"What? I don't remember the names of all your friends, and that's funny?"

"No, just the idea of Colt wrestling. He's the guy I met on the way to the Olympics. He was sitting in the seat next to me, and he had everyone's probability of winning all mapped out. He's a smart guy."

"He got you back here? But how could he have done that unless..." Eden jerked into a sitting position. "Were you on *Earth*?" She asked, gripping Xander's upper arm tightly. "*No*, no *way!*"

Xander smiled and nodded. "Yes, I was on Earth, but I just kept thinking about how I could get back here, back to you."

Eden laughed, because she didn't know what else to do when someone was saying something unexpectedly romantic to her. "You're here," she said.

Xander nodded. He was studying her extra intently, and Eden reached up to touch the ends of his hair that stuck out all over his head.

"You didn't have access to a comb when you were there?" she asked.

Xander reached up and pushed his hair back violently. It sprang back up. "Gee, thanks. I've come back from the dead, and all you care about is my messy hair."

Eden hugged him, burying her face in his neck, but he didn't smell the same. He smelled like a different person. She felt ecstatic that he was alive, but she also felt like there was so much she didn't understand.

After a moment of hugging, Xander pushed her back just a little and studied her face. "You seem different too."

Eden tugged at her own hair, pulling it together in the back before letting it bounce back around her face. "How?"

"I don't know. You seem more...confident? Maybe that's not the right word. It doesn't matter anyway. I'm glad I'm back here with you."

"But if you were on Earth, how did you get back here? And I like you a lot too, but why would you leave there to come here? I mean, so many people have just died because of-" Eden didn't want to finish her explanation. Her mind instantly started to spiral into if there would be a place for Xander to sleep and if he would be allowed to eat some of the precious food supply.

Xander leaned his head back against the wall. The light cast a shadow on his eyes so that she couldn't see their bright green color. "A lot happened," he said like he was summing up the story instead of beginning it.

"Like what?" Eden asked, looking at Xander's clothes. The shirt was collared, something she had never seen him wear in his life, except for the day when he was supposed to be called up on stage for the adulting ceremony. He looked like a different person pretending to be Xander.

Xander swallowed and shook his head. "Can I tell you the story later? Right now, we have work to do."

"Work? What do you mean?"

"The ship I came here in isn't going to self-destruct," Xander announced like he was revealing some grand secret.

Eden thought about that for a second, really soaking in the details. "So...it gives us more living space?" she finally asked, thinking now was the time to tell Xander about how he was too late. People had already been sacrificed, and her stomach turned over with a plop at the thought of how she had eaten some of the grilled meat.

"No, Eden!" Xander said, laughing as he scolded her. "We're going back."

"To...Earth?"

"Yes!" Xander said, nodding to emphasize his point.

"But..." Eden turned her head to the side, trying to understand how this could be possible. "Won't they... I mean, where will we live? We've been eliminated. They'll just throw us out or shoot us or..."

"No, they won't," Xander assured her. "A lot has changed since our Olympics. They gave me the choice to stay there." He took a deep breath and let it out. "We need to get everything together for the trip back, and then, we'll have a lot of time. I'll tell you everything then."

Eden didn't like being put off like that, told that she would be given information when he was ready, not when she wanted it. She pressed her lips together, though, and didn't say anything. A sudden desire to see her parents welled up in her, and Eden looked away so she could blink at the tears that came from nowhere.

"How do you *know* it's going to be alright? That we won't just be sent back here?"

"Because they don't want to waste another spaceship and all the gasoline?" Xander grinned. "At this point, if they sent everyone back, then it would be more of a waste of resources than keeping us."

"Doesn't mean they won't shoot us," Eden muttered. She remembered the guy in their group who had broken away from them as they were being led to the boat. He had run hard, but one of the officials had pulled his gun and shot him. With one bullet, he had fallen to the ground with a thump.

"Nothing's a guarantee, but I'm pretty sure. Look, I don't want to talk about this. I just want to enjoy seeing you again," Xander said. He leaned a few inches away from her, and Eden felt his eyes on her face. She didn't want to stare at him though with that dreamy look of love. She had a lot to process. She laid her head back on his shoulder so that he couldn't read her face.

Then, a guilty feeling about more than just eating other humans crept into her. She had *kissed* Simon, or he had kissed her. It didn't really matter which. She had been a willing participant. What would Xander think of that? Once that thought had processed, Eden realized that it wasn't so much what Xander thought of it, but that part of her really liked Simon, and she didn't want to just stop hanging out with him. She would have to explain things to Xander at some point, but that point was not right now.

"What are you thinking?" Xander asked.

"About...just what you're talking about. It's a lot to process. I thought you were dead," Eden explained.

"Sorry about that," Xander apologized. "I had no way of communicating with you." He was silent for a few moments, and Eden closed her eyes against the annoyance of the bare bulb's light.

"Anyway, now that I'm not, can you go with me to meet with these leaders? I'm not sure everyone will fit in the spaceship, but I think we can make it work even if it's uncomfortable for a little while. I mean, in exchange for being back on Earth, I would think some people could deal with not having their own space."

"Yeah, let's go talk to them," Eden agreed, standing. She opened the door and flicked off the light, listening as Xander unfolded himself and came closer to her. She moved so that he could pass through the door and watched as he looked up and down the hall like he was exploring new territory.

This was what she had wanted- Xander to come back. But now that he was here, things felt different than she had remembered.

Chapter 22

Xander sat at a round conference table and watched as three guys and a girl stopped their meaningful looks to each other as he settled. He glanced back to make sure Eden had come into the room with him.

She had acted strangely since his arrival, like she was in a complete state of shock and couldn't believe that he was Xander. She slowly lowered herself into the seat next to him and stared at the center of the table.

"So," Xander said, starting the conversation.

"Xander Coxon," one of the guys said. "I'm Brody, one of the leaders elected after we got rid of Roman. I'm sure Eden told you everything that's happened since you left."

Xander glanced at Eden. Clearly she hadn't, because he had no idea why there were four leaders and what Roman had done to lose his power.

"You told us not to shove the spaceship away, so if it blows up and kills us all..." Vince said, clearly showing he didn't trust Xander.

"It won't," Xander replied, trusting Colt. "It's not rigged like that. But, it's programmed to take us back to Earth, at least as many people as can fit inside it. I don't know how many people are on here, but I think it might be able to take us all, even if we are packed in there."

"The population is a lot smaller now," the girl leader spoke up. Xander didn't remember ever having seen her before, but she made excellent eye contact.

"Why?" Xander leaned forward, eager to hear. His first guess was an illness of some kind.

"They...volunteered to die," she said. "We were running out of food. Even now, we're barely scraping by until the garden is up and running again, and..."

She closed her eyes, and Xander could tell she was feeling some sort of pain. He glanced over at Eden, but she was still avoiding eye contact.

"I'm sorry," Xander said, because an apology seemed in order even though he had technically saved all of them by volunteering to take down the asteroid. He wasn't the kind of guy to bring that up now.

Everyone remained silent for a minute, and Xander picked at the paint chipping at the edge of the table, giving them time to work through their emotions. He didn't know who the volunteers had been, but he wasn't connected to anyone here except for Eden, and she was sitting right next to him now.

"So," he said. "We shouldn't wait long." Colt had told him that the longer it took him to return, the more likely he would be opposed, either because the Greenlanders would have had a chance to prepare for his arrival or because the little war with Alaska would be over. "We need to pack people onto the spaceship. The journey is less than twenty-four hours, so just some water for everyone, and we'll worry about food when we get there."

Brody spoke up again. "How many people can fit on it? Each year, it's been about a hundred of the eliminated."

Xander remembered the tiny prison-like room that he had been trapped inside on his first journey to the space station. "We could fit at least three people to a room," he said. "Then some people in the controls. I had a chance to look at them when I came up here. We could have people in the hallway too. I mean, wherever we can squeeze them."

The girl nodded. "People would be fine for a day, even if it's not a five-star hotel." She stood up and smacked the table. "If we can do three to a room, and the other hundred in the hallways, we can fit everyone. Let's make an announcement and plan to leave in..." she looked around at her fellow leaders, "...twelve hours?"

Xander glanced at the clock on the wall and realized that would be six in the morning. He wouldn't be sleeping tonight; that was for sure.

The other leaders leaned closer together and started discussing the ideal time to leave, but Xander didn't care about a specific time. Now that he had passed on the information, it was someone else's responsibility to get everyone informed and ready. He could relax and prepare for his final journey to Earth. He didn't plan to ever leave the planet again after his return.

"Do you need me to do anything else?" Xander asked, rubbing at one of his eyes.

"No, we'll call you over the speakers if we do," Vince told him. The four turned back to each other and continued their conversation. Xander stood and stretched. He had slept a little on his ride here, but he felt *exhausted.* He didn't want to waste his time with Eden sleeping, but then again, something about the idea of taking a nap next to her didn't sound so bad.

He took her hand, but he felt some hesitancy in the way she gripped it. Was she *still* having trouble believing he was really here?

"So," he said, once they were outside of the room. "Are you ready to go back home?"

"Yeah, I want to go," Eden said.

Xander sensed a "but" coming, and he waited for her to finish her thought. She didn't add anything. "You don't seem sure about it," Xander said.

"It's just...a lot," Eden said, yanking her hand out of his so she could move her hands as she talked. "It's like I've kind of gotten used to the new life, even though I don't like it very much. And then, I thought you were dead and here you are."

"You say that like it's a bad thing."

"It's not...a bad thing. It's just that my brain can't process it all. Now, we get to go back home, but I don't know what people will say when we get there. I need you to tell me everything that happened."

Xander's brain popped up flashes of what he had gone through traveling back to Earth, fighting to have the missile sent to save everyone on the space station, then the war breaking out with Alaska.

He closed his eyes and stopped walking now that they had reached Eden's door. "I need you to trust me. You'll be fine."

Eden didn't say anything as she pushed open the door to her room. The mattresses were just as they had left them, but this time, Eden leaned against the bed frame as Xander started to settle into the mattress on the floor. He gestured toward the open space next to himself. "I'm tired. Don't you want to sleep some before we have to go?"

"No, I'm hungry," Eden replied, still not sitting down.

Something was definitely wrong. She wasn't making eye contact, and it was hard to read her face in the bare light. Xander motioned for her to come closer again, but she shook her head and nodded toward the door of her room.

"I'm going to get dinner. The bell rang when we were at the meeting with the leaders, and I'm hungry." She gripped at her stomach, and Xander nodded. He had found some food stashes, though meager, on the spaceship, so he wasn't starving. Honestly, he didn't feel like moving either.

"Okay, I'll wait here for you. Then, we can talk when you get back."

Eden nodded, still standing there for another moment before finally moving to the door and closing it behind her.

Once she was gone, Xander stared up at the ceiling. He was here, back with Eden, which was what he had wanted. So why did it feel wrong? This should be one of the happiest days of his life, despite his uncertainty about how they would be received when they returned to Earth.

Xander didn't have much time to consider what was wrong, though, because he felt his limbs becoming heavy as he drifted into sleep.

"Ed-ah!" a girl's voice screeched, causing Xander to sit up half-asleep. "Hey, you're the guy who came back today!" the girl squealed again, her fright turning to excitement. "Why are you in here?"

"I'm Eden's, uh, boyfriend," Xander said, rubbing the sleep from his eyes. He couldn't have been sleeping that long, just long enough for Eden to get a meal. Where *was* she?

"Really?" the girl asked, bending over the mattress until she was too close to his face. "Huh, okay. Nice to meet you. I'm Nicole. Do you know where Eden is?"

"I think she's getting something to eat," Xander said, twisting so he could see the clock on the wall. He rubbed his eyes again and stared at it. Unless the space station's schedule had changed dramatically, dinner had finished an hour and a half ago. "Or not."

"Yeah, the dining hall is empty. Well, okay, thanks, and you're not planning on sleeping here all night, are you? I mean, that's my mattress."

Xander stood and shoved his shoes back on. "Go ahead. Take it. I guess I'll go search for Eden too," he said. He opened the door, and Eden was standing right there. She took a step back.

"Oh, hey, you're awake," she said at the same time he spoke.

"Where'd you go?"

"I checked on you after dinner, but you were sleeping, so I figured you must be really tired," Eden explained.

Xander felt Nicole taking a couple of steps closer to him so she could eavesdrop, and he slid over so that she wasn't pressed against him.

"Oh, Nicole? You're in here?" Eden asked, sounding confused, her eyes darting to Xander.

"Yes," Nicole answered, staring at Eden. "I met your *boyfriend*."

Eden glanced at Xander, then back at Nicole. "Yeah, yeah, I didn't know he was still alive. It's been a lot to take in," she said, mostly staring at Nicole.

Xander felt like they were saying more than what their words meant, but he couldn't quite figure it out. "Nicole, do you mind if Eden and I talk for a few minutes?" Xander asked.

"Yeah," Eden agreed.

"Sure," Nicole shrugged. She glanced at Xander, then leaned forward and whispered something in Eden's ear.

Xander tried not to hear what she was saying. Obviously, they wanted it to stay a secret, but what sort of secrets would Eden have from him?

Eden smiled, but Xander could tell from the way the corners of her mouth curved up too much that it was one of her fake smiles. "Thanks, I appreciate it. We can talk later."

Nicole flitted off, and once again, it was only Xander and Eden. Xander pressed his back against the door so that Eden could pass in front of him when he heard his name.

"Xander!" Connor shouted, running down the hall and waving.

"Oh hey, man!" Xander said, stress immediately dropping away as he stepped out of the room and embraced his old wrestling buddy.

"Dude, I thought you were dead."

"Yeah, sorry about that."

"Is it true that you're taking us back to Earth?"

Xander nodded.

"Good, because I don't know if I can keep eating this meat."

"Meat?" Xander's ears pricked up at the word, and his mouth watered.

"Not the kind you want, man. Human."

Xander shook his head, sure that he hadn't heard Connor correctly. "You…no, I'm not dumb enough to believe that."

"It's the truth, man, so believe it or don't, but it's what's happening."

Xander swung around to see Eden's face. She couldn't lie. It was one thing she was bad at, probably why she had gotten caught for cheating. "He's not serious?" Xander confirmed.

Eden dropped her eyes and did a weird combination of a shoulder shrug and nodding her head. Grateful that he had decided to skip dinner here, Xander looked around at the people walking down the hallways.

"Who?" he finally asked.

"Volunteers, man, no one was murdered, except for what Roman did."

"Roman?" Xander thought so much had happened to him while he was gone, but apparently the space station hadn't been dormant either.

"Man, Eden didn't tell you anything!" Connor exclaimed.

"Yeah, not really. I think she and I need to talk. I'll catch up with you later, okay?"

"Yeah, man, later," Connor agreed. He shook Xander's hand again and hurried off down the hall.

"What *happened*?" Xander asked as Eden stepped backward into her room.

"A lot," she sighed. This time, when Xander settled onto the edge of the floor mattress, Eden sat next to him. Xander placed his hand about her shoulders, but she hunched forward and wrapped her arms around her knees. "Roman tried to kill me," she finally said.

Xander shook his head, sure he hadn't heard her correctly. "He…no, no way."

"Don't tell me *no*!" Eden burst out. "You weren't there."

"Yeah, you're right. I wasn't there, but Roman is…was the leader."

"That doesn't mean he's perfect!" Eden's voice was still raised, and Xander tried to picture the scene. Maybe Roman had grabbed a kitchen knife and chased her around the space station, but this image turned into a weird sort of animated comedy piece.

"How?" he asked.

Eden didn't answer right away, and as Xander waited, he realized that it still bothered her to talk about it, even though Roman was clearly gone.

She needed someone to be there for her. Xander patted her shoulder, but she didn't react to his touch. Finally, she said, "He tried to strangle me. He had his hands around my neck, and Helena was there. She helped me get away."

She was only giving him bits and pieces of the picture, but Xander nodded, trying to accept it and validate her. "I'm sorry," he said after a moment. "I should have been there to take care of you."

"I shouldn't have needed anyone to take care of me," Eden replied, bitterness in her words.

Xander didn't know how to respond to that, so he stayed quiet even though he wanted to ask about the cannibalism that Connor had mentioned. "He's gone now," Xander said, landing on that cheerful and encouraging sentiment.

Eden shrugged, and Xander pulled her closer to him. She stopped resisting and laid her head on his shoulder. "I hate thinking about it, about how weak I was. There were bruises on my neck for a while, but they're fading now."

Eden pulled the neck of her shirt down, and Xander saw purplish marks. How had he not seen those earlier? Her shirt had been mostly hiding them, but he should have noticed.

"Sorry," he said again.

Eden moved her shoulder again, like it was no big deal. But it clearly *was* a big deal. Xander rubbed his hand up and down her back and scrambled for something else to talk about, to draw her attention away from her pain onto something else. He thought about the journey ahead, and his mind jumped to Colt waiting for them, hoping they were successful because he wanted to see his sister again.

"Oh, hey," Xander said, suddenly thinking of a good topic to use to distract Eden. "Have you seen Emily recently?"

"Em-i-ly?" Eden repeated, emphasizing each syllable like the name was an unusual one.

"Yeah, remember? Long blonde hair? I worked with her in the kitchen," Xander nodded, trying to think of another detail that would jog Eden's memory. "She had already been here a couple years, didn't come with us."

"Uh...." Eden said, and Xander felt her back tighten. He continued to rub it, pushing his thumb into her spine so it was like a mini massage.

"You know?" Xander asked. "I mean, I can ask someone else. They probably know where she is. I need to talk to her."

"Why?" Eden asked.

"Because her brother is Colt!" Xander revealed, still amazed at the fact that he had met them separately and never connected them. Now, he knew that of course they had to be siblings. They had the same whitish-blonde hair and face shape once Colt took off his glasses.

"Oh, so you want them to see each other or something?"

Xander nodded. "Do you know where she is?"

"Um, she's....Roman actually strangled her," Eden said.

A strange prickly feeling worked its way down Xander's spine as he processed this. "Is she okay or did she-"

"She's dead," Eden clarified. She reached up and touched the fading bruises that she had just shown him. "Someone asked me to help her, but she was already dead when I arrived."

"Oh," Xander swallowed. He had dangled Emily in front of Colt like a new microscope design in front of a scientist in order to convince Colt to help him. But now, Colt would realize that he had taken so many risks for nothing. "I don't know how I'm going to tell Colt that. Are you sure?"

Eden glowered at him, and Xander understood from the look that she didn't appreciate him questioning her. "I think I'm smart enough to tell if someone is breathing or not."

Eden leaned away from Xander and messed with something under the lower mattress. Xander clasped his hands together around his knees, his mind jumping back to what Connor had told him.

"Did you eat other...people?" he asked.

Eden stopped unfolding the piece of paper she had in her hands and gave him another dirty look. "I don't want to talk about it. It's not interesting or weird or...it's just what happened. And if we're really going back to Earth, hopefully it will never happen again."

Xander glanced over at the paper that Eden had been playing with, but now, she was folding it into a neat rectangle and tucking it back under the mattress. "Nicole wanted to talk with me," Eden said. "I should probably go see what she wants."

She didn't get up right away, but they didn't say anything for the next minute. For the first time ever in Eden's company, Xander felt awkward.

"I'm going to take a walk around the space station," Xander said when Eden didn't move to find Nicole. "I'll catch up with you later." Neither one of them specified a time or a place though, and Eden left first. Xander took an extra moment to put on his shoes, lacing them up tightly since they were Colt's and didn't fit quite right. He had done so much for Eden. Why, then, did they have this distance between them?

Xander forced himself to remain confident. Eden was just dealing with some personal stuff. They would get back to normal once they were on Earth. He was sure.

Chapter 23

Eden didn't actually want to talk to Nicole, but Xander's question about Emily in the wake of Eden's revelation about what she had suffered struck her wrong. How could she even feel jealous of someone who was dead? It felt wrong, but she couldn't change the way her stomach had twisted.

Hurrying down the hall, Eden took the stairs up to the third floor where Nicole had promised she would be waiting. She had almost given Xander the letter she had written, the one that had told him exactly how she felt. But then, she couldn't remember everything she had put in it, and she couldn't decide if she actually wanted Xander to know everything that she had laid out.

"Eden!" Nicole sang. "You're here!"

For being so late, the space station was amazingly busy. Everyone was running around, getting ready for takeoff in approximately nine hours. Eden's only job was gathering anything useful in her room and bringing it to the spaceship around four a.m. Even though they had no idea what they might need on Earth, it felt wrong to leave behind useful supplies. To keep the spaceship from getting too crowded with people trying to board at the same time, she had to stay awake until that god-awful hour.

She didn't think she would be able to sleep right now anyway.

"Ohmygosh! I can't believe Xander is back!" Nicole squealed. Her gossip index was high at the moment, and the squealing was even louder. Even though she could be annoying, Eden didn't mind it so much. At least Nicole wasn't hard to figure out.

"I couldn't believe it either," Eden said. "Still having trouble thinking it's real."

"So is it like your happily ever after? Or no, because now Simon is in the picture?" Nicole's face turned from a happy smile to a perplexed frown.

"Please don't make me talk about it," Eden said, settling onto the sofa in the lounge. Nicole had her feet up on a tiny footstool, and she flopped her head onto the back of the sofa.

"Okay, but will you *please* talk about it once we get back to Earth? I mean, I feel like talking about things helps you process your emotions properly. If you just hold it inside, the situation seems a lot more confusing than it really is."

"Thank you, Counselor Nicole," Eden teased her.

Nicole laughed, more joyful than normal, probably because of their upcoming journey back to Earth. Sure enough, as soon as Eden made it clear that she wasn't going to talk about Xander, Nicole leaned forward and started talking about the spaceship.

"Look, the reason I wanted to talk to you is that Avery doesn't want to come with us."

"What?" Eden asked, sure she had misunderstood. "You don't mean she wants to stay *here*, in the space station?"

Nicole nodded. "Yes, that's what I mean. She said it's not right to leave her twin in stasis, and she wants to stay with her, and I think it's suicide to stay. But she won't listen to me or Jazzy. I think the more people we have on board to convince her, the better. So, I need you to talk to her about it. Just don't tell her I told you. I don't know if I'm supposed to tell people or not."

Eden let her head hang forward as she tried to imagine someone wanting to stay in this place, outcast from the rest of the world. After a minute, she had finally wrapped her head around the idea. "I didn't even know anyone would want to stay here," she said.

"I think a few people do," Nicole said, waving her hand to show that they didn't matter. "But Avery is my friend. I don't care if she doesn't have any family left on Earth; we are kind of her family now."

Eden briefly wondered what it would be like to live on a mostly-emptied space station, but no way would she want to do that. No matter how confused she was about Xander still being alive but different, she knew for a fact that she was not going to stay here.

"I'll talk to her," Eden finally agreed, "but she's entitled to her own decision, even if you don't think it's the right one."

Nicole groaned. "Don't take her side! Eden!"

"I'm not taking a side, except that each person should get to choose for herself."

Nicole made a face, but Eden slowly pushed herself to her feet. "Where is she?"

"Probably her room."

Eden headed in the direction of Jazzy and Avery's newly-assigned room, briefly thankful for the opportunity to avoid speaking to or thinking about Simon and Xander. Or should she think "Xander and Simon"? Maybe she shouldn't think about them at all. Their names didn't sound right together.

Once they got back to Earth, Simon would probably go back to wherever he was from- Eden realized she didn't know where that was- and they wouldn't see each other again. That was reality, and Eden needed to accept it. But the sudden thought of not seeing Simon again bothered her.

When she reached the door to Avery's room, Eden knocked on it before letting herself in. These girls weren't her best friends, nothing like the bond she had formed with Helena, but she thought they were pretty nice.

"Hey," Eden said.

Avery sat up, and Eden realized she had been sleeping.

"Sorry," she whispered and started to back out of the room.

"It's okay," Avery said, pushing her long, brown hair out of her face. It stuck up in weird clumps. "I can't really sleep anyway. I'm too worried about everything."

"Worried about what?" Eden asked, taking the foot of the bed as Jazzy continued to snooze on the top bunk.

"About everyone leaving," Avery said.

Eden nodded. So, Avery *was* pretty set on staying, then. "Are you not coming?" she asked cautiously.

"No," Avery said. "I don't want to talk about it either, so if Nicole sent you here to convince me, no thanks."

Eden covered her smile, but Avery couldn't see her in the pitch-black space. Still, she must have sensed it.

"I'm right about Nicole, aren't I?"

"Yeah, she talked to me. I think you're brave to stay behind."

"Brave," Avery echoed. "Well, at least I won't be the only one doing it."

"Who else is staying?"

"My twin, Maya," Avery replied. She didn't add anyone else's name, and Eden imagined a future of Avery being the only out-of-stasis person roaming the space station.

"Well, it's been good to get to know you," Eden finally said.

"You too," Avery replied.

They didn't say anything for a few minutes, and the darkness had Eden's chin bobbing down to her chest with sleepiness.

"Are you tired?" Avery asked. "You can sleep in here if you want."

"I need to move the stuff from my room at four," Eden told her.

"I'll wake you up. I'm not going to be able to sleep anyway."

Eden didn't think she was that tired, but a few minutes later, she felt herself drifting into sleep.

"Time to wake up," a voice said softly in Eden's ear. She reached out a hand, for some reason her first instinct being to touch the person's face. As soon as she touched the cheek, she realized it wasn't Xander.

Eden forced her eyes open and started to sit up, her neck aching painfully from the awful position in which she had slept. "What's happening?" she asked, her brain slowly sweeping the cobwebs away from coherent thoughts.

"You have to move your things," Avery reminded her. "And then the ship is leaving in a couple of hours."

"Uh huh," Eden agreed, forcing her tired limbs to stand. She whipped her head around, but the only light in the room was from the glowing numbers on the clock. "Thanks," she said, suddenly wanting to be with Xander. All of the misgivings she had had the day before about why he wouldn't tell her what had happened had disappeared. She wanted to see him again.

"No problem...have a safe journey."

"Yeah, you too," Eden returned before realizing what she had said. Avery wasn't going anywhere. Oh well. It didn't matter. She was about to add something about seeing Avery soon, but that also didn't apply, so Eden left the room before she could say anything else dumb in her almost-four-o'clock-in-the-morning stupidity.

Stumbling down the hall, she found the door to her own room and hesitated before pushing it open. Would Xander be inside?

The bare bulb dangling from the ceiling showed Eden a busily-moving Nicole. She was sorting her portion of clothing, or at least the clothing that had been most recently laundered, and both mattresses were leaning against the wall.

"Good, you're here. I found this paper," Nicole said, dangling the paper that had Eden's note for Xander, the one she had never expected to actually deliver. "Sorry, I opened it up to see what it was, and..." she shrugged.

Eden snatched the paper from her and tucked it into her pocket, annoyed but knowing that Nicole hadn't meant to hurt her by reading it. She glanced at her own drawer of belongings and wondered if she should really bring them. She had no attachment to the clothing that hung unflatteringly from her body. She much preferred her dresser full of things back home.

But then, Eden realized for the first time that her parents might have already given everything away. What if they weren't the type of parents to keep her things for a year or two years or three in memory?

Shaking her head in disgust at her disappointing thoughts, Eden shoved the contents of the drawer into one of the shirts like a bag and carried it over her shoulder, pushing the mattress into the hall. A couple of doors down, someone else was doing the same.

"Hold the door for me!" Nicole called behind her. Eden blocked another bedroom door with her mattress as she went back to help Nicole.

A couple of people were calling up and down the hallway, and their enthusiasm was catching.

"One and a half more hours!" someone called out. Others were laughing about how they had wedged the top of their mattresses against the ceiling and couldn't get them moving again.

Eden glanced up and down the hallway, hoping to spot Xander. He wasn't there, though, so she continued to push her mattress down the hall with one hand as her other clasped the bag of clothing. Her letter for Xander felt heavy in her pocket.

The stairs were hard to navigate, and Nicole kept making jokes as they moved aside and watched someone expertly flip his mattress over the rail. Nicole and Eden copied him, then rushed down the stairs to grab them.

Finally, they were down the long hallway of windows, and someone was standing at the door, marking them off as they came.

"Everyone has to be settled in there by six, so if you want to find a room, you can go ahead and get settled."

"No," Eden responded immediately.

The guy looked up and frowned at her.

"I... I have to find Xander first," Eden said, not even wanting to go in the spaceship right now in case the door closed behind her, an irrational fear but one all the same.

"Please put your stuff in one of the rooms first," the guy instructed, ushering them inside and looking at the girl behind the two of them.

"I'll get it," Nicole offered. "You go find him. And if he's already on the spaceship, I'll find you and let you know."

"Thanks," Eden said. She needed to find Helena too. She hadn't seen her since the night before and suddenly hoped that she hadn't decided to stay behind.

Running back along the hallway, Eden started a thorough search of the space station, passing half-asleep people as they made their way down the hall and to the spaceship.

The speakers on the wall squealed, and Eden winced. Well, anyone who was still sleeping had to be awake now. "Everyone needs to be on the spaceship in one hour. If you are not on the spaceship in one hour, then the doors will be closed."

Eden didn't recognize the voice, but she hurried forward, clearing the first floor before taking the stairs at a run. Once she reached the second floor, no one was trying to be quiet anymore. Everyone shouted back and forth, asking questions and offering help. She witnessed teamwork like she had never seen before in her life, but Eden didn't care so much about how everyone was acting out a children's show on teamwork. She needed to find Xander.

Then, she spotted Connor up ahead, struggling as he tried to carry two mattresses above his head.

"Hey! Have you seen Xander?" she asked, ducking so he wouldn't smack her in the face.

"Xander? No, not since last night. You don't know where he is?"

At his obvious question, Eden rolled her eyes. No, she was just running around, calling his name for the fun of it. "I haven't seen him all night." She had also been hiding from him while she tried to figure things out in her mind about Simon, but Connor didn't need to know that.

"He's probably on the spaceship, teaching someone how to drive it or something."

Eden considered the idea. She didn't think spaceships needed driving, not like cars did, but maybe Connor had a point. Still, she didn't want to set foot on the spaceship before she had searched the whole space station.

Then, once she had ducked out of the way so Connor could continue, Eden saw Helena. "Hey!" she said, running forward and almost hugging her. Eden wasn't usually a hugger, but seeing Helena's face immediately made her feel just a little safer.

"Eden, what are you still doing here? I thought you were getting on an hour ago!" Helena said.

"What? I...I loaded my stuff, but I can't find Xander."

"Xander?" Helena looked confused.

"My...he was..." Eden shook her head, trying to clear her confusion with how to describe her relationship to Xander. "The guy who brought the space-ship," she finally said.

"Ohhhh!" Helena nodded. "I haven't seen him. He's probably in the bridge or something."

"You're coming, right?" Eden asked before hurrying off to check the bridge.

"Of course!" Helena reached forward and squeezed Eden's shoulder. "I can't wait!"

Then, Eden hurried to the bridge. For the first time since she had arrived there, the door was propped open. She could hear a conversation happening inside, but she wasn't trying to eavesdrop. "Hello?" she called out. "Xander?"

She popped her head around the door and saw a gaggle of people crowded around the computers. One of them turned and looked at her, but the rest of them continued with their conversation. A quick scan told her that Xander wasn't one of them.

"Sorry," she muttered and stepped back out. She didn't think he would be in the gym getting a quick workout in, but she didn't know where else to look. As she stood there with her head hanging, searching her mind for other options, she heard her name.

"Hey!" Xander said.

Eden's head snapped up, and she smiled at him. "Hey, there you are! I was looking everywhere for you!"

"Yeah, I ran into that girl again, the one you share a room with," Xander said. Clearly, remembering names wasn't something he could do at the moment.

"Nicole, yeah, I just wanted to make sure you were on the spaceship. I hadn't seen you in a while, so..."

Xander smiled. "Yeah, you kind of disappeared last night."

Eden swallowed, feeling guilty for hiding from Xander. "Sorry, I was thinking. I've had a lot going on in my head. Can we go ahead and get in the spaceship? I don't want them to shut the doors on us."

"Yeah, Nicole put your stuff in a room, so I guess I'll be in there with you."

Eden didn't completely mind sharing a room with Xander for the next however many hours it took to reach Earth. "Let's go, then," she said.

Xander grabbed her hand, and even though they hadn't spent much time as the cute, hand-holding couple, it felt right.

When they reached the long hallway that led to the spaceship, it was full of people shuffling slowly along as they were checked off a list. Eden and Xander joined the end of the line.

Some people were talking excitedly, but a lot of them were quietly waking up as they moved along. Eden fell silent, thoughts racing through her head once more.

She accepted a warm bowl of sludge and begrudgingly began to eat it. "You'll tell me everything once we're on there, right?" Eden asked when she had finished her portion and handed it to someone waiting just by the door of the spaceship.

"There won't be much else to do other than talk," Xander said. "I'll tell you everything." He looked serious as he answered her question, and Eden wondered if something bad had happened. Maybe it was his mother. As soon as the idea came to her, she knew that had to be it. His mother had been sick for a while, and she must have passed away while he was gone. She didn't ask, though, wanting him to tell her in his own time.

With each stair that she descended into the belly of the spaceship, Eden felt a tightening in her stomach that made no sense. They were on their way home. Everything would be right very soon, but right now, it still felt all mixed up.

"Which room has my stuff?" Eden asked Xander. He studied the hallway, slowing down as he neared the middle of it.

"Next one," he said, pointing to the right up ahead.

Eden turned into the doorway, one foot inside the tiny space before she stopped. She recognized the T-shirt bulging with clothes. But she hadn't expected to see another person in the room she would share with Xander.

"Hi, Eden!" Simon greeted her cheerfully, sitting up from his mattress.

Chapter 24

Xander frowned when he saw a lanky guy sitting in Eden's room for the trip back home. Sure, Xander didn't have "stuff" to reserve his spot, but he had told that person at the top of the stairs which room he had. A third person...but then, Xander remembered what he had told the leaders. He had said they could probably fit three people to a room. Apparently, they were testing that out.

"Hi," Eden said back.

Xander thought he had seen this guy around before, but he had never formally met him. "I'm Xander," he said, leaning forward and shaking the guy's hand.

"Simon," he replied with a strong grip.

Xander took in the one large bottle of water that had been placed in the room, similar to the way it had been set up when he had first arrived, except that this time there was a bucket clearly meant as a bathroom. He kept having to remind himself that he wasn't a prisoner like he had been on his first journey to the space station.

After a moment of processing everything, Xander turned to Eden's mattress to sit down and realized that this Simon guy had already transferred himself from his own mattress to Eden's. He was sitting on it, knees up by his face, and smiling at Eden.

Eden stared at him, and Xander could tell from the wide spread of her eyes that she wasn't comfortable.

"'Scuse me," Xander tried to say non-confrontationally as he sat next to Simon on Eden's mattress. "I don't have my own things to bring since I haven't been here during the last week."

Simon looked over Xander to where Eden was. "Do you know this guy?" Simon asked, and Xander experienced a strange feeling of being out of place, like he wasn't actually experiencing this but just watching it unfold. He didn't like the chummy way Simon talked to Eden over Xander's head.

"Er, yeah," Eden replied. "Yeah, Xander's a...good guy."

A good guy? What about "boyfriend"? That would be an easy way to put Simon in his place. But for some reason, Eden had chosen not to describe him that way.

"I see," Simon said with an icy edge to his voice.

Eden stood in the doorway for another moment before going to Simon's mattress and sitting down by herself. She hunched up against the walls and stared at them both.

"Is there no space for you in another room?" Xander asked Simon after a moment of awkward silence.

"Another room?" Simon looked confused. "Why would I go to another room?"

Xander was still trying to be polite, so he didn't explain exactly why Simon was unwanted.

"It's just been a while since I've seen Eden, so you know, it would be nice if we could catch up," Xander said, running a hand through his bushy hair to give his hands something to do.

"I didn't realize you two were friends," Simon said, looking back and forth between them.

There were so many things wrong with that statement that Xander didn't even say anything to Simon. He glanced at Eden, though, to see what she was thinking. She was folding back the edge of the mattress where it had come unsewn.

Part of Xander wanted to shout "yes," that he had thought they were dating, as much as you could date someone when they were stuck on a space station and couldn't actually *go* on dates, but the other part of him saw clearly what had happened. Eden had moved on. *That* was why she had been acting so strangely when he had gotten back. They hadn't even kissed since he had returned. The moment had never felt right, and she had been avoiding eye contact too much, like he made her uncomfortable.

"Yeah, we were," Xander eventually replied. Someone came by, glanced at the three of them, marked something, then slammed the door shut. Panic hit Xander with the sound of the door, and he stood up, striding to it. It only took two long steps to reach it, but it had melted into the wall. There was no handle on his side of the door, even as he tried to force his fingers into the tiniest of cracks.

He didn't say anything as he expelled effort toward getting the door open, then Eden was by his side, almost reading his panic. She grabbed his arm and pulled it gently back from the door. "They'll let us out when we get there," she said.

Xander turned and studied her wide, brown eyes. He felt the honesty behind them, but at the same time, he felt betrayed because she hadn't told him anything about this other guy. At least she could have just said she had moved on, even though it felt impossible for Xander to move on from years of friendship with her.

He took half a step back and studied the portion of the wall that represented the door. The room was about the same size as the complete rocket that he had shared with Matt. He could stay in this small space for a short time. The people in it would make it more difficult, but he felt confident that he could do it.

Xander sat back on the mattress that had been Simon's. Now, Eden was forced to choose between her own mattress where Simon sat or the other one with Xander. She stood there for a moment, glancing back and forth between the two of them.

Finally, she took a step toward where Xander was and sank next to him without saying anything. Xander felt the significance of her decision and wanted to wrap his arm around her, but Simon seemed oblivious to what Eden had clearly just done.

"So, what was it like back on Earth?" Simon asked. "It's been a year since I've been there."

Knowing that they were going to be in this tiny space together for a while, Xander decided to answer him. He had imagined sharing hours and hours of intimate conversation with Eden as well as a few kisses. But that wasn't going to happen.

"It hasn't been that long since I left, but Alaska finally did it. They attacked Greenland, right where the research center is... was."

Simon's eyebrows rose. "Alaska...attacked Greenland?"

Eden gripped his arm tightly and stared at him. Xander could feel her concerned gaze, but he avoided making eye contact with her.

"I'm from Alaska originally. Did you know that?"

"No," Xander replied, not mentioning that he hadn't known about Simon's existence until a minute or two ago.

"Maybe you should kick me off of this ship before I return and start fighting for them," Simon said. His face broke into a wide grin that showed he was joking, but Xander liked his idea. Getting rid of Simon would make this journey a lot better. He glanced at the closed door, but it was still firmly shut.

"Just kidding. Don't look so worried," Simon said.

Xander didn't see how Eden could like a guy like this. He was so different from Xander, but right now, Eden was being very quiet, like she didn't want to be in this room any more than Xander did.

Xander put his arm around her, some primal part of him urging himself to make it clear to Simon that he was more than a friend. But as his hand touched Eden's far shoulder, she flinched. Flinched!

A sinking feeling hit Xander's stomach, and he searched for an excuse to move his clearly unwanted arm. "Some bug," he muttered, waving at the air by her far ear. When he had waved his hand around a few times, he retracted his arm and gazed at the small strip of floor between the two mattresses.

It was the lamest excuse he could think of considering he hadn't seen any flies in his time on the space station.

No one spoke for a while, then Xander felt the ship begin to move. He should be out there, communicating with Colt if it were possible and helping direct their route. But instead, he was stuck in this tiny box of a room where he couldn't seem to say or do anything right.

The movement didn't last long as the ship seemed to shudder to a stop for another short while.

"So," Simon said after a long, long silence. "What competition were you best at?"

"I won a medal in wrestling," Xander said. "Gave it up for Eden." He nodded his head in her direction. He wasn't telling Simon this to exactly brag, but it didn't hurt if Simon realized how serious Xander was about her.

The ship shuddered to life again, and this time, Xander felt a small lurch as it jumped forward and the journey began.

Someone walked down the hallway, and Xander held his breath listening to the footsteps. The person said something that he couldn't hear, so Xander leaned closer to the former doorway. This time, the person's voice was closer.

"We have about twelve hours until arrival. We suggest using this time to sleep as it will make the time pass faster and only drink the water when absolutely necessary. I'll come by every hour to let you know how much time has passed." Then, the person was gone.

Xander sat back. Of course, there was already some system in place for managing everyone. "Did you hear that?" he asked.

Eden shook her head, so Xander repeated the gist of the message. She leaned back against the wall once she had heard him, and Xander touched it experimentally. "Remember how hot it got when we came here?" he asked.

Eden nodded and leaped away like it had just burned her. "Yeah, maybe it takes a while before it gets that hot. We should be careful and not fall asleep touching it."

Simon acted out getting burned by the wall as Xander stared at him with no appreciation.

"Eden, where are you from?" Simon finally asked.

"Sisimiut," she said. "Greenland," when Simon looked confused.

"Ooooh!" Simon said. "You two grew up together. That's how you know each other."

They all three looked at each other, then looked away again.

Simon stretched out on the mattress. "Didn't sleep much last night, so I'm going to try to sleep now."

Xander watched as he got comfortable and pulled a blanket over most of his body even though it wasn't cold in there. After a few moments, Xander glanced at Eden, and she was reaching into her T-shirt bundle of clothes looking for something. A few moments later, she pulled out a book.

"Glad I brought this along," she said, showing Xander the title.

"Yeah, because being stuck talking with me would be too boring," Xander said.

Eden smiled and put the book down, glancing at Simon as she did so. Xander also glanced at Simon and saw that his mouth was now slightly open. Had he really fallen asleep that fast?

"I didn't say that. I *like* talking to you, but I don't know."

Xander understood. Things had felt different since he had seen her again, and he wasn't sure why. He thought that a good talk would settle things back into place, though, and if Simon wasn't asleep, then he was doing a good job of faking it.

"Come here," Xander said.

Eden was already sitting on the same mattress as him, but she scooted a little closer. "What?" she asked as Xander continued to motion for her to move closer.

"I want to be close to you," Xander said. "I didn't know if I would ever see you again for a while there."

Eden scooted over again reluctantly, like she was scared of what might happen if she got too close. Finally, her leg was pressed against Xander's, sending a little thrill through him. He reached over and cautiously touched her knee, concerned she might decide to bolt in the other direction as soon as his hand landed on her.

"Matt didn't tell me what he was planning until we were already on the spaceship," Xander finally began his confession, with one last glance at Simon. "Matt knew how to work the controls, and I didn't, so he changed our course. I couldn't really do anything until we had landed on Earth, which by the way was hard because of how hot everything got when we got into Earth's atmosphere."

Eden covered her mouth and stared at him with raised eyebrows. "You really did almost die," she said in a reverent whisper.

Xander didn't mind the hero role, so he started to play it up a little. "Matt and I even got into a fistfight when I tried to get him to turn the ship back to the asteroid. It was actually kind of funny having a fistfight without gravity."

Eden's eyebrows went up, and she studied Xander's face. He watched her eyes dart back and forth before they dropped to where his hand rested on her knee.

"I...can't believe you went through all that."

"Things are bad on Earth," Xander confessed. "I didn't tell everyone exactly how bad, but there's war going on. Alaska and Greenland are going at it. I think Russia might just watch and pick up the pieces. Whatever is left will become part of Russia." Xander shrugged. "They have food though, more than enough food. It makes me wonder if these Olympics that everyone competes in each year... if they're really necessary."

"What do you mean?" Eden asked. She was reaching out and touching his hand, playing with his pinky finger.

"I mean...I know resources are limited, but that's why they put a population cap. No more than two kids a couple." Xander hadn't voiced this thought out loud before, so he took his time phrasing it, hoping it would make sense. "What if the Olympics are just a way to keep us under control? If we are focusing on the poor eighteen-year-olds, then we're not paying attention to what the officials or board members are doing."

Eden stopped plucking at his finger, but still didn't look Xander in the eyes. He wished he could understand what she was thinking. For a long time, neither one of them said anything.

Finally, Xander continued, fleshing out his idea a little more. "We've had shortages, sure, but would the shortages really be that much worse if a few hundred eighteen-year-olds weren't eliminated every year?"

"I don't know," Eden answered after another long pause. "I want to be able to trust the people in charge. Do you think they would...kill people if it's not necessary?"

"Maybe," Xander replied.

He glanced at Simon, but the guy's mouth was completely open now, and there was no question about him being asleep. A soft whistle escaped his nose every few moments.

"Who is this guy anyway?" Xander asked. "I don't remember him from when I was on the space station."

"He's...a friend," Eden replied, but Xander sensed the hesitation in her words, like she wasn't sure if she should classify him as a friend or a.... What else had she been considering? A boyfriend? No way. It wasn't possible that Eden had moved on so quickly.

Xander's heart raced, and he had to know that moment.

"Don't squeeze my knee," Eden complained, and Xander let go of the pressure he had been applying.

"Sorry. What did Roman or whoever tell you about me?"

"What do you mean?"

"I mean, when I left. Obviously, we didn't hit the asteroid the way we were supposed to, so they must have said something, right?"

"Uh, Roman asked me if I knew what you were planning. He was all mad, but I didn't know what he was talking about. I knew that the asteroid wasn't hit when they thought it would be, but then it was destroyed. There was a huge celebration. And...I just thought you got off course or something. When I heard it had been destroyed, I knew that you couldn't have survived." Eden wiped at her eyes.

"You really thought I was dead," Xander echoed.

"Yeah, and it was hard. I thought you were gone. I cried a lot," Eden admitted with a weird king of chuckle.

Xander wrapped an arm around her shoulders, and she didn't duck away now. She laid her head against him, and he played with the ends of her hair. "I wanted to communicate with you, but it was impossible."

"Sorry," he added after a minute.

"Sorry," Eden echoed, and Xander studied the top of her head.

"What are you saying sorry for?" he asked, thinking she was apologizing for crying. He had seen all of Eden's emotions, especially in the month before the Olympics, so he didn't see why she was apologizing now.

Eden took a deep breath. "I kissed Simon," she said.

Xander blinked a couple of times, taking the words like a punch to his stomach. He immediately wondered if Eden had thought about him when she had kissed Simon, and if their kisses had compared. Had it been more than once?

"Oh," Xander said after a second.

Eden rushed to give her excuses. "I thought you were dead, and he was there when I needed a friend, and so...it kind of happened."

"So you like him," Xander stated. If he asked it as a question, then he would have to hear her answer. He wasn't sure he wanted to be punched again.

"I..." Once again, Xander heard her hesitation, and it bugged him. "He's a good friend, but..."

"I don't kiss my friends. I mean, you can ask Connor if you don't believe me." Xander wasn't sure where the nasty comments were coming from, but he suddenly felt like he needed some space. He retracted his arm and stood.

As soon as he moved, Simon shifted to his side, and the whistling noise stopped. Xander stared at Simon hard, wondering if he were awake. He hoped not, but he couldn't be sure.

There wasn't much space to pace, so Xander just shifted back and forth, kind of an awkward march in place. He stared at the wall, because it was easier than staring at Eden. Finally, when he thought he had his disappointment under control, he sat back down on the mattress, keeping his hands to himself.

He dared a glance at Eden. She was staring into her lap like a child about to be scolded. The easy conversation from before was gone. It had never really reappeared since Xander had come back, and Xander wondered if the thing he had worked so hard to get was gone forever.

"You thought I was dead," he finally said. "It's no big deal. You can like whoever you want to like." He lifted one of his shoulders in what he hoped was an easygoing shrug.

"Then why do you look like you're mad?" Eden asked.

Xander studied her wide, brown eyes. He didn't even think she was making that puppy-dog, pleading look on purpose. "I'm just surprised that you moved on so quickly. I mean, I was gone..." he tried to do a quick calculation. "A week or so? And you've got a new boyfriend." He shrugged again, knowing that even though he was trying to hold it back, the bitterness was coming through.

"He's not my..." Eden glanced at the sleeping SImon and lowered her voice, "...boyfriend. He's just...okay, I kind of like him, but not as much as I like you."

Then why didn't you look excited to see me? Why did you disappear all night last night? Xander wanted to scream at her. He had assumed Eden was with Nicole, but suddenly he wondered if she had spent the night with Simon. Maybe *that* was why Simon was so tired.

Xander felt like he was going to be sick. Once again, he stood and started trying to pace. He couldn't get very far, and the frustration in him felt like it was going to burst out. This wasn't the way he had imagined his reunion with Eden. He should have just stayed on Earth and left her in the spaceship with her boyfriend, Simon.

Chapter 25

Eden had assumed she would spend the whole ride back to Earth eagerly exchanging stories with Xander. She hadn't counted on Simon being in their room, and she hadn't counted on the strange feeling of discontent that had welled up in her.

Eventually, she had decided that faking a nap would be the best way to avoid the awkwardness. Because there was so little room, Eden had curled up on her side while Xander sat at the end of her mattress. Simon was so tall that he spread out over his entire mattress.

Eden lay looking at the wall, staring at the metal. She could feel the heat rising off it and wondered why the ships were designed so poorly that the walls became piping hot whenever it was in use. Every time Xander shifted, Eden's thoughts jumped away from her mundane wonderings to him.

Did he hate her now? She'd *had* to tell him about kissing Simon. It was only right, and honestly, it wasn't like she had been cheating on him. Sure, they hadn't broken things off before he left the space station, but she had thought he was *dead*. If she had even doubted he was for a second, then she never would have opened herself up to Simon.

Eden closed her eyes and took a couple of deep, calming breaths to try to center herself and calm down her racing heart. Surprisingly, a feeling of calm rose within her, so she took a few more deep breaths.

Everything would be alright. Things would work out. She was going to be a regular citizen of Greenland, and...

She instantly became alert when she heard some movement behind her, but something told her to keep her eyes closed.

"Eden's sleeping?" Simon asked, yawning so loudly that no one within twenty feet of him would be able to keep sleeping.

Eden tried to keep her face neutral, even though eavesdropping felt like a crime. She wanted to know if Xander would say anything to Simon. Now that he knew who Simon was and what had happened between him and Eden, would he care enough to speak up?

"Yeah," Xander responded after a second.

There was more rustling around, and Eden felt her muscles remain taut as she waited for something else to be said.

"I'm gonna pee," Simon said. "That's what this bucket is for, right?"

"Yeah," Xander said again.

Eden heard the sounds of peeing and tried to keep her mind focused on the images of reaching Earth, the ones that had been filling her mind earlier, but it was hard to focus on picturing her mom greeting her with the musical noises happening in the background.

Finally, they stopped, and Eden heard Simon settling back into the mattress.

"I brought a deck of cards," Simon announced. "Want to play a game?"

Xander agreed, and Eden heard the flicking noise of the cards being shuffled. Then, everything got quiet, except for the occasional slap of a card hitting the floor. Neither one of the guys spoke, and Eden wasn't sure how they even knew what game they were playing. She had been listening carefully, and no one had said the name of one.

Simon grunted, and Eden heard some more cards hitting the ground. Her eyes darted back and forth under her eyelids, and she knew she wouldn't be able to fake sleeping much longer. She stirred for a moment, and the sound of the cards stopped. She could almost feel both Xander and Simon looking at her.

All she had to do was pop her eyes open and say, "Hi," but then what? She would have to make conversation with them for the next however many hours. The room suddenly felt too small, so Eden stirred again and kept herself firmly facing the wall. Staring at the back of her eyelids was better than figuring out what to say to the two of them while they were all in the same room.

Xander...she wanted to be with him, but she couldn't deny the spark that she felt with Simon. Would it just go away if she ignored it? And if she did, how would she explain that to Simon?

Finally, Eden must have drifted off to sleep, because she was waking up to the sound of someone pacing two steps forward and back right behind her. She yawned silently, then turned around to see what was happening.

Xander was pacing back and forth in the tiny aisle between the two mattresses, and Simon was playing what looked like a game of solitaire on the other mattress.

"Hey," Xander said, pausing in his movement.

"Good morning," Simon greeted, glancing at her before studying the cards facing him.

"Hey," Eden said, drawing out the word and yawning again. "How long has it been?"

"We're about four hours away," Xander answered.

"Oh!" Eden grinned. "That's so close!"

"That's why I napped," Simon said. "I wish I could have slept more because it really helps pass the time."

Xander settled next to Eden on the mattress again, and Eden didn't like the way he was hovering by her, like he was claiming her. Normally, she would have loved the possessiveness, but everything felt wrong.

Eden stood and stretched, feeling a sudden, strong urge in her bladder. She glanced at the designated bathroom bucket, which was already half-full and smelled acrid. She mentally steeled herself to wait the next four hours, but as soon as she sat back down again, her body told her that wasn't going to happen.

She glanced at first Xander, who was watching her closely, then at Simon, whose cards were facing the bathroom bucket.

"Do you...mind?" Eden asked. "I kind of need to use the bucket."

"What?" Simon asked, distracted from his cards. "Oh, oh, yeah, no worries. I'm not watching or anything."

Xander made a show of turning his back to the bucket. Simon was staring at his cards but still facing the bucket.

"Can you just...turn around?" Eden asked, using her fingers to emphasize her meaning.

"Oh, yeah, sure," Simon said, turning on his mattress to stare at the wall. Now, both of the guys were staring at the wall, but Eden still felt awkward as she began to use the bathroom bucket. Now that they had nothing to do but stare at the wall, they were probably *listening* which was almost worse.

Her face reddening from embarrassment, Eden quickly pulled up her pants. She plopped onto the mattress next to Xander. "Done now," she said, when neither one of them turned around.

Simon rotated back to his cards, and Xander sat watching her for a few minutes, his green eyes calculating, like he didn't know what to expect from her. Eden glanced at Simon then back at Xander. She wanted to ask what he was thinking, but it was awkward with someone else listening to their conversation.

Instead, she chose to sit in awkward silence, only responding to Simon's occasional remarks about his cards.

Four calls from the hallway later, Eden felt a difference in the way the spaceship was traveling. She suddenly felt heavier, and the spaceship started to move more quickly. She glanced at the wall like a window might suddenly appear and give her a chance to see their progress.

"We should probably sit down," Xander said, "in case the landing is bumpy."

Eden glanced at the bathroom bucket and scooted away from it a little bit, hoping it wouldn't slosh too much when they hit the ground.

"Where are we landing?" Simon asked, finally pushing the cards back into a neat pile.

Xander shrugged. "I guess back near the research center. I'm not sure what Colt programmed in."

"I just hope Greenland doesn't kick me into the water and make me start swimming for home," Simon said.

For the first time, Eden imagined an unwelcoming group of officials waiting for them. No, Xander wouldn't have brought them back if there wasn't a place for them.

Xander reached an arm around her shoulders. He didn't say anything, but his arm was exactly what she needed at that moment. She sat in Xander's circle of comfort as the spaceship slowed, then bumped down haltingly.

Eden caught herself from tumbling forward and pushed herself back into a sitting position. She felt kind of sick, her stomach turning over. She stayed still, waiting for the feeling to pass, but it didn't.

When Eden glanced at Xander, then at Simon, they both looked queasy too.

Finally, after what felt like a long time, the seams for the door in their wall appeared, and the door slid away.

Even though she didn't feel well, Eden stumbled toward the open space clutching her bundle of clothing. She was desperate to be free, to see Earth again, to make sure that everything was real.

Other people were stumbling out of their rooms and looking sick as well. Remembering her journey in the spaceship just a few weeks before, Eden stumbled down the hallway to the set of stairs that would lead her outside.

"Eden!" she heard behind her, and Eden reluctantly waited as Xander caught up to her. Simon was right behind him, then there was a crush of people, all hurrying them forward. Eden almost fell on the steps, but Xander grabbed her shoulder when she pitched forward and helped her stay upright.

The door at the top of the stairs wasn't open, and when Eden tried the handle, it was locked. Someone behind her pushed forward to try it too, but it wasn't opening.

"We're going to die in here!" someone called out.

People pushed forward, squishing Eden against the door, when something clicked. She tried the handle again, and the door opened. She was barely able to shuffle backward enough to pull it. But through the gap, she could see the light blue sky with fluffy, white clouds dancing across it. This was the way she was used to seeing the sky, not as a dark, starry blanket.

Eden had been taking her time pulling the door open and stepping into the fresh air, but the people behind her pushed her through. The scent of pine needles filled her with nostalgia as she took her first few steps on Earth again.

"Line up right here!" an angry voice shouted.

Eden's eyes snapped open, and she turned to look at the person who had shouted. He was pointing a gun directly at her, his eyes angry pools of darkness. Eden glanced at the officials she had registered briefly before focusing on the wonder of being in a breathable atmosphere again.

She glanced behind her to make sure that other people were seeing this too.

"Move slowly. Right there," the man said. The gun he had was long and intimidating. Eden had never seen a gun like that, and she wasn't sure she would be able to make her feet move.

Suddenly, Xander was behind her again. He grabbed her hand and steered her in the direction the man wanted, and everyone else followed their lead. When they had marched the length of the spaceship, the man with the gun following them commanded them to stop.

Eden slowly revolved on the spot until she was making eye contact with the man carrying the gun again. She slowly leaned her face back until she could whisper in Xander's direction.

"I thought you said they were going to be friendly."

"They should be," Xander responded, not looking at her.

"Well, they aren't. What if they shoot us?" Eden recalled the terrible noise of someone being shot when he had broken away from their group of eliminated.

"That's not going to happen," Xander replied with a determination he couldn't really feel. Eden's hands felt sweaty, and she wiped them on her shirt, wondering how many minutes or hours she had left. This was all Xander's fault.

Chapter 26

Xander watched and waited, trying to understand the purpose behind lining everyone up like they were prisoners. He glanced at the officials' faces as they passed in front of him, trying to see someone he recognized.

The line had to shift down as more people came out of the spaceship than the official had first anticipated. Now, they were past the end of the spaceship, and Xander could see the road that led to Sisimiut stretching in front of and behind them. The ocean lapped at the rocks just a few yards away.

Eden clenched her arms around herself, and Xander could tell that she was worried. Worse, he was pretty sure she thought this was his fault, and wasn't it, kind of?

"Excuse me!" Xander called.

An official with a pistol immediately swiveled and gave Xander his full attention.

"Can I speak to..." Xander didn't want to call him Barrel like he had in his mind, so he scrambled to remember the guy's real name. "Sergeant Flynn?"

"What do you want to say to him?" the official asked, his pistol lowering a notch or two. Xander still didn't feel safe, knowing that a twitch of the man's finger could send a bullet through his chest.

"I fought against the Alaskans when they invaded," he said, hoping that the man would believe him since he had information that no one just landing would have.

The official continued to stare at Xander. "Fine, I'll take you to him," he decided. He called to one of the other officials, and they had a quick, shouted conversation about where he was taking Xander.

Xander squeezed Eden's arm for comfort, then slipped out of the line and walked ahead of the man with the pistol.

When they were a short distance away from the spaceship, the official started asking him questions. Xander noticed that he wasn't leading him to the entrance Xander had used before.

"How do you know Sergeant Flynn?"

Even though he wanted to be irritated, Xander just repeated the same answer he had given before. "I fought with the Alaskans when they sent that plane in for an attack. He gave me and a bunch of others guns with blanks."

The official didn't say anything for a few minutes, and Xander couldn't turn around to see his expression. "Right," the official said after a second, finally agreeing with Xander. After a few more steps, he barked again, "Turn right!"

"Oh," Xander had thought he was agreeing, not commanding.

Xander turned right and started picking his way slowly through rocky outcroppings, not sure where he was being taken.

"You're the one who stole the spaceship then," the official finally concluded.

Xander tilted his head back and forth, weighing his options. "Yes," he finally said. He didn't want Colt to get blamed. Colt was too useful, and he wouldn't know how to deal with a stressful, questioning situation.

"Huh," the official said, almost laughing. Xander stumbled on some rocks and caught himself. When the official chuckled, Xander wanted to turn around and show him something funny. But he didn't. This guy had a firearm, and he probably knew how to use it. If he hadn't, Xander was confident that he would have been able to easily take him down.

"There," the official said, motioning to a rock wall. Xander stopped and studied it, then noticed a fracture in the rock that could indicate where a door was. The official stepped forward and for only a fraction of a second had his back to Xander.

Then, the door was open, and Xander was being ushered inside.

The sudden darkness shocked his eyes, and he squinted and blinked, unable to move until he was no longer blind. Finally, he realized that a dim light was outlining everything.

"You can wait for Sergeant Flynn there," the official said, motioning to a doorway just off the barely lit hallway.

Xander stepped into a room that looked like a prison cell. There were no windows, and two of the walls were made out of rough rock. The official shut the door behind him, and Xander was alone.

This room was slightly bigger than the one he had shared with Eden and Simon on the way back to Earth, but one of the walls darted up to the ceiling at a strange angle, making the corner unusable space. Xander ran his hand along the rock wall, and it felt cool under his touch. The whole space was at least ten degrees cooler than it had been outside, and Xander didn't see any sort of air conditioning device in the room.

Assuming he would be waiting for a long time, Xander settled in with his back against the cool, rock wall. Just as he had gotten comfortable, the door opened, and Sergeant Flynn filled the doorway. He stared at Xander as Xander leaped to his feet and narrowly missed hitting his head on the ceiling.

"Xander Coxon," Barrel said, his eyes evaluating Xander slowly. "You are a troublemaker. I should have guessed it when you accused me of giving you blanks."

Xander wanted to point out that accusing someone of doing something he had actually done didn't make him a troublemaker, but he kept his attention on the real problem at hand. "I'm not here to cause trouble, Sir. I'm here to help." A little respect never hurt, so Xander threw in the "sir."

"Let's have a conversation," Sergeant Flynn said. He signaled toward the doorway and led Xander to another small room. This one had some chairs in the cave-like space, the kind of armchairs Xander might see in his grandmother's house. Their style was so unexpected that Xander didn't know what to say at first.

Sergeant Flynn flopped into one, sighing loudly, and Xander took a deep purple one with tiny white flowers on it. The chair hugged him like a long-lost friend, and the comfort made Xander want to close his eyes and curl up for a little nap.

"When you and I last talked, you were looking for more help against Alaska," Xander started when Barrel didn't say anything. "I've brought help against Alaska."

The man studied him critically for a minute, then laughed. "*Those* people are my *help*? They look like an underfed lot of misfits. None of them know how to fight, that I'm sure of."

"They may not be trained like officials are, but some of them competed in wrestling. Some of them would be really good, and a lot of them are willing." Okay, Xander was really stepping out and volunteering information he didn't know here, but he didn't know what else to say. If he didn't present them as offering something worthwhile, then Sergeant Flynn might just decide they were extra work. He had seen the way the officials were brandishing their guns toward them.

"And even more important than training," Xander added when Barrel didn't say anything, "is willingness to fight. They have been stuck on a spaceship for years. They may not know what sunshine feels like on their skin anymore, but they know they want the chance to feel it. They'll fight if it means they can earn their place here."

"Huh," Barrel said again, clearly not in a talkative mood. "And you're here to make sure they don't lose their lives for throwing away the one chance they were given to live after elimination."

Xander tilted his head to the side, conceding Barrel's point. They both sat in silence for what felt like a long time as Xander forced himself to keep his thoughts inside. He would seem stronger and smarter if he just waited out Barrel.

"I would need to hear from them that they're willing to volunteer," Barrel finally said.

Xander nodded, sure that at least half of the people who he had rescued from the space station would volunteer if they understood what was at stake. "I understand."

Sergeant Flynn squinted at Xander, screwing his face up like he was about to ask a distasteful question. "I would give them blanks. Can't trust you all wouldn't turn against us."

This made it a little harder for Xander to agree. "Would you *tell* them that you're giving them blanks?" he asked. "If they are risking their lives, then they should understand how their weapon works."

Barrel didn't answer right away. Instead, he rested his hands across his ample chest and studied Xander some more. "If they know they have blanks, they won't be willing to fight." A pause. "I just sent two hundred of my best boys to Alaska. They had *real* weapons with *real* bullets, and we've got more injuries and fatalities than healthy ones left."

Xander's stomach turned over as his mind started calculating the math behind that. "That number will be higher if you don't give them real weapons," Xander pointed out. "Some of them may be originally from Alaska and not be willing to fight for a government that doesn't supply them correctly. And I *will* tell them if they've been given blanks."

The air between them grew tense, but Xander didn't want to be responsible for putting everyone on the spaceship in a bad situation. He thought back on the few that had remained, determined to stick with the evil they knew versus the evil they didn't. He had thought they were dumb, throwing away a chance to live, but now, he envied the predictability of their next few weeks, months, years.

"I'll ask for volunteers. Those who don't volunteer will be put somewhere safe until all of this is over."

Xander nodded at the sensibility behind the plan. "I'll be the first volunteer." Even though he didn't want to go to Alaska, especially if that meant entering a losing battle, he would do it if it meant that there was a chance the battle would end and life could go back to the normal he had enjoyed before. "But you have to agree that these eliminated, the ones who have come back with me, will be allowed to live."

"Not if they don't volunteer," Barrel decided.

"Trust me," Xander said, trying to remain calm. "You don't want everyone from that spaceship to be holding a gun, even if it only has blanks in it. Some of them..." he let his sentence trail off so Sergeant Flynn could imagine how badly things would go. All Xander had to do was imagine Colt waving a gun around, and he knew what he was saying was right. Not everyone from the space station would know what to do if armed.

He spoke again when Sergeant Flynn didn't look like he was going to agree. "The ones who volunteer will be the ones who are willing to make a sacrifice. They'll be the ones you want fighting on your side, not someone who might turn around and run away."

"If they run away, then why should we save them?" he asked.

Xander held in the puff of frustration. "Not everyone is fighting material. Not everyone wanted to win a medal in wrestling or even tried to compete in it. It's not their talent. That doesn't mean we don't need scientists or teachers or whoever else."

"I'll see how many volunteer, then I'll make my decision," Barrel said, hefting himself to his feet. He didn't give Xander any instructions, but Xander followed him out of the cave-like room. He hoped that at least half of the space station inhabitants would be willing to fight for their new chance at life.

Chapter 27

Once Xander had left Eden with the armed men, she wrapped her arms around herself. The sun felt warm and welcoming, but she still had goosebumps. Something bad was going to happen. She could feel it.

It took a long time for everyone to pile out of the spaceship. The line started slowing, and a couple of officials entered the spaceship and came out with about fifteen more people. They had clearly figured out what was happening and thought they would be safer hiding in the spaceship than facing the guys with the guns.

"You alright?" a voice asked just above her ear.

Eden turned and saw Simon standing behind her. She instantly felt a little relieved, just knowing that she wasn't alone. She had seen Helena climb out twenty minutes after she had, but there were many people between the two of them.

"Fine, just don't know what's going to happen," Eden replied.

"It will work out. They won't send us back. Wasting another spaceship would be stupid."

"That's not what I'm worried about."

Eden had never seen so many guns in her life, and she wondered if the officials were planning to use them or just carry them to scare everyone into obedience.

Simon laid a hand on Eden's shoulder and squeezed it gently. Eden stared resolutely ahead, her stomach churning as some of the officials conferred.

"You can sit down!" one of the officials shouted out. His order was repeated down the line. "You'll be waiting awhile!"

Eden crossed her legs and sat down, running her hand through the grass. It tickled her skin in a familiar way, and she suddenly remembered the many times she and Xander had lain in the grass and stared at the clouds, discussing what would happen after they both won medals in the Olympics. Back then, it had seemed obvious that nothing bad would ever happen to either of them.

Simon's voice brought her back to the present. "What do you think they'll do now?" he asked.

"I guess we just have to wait." Eden gazed off in the direction Xander had gone and wondered if he would be able to fulfill his promise of them having a safe life here even though they had been eliminated. As she strained her eyes to see if anyone was approaching from that direction, she realized that the time was never going to pass if she kept waiting for movement.

To distract herself, she turned and faced Simon. "I hope we don't get burnt waiting out here, though. A lot of you haven't been in the sun for years."

Simon looked up and down the line of people in various states of sunbathing and nodded. "Good point." He looked down at his own pale arm. "Too bad they aren't passing out tubes of sunscreen. Maybe I should do something about it." He stood up, and Eden reached for the hem of his pants to tug him back down. No way was Simon going to abandon her too.

"Don't go anywhere," she told him, in case he hadn't gotten the first hint.

"Who said I was going somewhere? I'm becoming a tree to give you shade," he said, stretching out his arms and balancing on one foot like some sort of awkward flamingo.

"I'm not the one who needs protection," Eden said. "I wasn't up there long. I'm sure some others would appreciate your flamingoness."

"Flamingo? No, no, I'm a *tree*."

"Well, *tree,* you're missing leaves and roots and other important things."

Simon finally flopped down again, and Eden noticed that his skin was already taking on a pink tinge. Someone down the line started complaining of hunger, and Eden's stomach rumbled too. Still, she kept quiet, not wanting to draw any extra attention to herself.

"So you and Xander used to be a thing?" Simon asked.

Eden was about to correct him on that "used to" phrase, but the truth was that they hadn't really clarified their status since Xander had come back to life. Maybe "come back to life" wasn't the right way of calling it either, but she kind of felt like his reappearance was a miracle, one that had come without time to prepare.

"We...said that we would date if we both won medals," she explained. She and her mom had been close, but not close enough that Eden had wanted to squeal over Xander with her. Whenever he had done something sweet or kind or whatever, she had just squealed to herself. She hadn't really talked about her feelings for Xander *with* anyone, especially another guy. This was kind of weird.

"But neither of you did," Simon clarified.

"Actually, we both did," Eden said.

Simon looked confused, so Eden tried to explain their story as succinctly as possible. She had spent a lot of time with Simon just talking about what happened on the space station, not about what had happened before. This was a new experience. "Basically, I cheated in the running competition, then later won a medal in the science competition. I don't even know how I won one, to be honest. But they found out I cheated, and they took my medal away. Xander gave his up so I wouldn't have to be eliminated alone."

Simon's eyebrows rose. "Wow. Bold move."

Eden shrugged and bit at her bottom lip, thinking about the second time Xander had chosen to give up his life. He had escaped death two times, times he shouldn't have. Would they really be lucky a third time?

"I get it then. Now that he's back, you're hoping you can start a normal life here, with a relationship and everything."

Eden felt like Simon was fishing, wanting her to admit something. She pressed her thumb into her arm to see if her skin was burning yet. "The weird thing is that I don't know. I used to have my life all mapped out, how it was going to go. If I didn't win a medal, then that was the end. But if I *did*, then I had a life kind of already imagined. It sounds dumb now, I know..."

"It's not dumb," Simon assured her. "I thought even though I didn't stand a chance, I would still win a medal somehow." He shrugged. "But I didn't. And I'm here, and here isn't so bad."

Eden smiled at him and finally nodded her agreement. "Yeah, it's not." But then she remembered where she really was, and she glanced back at the pacing officials, each of them carrying a different-sized gun.

Simon nudged her, and Eden turned back to him. "Yes?" she asked.

"You were saying here isn't so bad," he reminded her.

"Yeah," this time, she didn't sound as sure, more like a dejected sigh. "I mean, I made friends I never would have if I hadn't been eliminated. I'm just worried about what's going to happen now."

"Worrying about it won't change it," Simon said in a rare moment of seriousness. "Focus on something else."

Eden raised an eyebrow at Simon, trying to tell him that it wasn't as easy as just deciding to shift her focus.

"Like me," Simon said, wiggling his head back and forth on his neck.

Now, Eden laughed. He was being so ridiculous, but ridiculous was what she needed at the moment.

"Yeah, okay, I'm focusing on you," she said, moving her head to follow Simon's path. It was crazy how something so little, so silly could release some of her nerves.

"And now," Simon said, holding an imaginary microphone up to his lips, "you'll strike the turtle pose." He pressed his hands into the grass and craned his neck upward.

Someone nearby was watching Simon and started laughing. Feeling self-conscious, Eden sat back a little so that it was clear that she had not started this ridiculous animal yoga.

Simon laughed as he sat back in a much more normal pose. Eden looked in the direction of Sisimiut. The rubble of the nearby buildings did nothing to help orient her, but she could see the road that ran along the cliff, the road that she and Xander had spent hours pedaling along. She missed her bike and wondered if it was still there, leaned just inside their apartment door.

"What are you thinking?" Simon asked.

Eden hesitated. Normally, she wouldn't share her thoughts just like that. But part of her wanted to reminisce out loud. "I used to ride my bike along this road, not right here exactly but further down."

Simon nodded, and Eden continued, feeling like he was really listening.

"Riding my bike made me feel so free. I loved the way it felt like I could outrun whatever was bothering me." She shrugged. "I know that's dumb."

"It's not. Don't say it is. I used to spend a fair amount of time on my bike too," Simon said.

"Really?"

"Yeah, it was a lot easier to get to school like that than walking. I don't know about here, but in Alaska, school buses are seen as a waste of petrol. You have to figure out your own way of getting to school."

Eden nodded at the similarity of life in different countries. "Same here. Almost no one has a car except for a few important people. My dad used to walk to work, but my mom would always ride her bike."

"I wondered what it would be like," Simon said after a short pause, "having a regular job somewhere. Part of me thought it would be boring, the adult life. But of course, I would prefer that to no life at all."

"What did you see yourself doing if you won a medal?"

"I wanted to be a teacher," Simon said, "but of the little kids. They get to have more fun. When you get older, it gets too competitive. Everything is so serious. But the little kids still have fun in school, and they barely even think about the Olympics unless they have a much older sibling."

"A teacher," Eden said, considering what Simon's career would look like. "You'd be a good teacher. You would always make them laugh."

"Oh yeah?" Simon asked, his mouth curving upward.

"Yeah," Eden nodded, too focused on Simon's mouth. "You would." She said the words, but she couldn't really focus on their meaning. She was thinking about this little life Simon had just painted for her. He was a teacher at an elementary school, and Eden was a health coach since she couldn't be a professional dancer.

They would go home to their own apartment, and then...

Eden wasn't sure how it happened, but she realized she was leaning toward Simon. She tried to slow down the movement, but it was like her thoughts couldn't reach her brain very quickly.

Then, she and Simon kissed. It was nothing as intimate as their first kiss, but still, Eden felt the spark of something. She pulled back immediately and glanced around, sure that Xander was staring into the back of her head. But he wasn't. No one was paying attention. They were all wrapped up in their hungry stomachs and approaching sunburns.

When Eden made eye contact with Simon again, he was looking at her through confused, brown eyes. He wanted to know what the kiss meant, but Eden couldn't tell him. The last few years, she had only dreamed of being with Xander. But now, she had to admit that she liked spending time with Simon too.

She avoided eye contact, her lips still stinging with the remembrance of Simon's touch. Her brain jumped ahead, telling her that Xander wasn't the only one who cared about her. A flash of a simple life in a newlywed apartment jumped into her brain, but Eden pushed it away before she really got the chance to pull it out of its place and examine it.

"I think something is going to happen," Eden said, clearing her throat and looking expectantly in the direction of a group of five men coming toward them. As she squinted against the sun, she recognized that one of them was Xander, and she felt relieved that he didn't have handcuffs on. He had clearly known what he was talking about when he said there was space for them. Why was he so serious though?

Chapter 28

Barrel stood back and let Xander make his way down the line first, explaining what was happening. On their walk to the group of eliminated, he had made his case for explaining the situation to them first before demanding that they fight. Barrel had just grunted his response to that suggestion, but at least he had agreed.

Xander searched out Eden and found her eyes trained on him from the far end of the line. Even though his feet pulled him in that direction, Xander decided to start at the other side so that he could finish near Eden and be able to stay next to her for as long as possible.

Then, his eyes jerked upward, and he saw Simon right behind her, staring at Xander solemnly. Xander wasn't sure why he disliked Simon so much. Nothing that had happened between Simon and Eden was wrong. They had kissed, sure, but Eden had thought he was dead. That was partly Xander's own fault. No matter what his brain wanted to suspect, he didn't have any proof that anything had happened *after* he had returned to the space station.

Xander turned his attention to the first group. A few extra broke free from the line to crowd around him and make him explain what was happening. "We have been granted the chance to live here, even though we were eliminated," he started explaining. "However, the- er, Sergeant Flynn needs some volunteers to complete his army. A war is happening with Alaska, and he needs more people willing to stand up for Greenland. He said not everyone has to fight, but he needs a lot of volunteers. That will seal our chance to live here."

Xander looked around, hoping that people would volunteer right away. Instead, they shifted uneasily and looked at each other. He noticed a sudden space around him where none had been before. They weren't so eager to listen to him now.

"You have a little bit of time to think about your decision," Xander said. "But we need some willing volunteers." He considered whether to mention the guns and the blanks, but decided it was better just to leave things at that.

As soon as he started moving to the next group, he heard those behind him start whispering, talking about what he had said. Xander gave the same speech with a few adjustments to the second group. This time, someone started a discussion with him.

"How many volunteers does he need?"

"He didn't give me a number, but I get the feeling that the more, the better."

"I've never had any training," someone else said.

"He'll show you what you need to know. And if you still feel underprepared, find me. I won a medal in wrestling, and I would be happy to show you some moves." Though as soon as Xander made the offer, he wondered how useful it would be. Wrestling wouldn't happen if everyone was equipped with a gun.

He continued moving down the line, explaining what was happening and urging everyone to consider if they could do this and volunteer for those who weren't physically capable of it. Xander already knew that he didn't want Eden participating at all. She had no training in this sort of thing, but even if she did, he didn't want her putting herself in danger.

Finally, Xander arrived at the last group. Feeling Eden's eyes on him, he explained what was happening. "Sergeant Flynn needs volunteers to fight the Alaskans in the battle that started a couple of days ago. If he gets enough volunteers, then everyone else will be allowed to stay here and take jobs and live their lives like normal."

Some people started excitedly chatting about what that life would look like.

Xander urged them, "Consider if you can volunteer and don't just wait for everyone else to volunteer or no one will." He made eye contact with the people watching him, his eyes jumping from one to the other slowly... slowly... waiting to see if anyone had questions.

At last, his eyes landed on Eden, and her big, brown eyes were wide with anguish. Xander grabbed her arm just above her elbow and steered her a few steps away from everyone. Eden glanced back at them, and Xander followed her gaze to see Simon's eyes following their movements. Xander gritted his teeth and purposely turned Eden so that her back was to Simon while Xander could keep an eye on him.

"Tell me what you're thinking," Xander said, keeping his voice low.

He glanced at Sergeant Flynn, hoping the man wasn't becoming impatient. He had his back turned to Xander and appeared to be speaking to one of the officials.

"I know you're going to volunteer," Eden said.

Xander was surprised to hear her almost crying. He turned his focus back to her, and her eyes were shining with tears that hadn't been allowed to fall.

"I have to," Xander agreed. "I have to set an example. If I just think about myself, then of course, I just want to stay here with you. But if I think about everyone else, then... I know it's only fair if I volunteer."

Eden looked at the ground and wiped at her face with the heel of her hand. Xander rubbed his hand up and down her shoulder.

"It's not like I think you don't know how to fight," Eden said, sniffing and looking at Xander in the eyes again. "But some of those guns are...big."

"I realize that." Xander glanced at the nearest official who was doing nothing to hide the presence of his gun.

"I wish I didn't have to," Xander spoke again. "But I do. It's only fair. I know how to fight. I actually won a medal in wrestling, and..."

He didn't finish what he was saying because Eden wrapped her arms around him and buried the side of her face in his chest. "I feel like the worst friend ever," she said. "You were busy working out a deal, and I... I..."

Xander rubbed her back, waiting for her to finish getting out her words so he could comfort her.

"I was just thinking about myself," she finished. "I still am. You're so brave. I don't even deserve you."

"Oh, don't say that," Xander said.

"No, but seriously, this is the *third* time, maybe even the fourth that you're throwing away your life, and you're doing it so I can have a chance to live. That's too many. You won't get lucky again," Eden said.

"Since when did you take up fortune telling?" Xander asked, trying to keep things light.

Eden wiped at her face again, her grip on him loosening. He didn't want to admit how much her words bothered him. "I just don't know if you'll be okay," she said.

"Me neither. We can never know." He shrugged, searching for some way to comfort her. "It could even be safer fighting Alaska than just staying in one of the towns. I'll have a weapon." He clenched his jaw at the lie. Sure, he would have a gun, but it might not have any bullets in it. Still, his hands were better weapons than almost anything. He recalled the fight in the research center with the ten officials. He had done pretty well, and he had only had a container of water and a lamp as weapons then.

"I don't want you to worry about it. We'll take care of this so that Alaska is out of the way, then we can actually start our lives like we always planned."

Eden nodded but wouldn't meet his eyes. "Please be safe," she finally begged, looking up at him. Her eyes were still shining, and Eden reached up and ran a hand through her hair.

"I'll do my best. Believe me, I'm not ready to die."

Sergeant Flynn pressed a button on his radio that sent out a piercing screech. He had everyone's attention as he gave the official call for help. "We need volunteers if we want to put Alaska in its place. They have attacked us and started a war, and Russia is not backing us up like they promised. If none of you volunteer, then you all die. If half of you volunteer, then the other half can stay."

Xander winced at Barrel's use of the word "die." Why did he have to put it like that? Couldn't he just say that they would keep waiting around until they got more volunteers?

Xander squeezed Eden's hand, even though it didn't seem like enough, and stepped forward. He needed to be one of the first volunteers and set an example. The first step was difficult, but after that, his legs continued to propel him forward without much thought on his part.

Soon, he was standing in a line with another official and Sergeant Flynn. Xander slowly pivoted until he was facing everyone else. Eden's distraught face stood out to him, but what bothered him more was the way Simon was patting her shoulder. Just as Xander started thinking about how he would put Simon in his place, Simon said something to Eden, then stepped forward and joined Xander.

Simon's lanky body made him stand out from the more muscled officials, and it seemed to be some sort of signal for everyone else that the volunteers didn't need to be trained for this. Xander's eyes continued to trail down the line of people he had brought back from the space station, and he felt personally responsible for each one. He could have taken the easy route out once he had made sure the missile had destroyed the asteroid and stayed down here building a life for himself.

But no, he had taken a risk, a risk for Eden, and all of these people had benefited. At least, he hoped they would benefit. He hoped that things would turn out like they were hoping.

A few more people started to drift across the gap between the officials and everyone else, slowly infiltrating the group with more and more un-trained individuals. Xander knew they hadn't reached half yet, but they had a good start. He noticed an official asking each person's origin country and sending a couple of willing volunteers out of the line.

Xander strained to hear what Simon would say. Hadn't Eden mentioned he was from Alaska. But when the official reached him, he said "Russia" with such confidence that Xander was sure he had gotten confused.

As he waited for more people to feel the tug of their consciences, he turned his gaze back to Eden.

She wasn't trying to hide her tears anymore. She just wiped at them as they leaked out of her eyes, and Xander wished he could wrap his arms around her. In fact, he decided as he stood there that he wouldn't just turn and follow Barrel back to the cave or the underground lair or wherever he was planning to take his new recruits. Xander had to say one more goodbye to Eden.

An official marched down the line, moving his lips as his finger jumped from person to person, and Xander waited while they were counted. He knew about how many people had come in the spaceship, so he started counting the line opposite, sure that they were just twenty people or so away from being even.

The officials conferred, but Xander couldn't hear what they were saying. He glanced at the approximately two hundred people who hadn't moved.

Many of them were avoiding eye contact and trying to make themselves look smaller by hunching over on the ground or folding themselves into small balls.

"We have enough volunteers!" Sergeant Flynn barked out. "Follow me!"

Xander darted across the gap back to Eden, his heart pounding with the daring as he wrapped his arms tightly around her. There was no hesitation as she wrapped her arms back around him, hers fitting perfectly under his. Xander laid his cheek on the top of Eden's head for the briefest moment, and her words about him being lucky so many times ran through his brain. She had a point. Xander had survived a lot. Would he keep surviving?

He wanted to say something important, something lasting, but the group was marching forward. He had to go. It was time for him to go, but he stayed another second or two. "I... bye," he finally said.

Eden licked her lips, but didn't say anything back. She just waved at him, then Xander had to turn away and run to catch up with the group. He forced himself to keep looking forward and not look back. If he allowed himself to look backward then he might not be able to keep going. The sight of Eden so upset made Xander question the decision he had made. But no, he couldn't do that. He had to set an example, and he had to fight Alaska if he and Eden were going to have a chance to live their lives together.

Almost no one talked as they marched to the door in the wall of stone. There were a few murmurs of surprise as they entered the cave's structure, but Xander didn't say anything. He watched everyone else as they reacted to each thing. For those who had grown up near Sisimiut, they started talking about how they had no idea that all of these things were right here, so close by.

Connor threaded his way back through the crowd until he was walking back to Xander. "You okay, man? I saw your girl crying and everything."

"Yeah," Xander responded with a shrug. He wasn't going to talk about *feelings* with Connor, no matter how upset he was. Connor just wasn't that kind of guy.

"This is kind of cool, though, right? I mean, we both wanted to be officials, and now, we're going to be."

Xander opened his mouth to mention the blanks, but he closed it again without saying anything. He wanted them to know, but he didn't know if Barrel would actually do it. If they still had a chance to desert and word spread that they would be fighting real weapons with fake weapons, the group of people might just turn around and go back out through that door. Maybe Xander had been convincing enough to have the Barrel give them real guns.

The movement stopped, but Xander couldn't see what was happening up ahead. He was forced to listen to Connor's attempts to make conversation.

"I thought you were going to bunk with me on the ship back, man, so we could catch up, but I guess you wanted a private room with Eden, huh?"

"We didn't have a private room," Xander responded, annoyed that Connor was trying to pry into Xander's privacy like this.

"Sure? She seemed all connected to you like, 'Don't fight!'"

"Can we listen to what's going on?" Xander asked, turning his ear toward where a lower official was talking to some people ahead of them. He could only catch a few words, but from the movement, it seemed like they were being divided into groups.

"They'll tell us what's happening soon," Connor said. "Man, you're uptight today."

Xander gritted his teeth but kept his mouth shut. Connor had always been a good friend, if annoying sometimes, so now was *not* the time to share his frustration.

Finally, the official made it to them and motioned for ten of them to be a group. "You ten," the official instructed, "are going to be with those of us who are guarding Sisimiut. We have ears in Alaska, and they are planning to infiltrate the capital and kill anyone they find. We need to block as many main thoroughfares as we can and protect the board members."

Xander thought of his mother. She would be safe, right? She wouldn't leave their apartment, and who would single her out to attack? Still, his mind started parading forward, thinking of how he had said goodbye to Eden, but not to his own mother.

"When do we leave?" Xander asked.

"We'll get you equipped, and everyone going to Sisimiut will be put on a bus. It might take a few loads, but we will get you there. You'll be partnered up, never alone."

Connor started to reach for Xander like they were being assigned a science project for school, but the official finished explaining the partner system.

"You'll be partnered with an official who had real training," the official said, giving Connor a pointed look. "You'll listen to your partner no matter what he or she tells you to do, because all of us know what's going on."

Xander appreciated the fact that they weren't just throwing these volunteers out on their own.

"Wait for your partner to come find you and equip you."

"Will we be equipped with blanks or real bullets?" Xander asked, his throat feeling dry as he voiced his concern. It was now or never.

Several heads swiveled in his direction, but the official stared him down. "You can choose to go into battle with blanks or with no weapon at all. What do you choose?"

Murmurs echoed up and down the line as the volunteers realized what they were really going to be doing. Xander's heart pounded loudly in his chest. "I'll take a gun, blanks or not," he said. "The enemy won't know it's useless."

The official nodded at him, and Xander settled against the cool cave wall to wait. He had done his job of alerting the volunteers of the real situation. They had a choice to take a gun or not, but at least they knew that it was filled with blanks.

Part of him felt excited; part of him felt a premonition that this wasn't going to end well. Xander could only assume the best and focus on the positive. He was going to be fighting whether he was ready or not.

Chapter 29

An official led Eden's group into a shaded area and started explaining what was going to happen. There was an underground hiding area, apparently, but there wouldn't be enough room for everyone. Half of them could go there, and half of them could go to Sisimiut. The officials would do their best to find hiding places for them, but he couldn't promise the safety of those places. Greenland was in a state of emergency until further notice, but once that passed, they would be assigned jobs.

Eden studied the ground for a minute. She didn't want a hiding place. The sudden excitement of being able to see her mom bloomed within her. As soon as the idea had occurred to her, she couldn't think of anything else. She *had* to see her mom. So, when volunteers were asked who would be going into Sisimiut, Eden raised her hand immediately.

Then, she spotted Helena across the circle, making eye contact and slowly raising her hand in response as well. Eden tried to remember if Helena had told her which country she had come from, but Eden couldn't hold onto concrete details in that moment.

The official nodded and motioned for another official to take the group that would be staying in the underground hiding spot. Eden watched the group leave, wondering if she was stupid because she was taking the less safe, sentimental route.

A couple of officials remained, and one of them pointed in the direction of the road. "Turn left and keep walking," he said. "It will be dark in six hours. You should be there and in hiding by then."

Eden's eyes widened. That was it? They were just leaving them to their own devices? After the moment of shock passed, Eden darted forward and wrapped her arm around Helena, tugging her away from everyone else. She could really go anywhere she wanted, and she wanted to see her parents. She wasn't sure how many miles the research center was from where she used to live, but she knew that they could make it if they hurried.

"Where are we going?" Helena asked as Eden was one of the first people to set foot on the road.

"My apartment," Eden said. "I haven't been there in *so* long."

Annoying tears popped up, but Eden swallowed them out of her throat so she could keep talking.

"I thought I would never see my parents again. You'll love them, and they'll love you. And I think if we're just there, in an apartment, not standing out from anyone, then we'll be safe... you know, not any sort of target."

Helena nodded, and Eden glanced at her friend as the dusty road stretched out in front of them. Even though they were the first two to get moving, everyone else was peeling out in groups as they headed for Sisimiut. Some talked excitedly, clearly natives of the area, while many others remained silent, trooping forward like they were completing a duty.

"Are you okay? How are you feeling after landing here and everything?"

Helena squinted up at the sun. "It's strange, like I almost believed that thing didn't exist anymore. And here it is."

Eden stretched her arms out so that the sun's rays bounced off the back of them. "I know what you mean. I had kind of accepted that I would be on that space station forever. But now..." She didn't want to keep talking about her parents and bore Helena, but she was so excited to actually see them again.

When Helena didn't say anything to fill the silence, Eden's thoughts hurried ahead to what it would be like to enter her apartment again. She hoped her bed and room were still set up how she had had them. All she wanted to do was curl up under the covers and let everything that had been bothering her drift away.

"I wonder how long they will consider Greenland in a 'state of emergency,'" Eden said, copying the phrase the official had used. "And what job they will give each of us when everything has passed."

"You do realize that there's a possibility it won't pass," Helena said. "Did you see the destruction in that area? I don't know if Alaska has access to missiles, but they did something to destroy *buildings*."

Helena's negative mood was wiggling into Eden's excitement. She didn't want to think practically, especially about missiles. "But if Alaska wanted to really kill everyone off, wouldn't they have aimed a missile at the bigger cities? The officials didn't say anything about a missile hitting Sisimiut or any of the other major population areas."

"Maybe the first one was just a warning," Helena said. "And now that Greenland isn't backing down, they're going to start really hurting us. I don't think we're safe anywhere."

Eden swallowed and imagined a missile falling and destroying her apartment building. It seemed almost comical, it was so strange. Surely, the war wouldn't come to *them*.

"We'll be fine," she said, though she had no way to back up her words.

"How can you *know* that?" Helena asked.

"I mean, I just…it doesn't seem right that we would come all the way here just for a missile to…"

"Nothing about this life is right or fair. I've learned that from living in the space station," Helena said, her tone dour.

Eden didn't respond. What was she going to say to someone who was determined to see everything in the most negative light possible? Keeping her mouth shut even though she wanted to chatter excitedly, she thought about her parents and her apartment and her old life before cheating in the Olympics had ruined everything. A couple of times, she opened her mouth to share a detail with Helena. But then, she glanced over at her and saw her sour mouth turned down at the corners, and Eden shut her mouth again.

Eden glanced up at the sun that had now shifted decidedly to the right. It would be setting in another two to three hours if she had to guess. When she placed a hand on her shoulder, the skin was aflame beneath it. She *knew* that she was going to be burnt for the next few days or even a week. But it was worth it.

Glancing behind them, Eden realized that not everyone had kept up with their steady pace forward. Some people had dropped back or scurried under the shade of the trees for a chance to rest. Eden knew that if she stopped moving, though, it would be difficult to start back up again.

The buildings of Sisimiut had been visible for the last thirty minutes, and they were starting to pass a few houses on the outskirts of the city. Eden smiled at each one. The route was more familiar now. She had often ridden her bicycle out this far and back to her apartment.

Some of the others, clearly not from Sisimiut, appeared lost as they stalled at the edge of the city, but Eden's pace sped up as she realized how close she was to her home.

"It's probably only thirty more minutes from here," she told Helena, her mouth feeling dry as she spoke. If she thought about it too long, her dry tongue started to swell in her mouth, and the fuzzy feeling of needing water after so much exertion started to take over. She would be able to have as much water as she wanted once they reached her apartment. She continued to remind herself of that fact as they moved forward.

"Turn here," Eden directed, glad of something to say as she cut up a side street. The parade of people behind them petered out as they began looking for places to hide.

"At least we have a place to go," Helena said as they climbed the hill to Eden's apartment.

Eden nodded, now too tired for conversation. She could almost see the look on her mom's face when she realized Eden was standing in front of her. That picture infused energy into Eden, and Eden hurried forward, leaving Helena a bit behind her.

Her feet took the apartment steps two at a time. Then, she was standing in front of her old home, heaving with the effort of reaching it, her skin on fire from the relentless sun.

Eden took a couple of deep breaths, and she faintly registered Helena thumping up the stairs slowly. Then, Eden watched as her own hand moved forward and tried the handle. It didn't open. She tried it harder for a second, thinking that she just hadn't expended enough effort, but it was locked.

A wild, panicky thought passed through her head that her parents weren't home after all, and Eden would have to wait hours for them to return.

"Knock," Helena suggested calmly.

Eden made a fist and knocked soundly on the door, straining her ears to hear any sign of life behind it. Then, she did, and nothing else mattered besides the sound of movement getting closer to the door,

The door flew open, and Eden stared at her mother. She hadn't changed at all since Eden had left. The familiar ponytail and the curve of her cheeks made Eden stumble forward without a word, wrapping her sensitive, sunburnt arms around her mother.

"E-den?" her mother said, clearly not believing that her daughter was alive.

Eden found that she couldn't speak. Nothing seemed right, and the familiar smell of her mother's clean clothes made Eden want to cry. She remained in her mother's arms like that before she realized that the apartment was cooler for a reason. A/C! Eden stood on her own two feet again and stumbled further into the apartment.

Everything was exactly where it was supposed to be, and Eden's gaze jumped eagerly from item to item. The dirty dishes were in the sink just like they always were. The four wooden chairs, three more worn out than the last one, were pushed under the table. The door to her room remained firmly shut, but Eden walked toward it slowly, wanting and not wanting to see her space at the same time.

A voice reached her from far away, and Eden stopped with her hand on the doorknob. She rocketed back into the present, her mom halfway between the still-open front door and Eden.

"Oh," Eden said. "Helena's my friend. We need a place to stay, and I thought she could stay here since she doesn't know anyone here."

"Y-yeah," Eden's mom responded, "but *how* are you here? It's been...weeks since the Olympics. And..."

Eden dropped her hand from the doorknob and came back to the living room, saving the visit to her room and her bed like a strange treat. She sat on the couch, and even that felt right. "Helena, come sit with me," Eden said. Helena was hovering just inside the doorway, clearly uncomfortable with making herself at home.

Helena glanced at Eden's mom who seemed to understand what was happening. She motioned for Helena to come inside even though she didn't take her eyes off Eden.

"Let me get your father," Eden's mom said, moving to their bedroom door. Dad was home during a weekday? Eden didn't have much time to think about the strangeness of it as Helena perched on the couch next to her.

The door to her parents' bedroom flew open. "I was trying to take a nap, and you-" But he stopped in the middle of his "interrupting my nap" tirade. He stared at Eden the same way her mom had, ignoring Helena completely.

Then, her dad blinked, glanced at her mother, then back at Eden.

He crossed the floor in less than a second and had his grizzly, hairy arms around her. Eden reveled in the familiar feel of his too-strong hug. "Dad," she managed, her voice coming out as a squeak.

"You're alive!" her dad choked out, clearly trying to hide his emotion. "What happened? Is this related to the war with Alaska?"

"Let's...sit down," Eden's mom suggested, reverting back to her comforting role. "I can get everyone something to drink. Do you want..."

"Yes, please!" Helena agreed before Eden's mom had had a chance to trot out all the options.

Eden's mom smiled. "Are you hungry too?"

Eden nodded, finally allowing herself to feel the hunger pains in her stomach. "So hungry, Mom."

"Okay, give me just a minute. I'll get something quick ready." Her mom started opening the fridge, then the freezer, and pulling things out onto the counter. Helena moved into the kitchen area and offered her help.

Eden just stared at her dad and noticed a little difference with him. He had lost some weight. He had a couple of gray hairs peeking through his normally-dark hair. He had never looked old before. But no, something had changed. Eden stood up and hugged her dad again, because one hug didn't feel like enough.

"Don't say anything yet!" Eden's mom commanded from the kitchen. "I want to hear everything."

Eden and her dad shared a secret smile, the way they always did when her mom did something that was just like her. So, they sat in silence on the couch, Eden watching as darkness fell out the window and wondering where all the other eliminated had decided to roost for the night.

Finally, her mom brought over warm chicken sandwiches, and Eden bit into one, trying to make herself savor the bite and really taste it. She couldn't control herself though. She took three more bites before pausing for a breath.

When she glanced over at Helena, she was treating her sandwich the same way. "This is good. Thank you so much," she said.

Oh, manners. Eden had forgotten about those in her eagerness to fill her stomach. She felt her mom's and dad's eyes on her as she ate. Finally, with only a couple of bites left, she felt like she was able to slow down enough to talk.

"I was eliminated," she said. "But I actually won a medal in science!"

"We saw you!" her mom said, her voice a mixture of excitement and disappointment. "And when you called and told me what had happened, I couldn't believe it."

Eden remembered the phone call that the official had allowed her after he had stripped her of her medal. She couldn't remember much of what she had said, but she just remembered that overwhelming fear, wishing her mother could fix everything the way she had been able to do when Eden was little.

"So, after the adulting ceremony, we were basically led onto this huge boat, like a yacht, kind of." Eden had never seen a yacht in her life, but the word seemed right.

"You too?" Eden's mom asked Helena, taking her eyes off her daughter for once.

Helena shook her head. "I was eliminated last year."

Eden's mother blinked a couple of times, and Eden rushed to fill in the blanks of what being eliminated really meant. "I think they drugged us, because I don't remember anything except being on the boat next to Xander."

"How did he get there?" Eden's mother asked. "I visited his mother last week. She's so sick now, and I talked to her about what had happened. She didn't seem to know anything except that he never came home after the Olympics. Everyone she asked seemed confused about it. Are you saying he's still alive too?"

Eden nodded, though she wondered if Xander would still be okay with everything that was happening. Would he be shipped off to Alaska or stay here? Would they at least give him one of the weapons they had been holding?

"He's... he came with me." She rushed ahead to tell her painful story, not wanting to relive the moments of confusion. "We woke up on a space station. It orbits Earth, but it doesn't have an engine or anything. It can't control its movement. Apparently, every year, some of the eliminated are shipped there.

I don't know why, but anyway..." She trailed off as she thought of everything that had happened on the space station. How could she compact things?

Helena put an arm around Eden's shoulders, and Eden blinked, remembering where she was. As she shoved the last few bites of her sandwich into her mouth, she began to tell every detail, every painful detail, of what had happened to her on the spaceship, including Xander's volunteering to destroy the asteroid and the forced cannibalism.

By the time she was done, it was pitch black outside the window. Eden felt exhausted, and she kept glancing toward the bathroom, thinking about what it would be like to have a long, long shower without anyone waiting outside the shower stall.

Suddenly, her mom's and dad's phones started blaring at the same time. They both reached for them and stared at the notifications on the screens.

"It's started," Eden's mom said in a tight voice.

"What?" Helena asked.

"We need to turn off all the lights and cover the windows," Eden's dad commanded, immediately moving around to do just that.

"Why?" Eden's heart started pounding as her mom ushered Helena and her behind the couch that was at the center of their apartment.

"They're coming," her dad said. "They're coming straight for Sisimiut."

Chapter 30

Xander had spent the last five hours prepping for the upcoming battle. It seemed so prehistoric, this man-to-man fighting, but with most of the major weaponry having been wiped out years ago, this was one of the few options left.

Xander had been paired up with an official named Greg, who was at least fifteen to twenty years older than him. The man had a paunch that said he hadn't ever needed to engage in a physical fight. He had short-cut, gray hair and a serious look.

As everyone piled onto a bus next to their partners, Xander stared out the window, excited to see Sisimiut again, even if it would only be through a window. Intel had it that the Alaskans were flying over Sisimiut, and they would be dropping officials into the city via parachute. The officials who had been equipped with real guns would be responsible for shooting them. The volunteers, like Xander, would be responsible for catching and engaging them if they made it past that.

Almost everyone on the bus was silent as they rumbled the few miles into Sisimiut. Xander saw the familiar main road in front of him, and wondered if anything would be the same when this battle ended. Would he be able to have a normal life? For some reason, after working with Barrel, Xander had no desire to go through the correct training and become an official anymore. Still, he had no other skills, so it was probably what he would end up doing.

The bus swerved to the side, and Xander realized that there was a group of people walking along the side of the road. He watched them for a moment, observing that some of them should have put on sunscreen. As he wondered where they were going, he realized that he recognized a few of the faces. He pressed himself against the window trying to see better, but the bus had already moved on. Were those... it had to be! The people he had traveled with from the space station had been *walking* to Sisimiut. Had they been walking all these hours and where was Eden?

The bus squeaked to a stop, and the front half began to unload. Xander's partner who was squished onto the bench next to Xander didn't move. Finally, the bus started up again, and they continued around the coast to the southernmost part of the city that Xander didn't know. He kept his eyes open, but he knew where Eden would have gone if she had walked all this way. He had already passed the turnoff to her apartment building.

Xander's partner grunted and slid out of the seat, leading Xander off the bus. It was just starting to grow dark outside, a strange sort of twilight that made the whole city look like it was coated in gray paint.

"This way," his partner grunted again, and he and Xander peeled off from the group. Xander hadn't seen a map or an assignment, but he trusted that his partner knew where they were supposed to wait this thing out.

They walked along a thin street that Xander had never seen before. Suddenly, a shout behind them alerted Xander. He pulled up his pistol, even though it was only loaded with blanks, and hurried back to the corner they had just turned.

Despite his out-of-shape state, Greg appeared behind Xander in a matter of seconds, also scanning the sky. He swore. "They're coming in early. We're not ready."

Xander didn't know what he meant, but suddenly, he saw something moving in the gray sky. It wasn't quite dark, but it was dark enough that he had to strain to make out the shape.

It was falling too fast. Xander was sure the thing would shatter falling at that speed toward the ground. That was when he realized it was a person. Suddenly, when the man reached the height of the tallest buildings, a parachute bloomed around him, slowing his fall.

Greg aimed at the man, but someone else must have got him. He yelped, and his movement changed from fluid to wildly flailing. Another shot stopped his movement all together. Xander wasn't a kid, but watching someone die like that, someone who was just following orders like Xander was... it felt wrong.

"This way," Greg commanded and started moving immediately, going down the street he and Xander had originally been following. Xander picked up his pace, glancing behind himself.

They turned a corner and headed down another street to an area that provided an open view of the sky. There wasn't much cover, though, and Xander wondered if someone parachuting down would be able to shoot before landing.

Then, he saw one to the right and pointed it out to Greg. With the strange lighting, it was nothing more than a fast-moving shape, but after seeing it once, Xander knew how to recognize it. Calling the Alaskan an "it" made it easier to fulfill his duty. Greg took aim, and Xander moved in the direction of the man's predicted trajectory. Once the parachute blossomed out on either side, and he slowed, Xander tightened his muscles, waiting for the sound that he knew would come.

Sure enough, four seconds later, the *pop* behind him told him that Greg had done his duty. "Far left," Greg's scratchy voice said, but Xander was already moving to where the parachute was falling. He had to make sure the Alaskan was dead. It had seemed a simple task when he had received it. But now, it felt impossible. He didn't want to finish off the job himself.

The parachute was huge as Xander got close to it, probably as big as his whole apartment. As he approached, he paused on the edge, looking around. He couldn't let himself miss something that was happening around him because he was too intent on the job in front of him.

Nothing. Xander took a couple of steps forward, kicking the material aside as he went. He could see a distinctive lump under the heavy fabric, but it was getting harder and harder to see. None of the street lights had come on, and Xander wondered if that was planned or if someone had cut some lines.

Xander paused again to look around. Still nothing. He took another step forward, moving more fabric with his foot. But as he moved his foot in the sweeping motion, it caught on something. Xander yanked his foot back, but it wouldn't come. The movement threw him off balance, and he fell, catching most of his weight on his butt. He winced at the sudden pain, but tugged his foot free from the cords, holding his gun in one shaking hand.

Just as he was getting to his feet again, a hand flashed out from underneath the fabric and pulled him down. It happened so quickly that Xander dropped his gun as fabric suddenly covered his face. Someone pressed down on him, trying to suffocate him in the yards and yards of fabric.

The other person grunted, and Xander's instincts kicked in. He kicked out, hit something, and loosened the fabric from around his face. He couldn't see and couldn't breathe. He wouldn't be able to fight properly here, so he turned and tried to scramble out from under the fabric.

The hand came again and locked itself around his ankle, refusing to let him breathe the fresh air.

Xander turned and grabbed the fingers, pulling them away one by one. He heard a pop and a yell, then grabbed the wrist of the person and pulled him out from under the parachute. It was surprisingly easy to get him into the open air, the person just slipping along.

It was only once they were out in the still-not-quite-dark air that Xander realized why. Blood was pumping out of the person's leg like a fountain of juice, and Xander's stomach turned over. He tamped down the urge to ask if the person was okay, and just stood over the person.

He looked into the person's face and realized it was a girl. Was she...? Yes, Xander recognized her. He had seen her in the hallways during the Olympics. That meant she had barely had any training after winning her medal before being tossed into an airplane and sent here.

They both looked at each other, and the girl finally seemed to realize that Xander wasn't about to attack her again. She closed her eyes and let out a low groan, voicing her pain.

Xander once again clenched his mouth shut to keep from saying something to comfort her. He couldn't. It was wrong. But... who would know?

With that thought, Xander was down on his knees, using a corner of the parachute to wrap it around the girl's leg and stop the flow of blood. She watched what he was doing, until he had a tight tourniquet in place. There wasn't much else he could do.

"Sorry," he said.

But before he could say more, the shots that had been ringing out far away came closer. A burst of pain in Xander's back told him that he had been hit, and he fought against the pain, trying to stand, trying to move away, trying, trying, trying to do anything to get himself to safety.

"Stop!" the girl called out. "He helped me. Don't hurt him!"

Chapter 31

Eden huddled on a couch cushion on the floor with a blanket around her shoulders. She wasn't cold, but she felt safer with its familiarity surrounding her. No one talked much as they listened to the noise through the windows.

She had heard only one gunshot before, when the boy had tried to escape his fate as an eliminated, but Eden had now heard too many shots to count. The *pop pop* of the guns was burning through her ears and into her brain. She buried her face in her knees and waited, hoping the horrible noises would stop soon.

Someone screamed, a heart-wrenching, primal scream, and a silent tear made its way down Eden's face. Where was Xander right now? Was he safe? She knew that Xander could be relied on in hand-to-hand combat, but involving guns made the whole thing a deadly mess.

Eden's mother put her arm around Eden's shoulders, her fingers stroking through Eden's stringy, brown hair. She hadn't been able to take a shower as she had planned, and she had sweated through her shirt during their walk into the city. She felt disgusting, but that was only a vague feeling at the edge of her mind at the moment.

"What do you think is happening?" Eden finally asked after no one had said anything for a long time. She could feel Helena next to her in the darkness, and she thought Helena might have fallen asleep. Sure, they had walked for a long time, but Eden couldn't slow her mind down enough to sleep.

Her father answered. "We were told this might happen after Alaska's surprise attack on the research center. That's why everyone is home and hasn't gone to work for the last three days. They weren't sure when it would happen."

Eden was already tuning out part of his explanation as she imagined Xander shooting someone from Alaska. Eden had friends from Alaska, now that she had lived on the space station with so many different people. And honestly, she wouldn't be able to pick them out from those who came from Russia or Greenland. They were all the same. She didn't know what anyone was hoping to accomplish by attacking them now.

Everyone remained silent for a long time again, the noises outside the window exploding Eden's imagination with gory images.

"We found the video on your phone," Eden's mom said in a whisper. "It was beautiful."

Eden remembered the dance she had created with the special song for her parents. It felt so long ago that she had filmed herself and left it for her parents. Her hands suddenly itched for her phone.

"Do you still have it?" she asked.

"Of course!" her mother sounded offended that Eden thought she might have deleted it. Crouching, her mother peered over the back of the couch at the curtained windows. Then, she scurried to their bedroom and came back a moment later, pushing the clunky box with its clear glass screen into Eden's hand.

She pressed the button on the side, and the screen flared to life with the time, almost 10:00. When she had been going to school, ten had been her bedtime every night. She had wanted her eight hours without interruption. As she pressed in the easy password, Eden was filled with a desire for the past. She had loved the routine and predictability of each day. Now, she had no idea what awaited her.

Would she really be given a profession and a place to live after all of this or would the official say that he hadn't been serious when he had offered that to them, just desperate for more volunteers?

Eden clicked on the video, the only thing left in the gallery and watched the dance she had created for her parents. She felt her mom watching over her shoulder as the tiny Eden twisted and turned on the screen. Without meaning to, Eden started critiquing her technique. By the end of the song, she had resolved never to film something again if she wasn't going to do the routine perfectly.

"It's just so beautiful," her mom said, wiping at her eyes. "I think I could do it now with how many times I've watched it."

Eden laughed at the idea of her mom performing the dance routine, and Helena stirred and looked up. Eden shut off the glaring phone light and stared at her friend in the dark, wondering if and when Helena would be able to reunite with her family. She had been so busy experiencing tonight through her own eyes that she had mostly forgotten about what Helena was going through. Had she ever told Eden where she was from? Eden's thoughts were scattered at the moment, and she couldn't remember if they'd had that conversation.

Suddenly, the whole building shook. Eden squeezed the blanket so hard that her nails cut into the palms of her hands. She looked at her mom as she always did, and her mom's face reflected her fear.

"What happened?" Eden asked in a whisper, but no one answered her.

Her mom crawled to one of the windows, and Eden held her breath as she looked out. After four or five seconds, her mom ducked back down, the curtain falling into place.

Suddenly, the window that looked out on the landing shattered with a loud *crash*, and something was catapulted into the room.

Even though Eden's first thought was a curious, "Huh, what's that?," she knew that they had to get out of there as quickly as possible. The escape route that she had always planned but never taken would now be put into use.

"Here, here," Eden said, grabbing the half-asleep Helena's arm and running toward her room. Her parents stumbled afterward. There were some screams on the floors beneath Eden, and she knew something bad was happening.

Once everyone was in her room, she slammed the door and yanked the comforter off her bed to shove it under the crack.

"What is..." her mom started to ask, but Eden didn't have an explanation. She just knew that their building was under attack.

"We have to get out," Eden said, shoving her bedroom window open. She had barely had a chance to register her room. It looked the same, just a bit more bare. She didn't have time to play the "what's different?" game.

"Down to the overhang roof, to the tree, and to the ground," she instructed, her eyes bouncing from place to place in the moonlight. She had sat here imagining how she would do it if she were one of those kids who snuck out. Now, she had to try it for real, and the drop to the overhang roof looked long.

"Come on," she said, trying to sound brave.

A strange smell was infiltrating the room, and Eden knew there was no more time to hesitate.

She turned, and gripping the windowsill tightly, she jumped down, a sick lurch in her stomach as she dangled in the open air. She strained to turn her head and see beneath her. She was only a few inches above the overhang roof, so she dropped with a tiny *thunk*. Then, she reached for the tree branch which was steadier than she had thought and disappeared into the leaves of the tree.

Once she was close to the trunk, she turned around so that she could watch whoever came next. Helena appeared, her braids swinging with the movement like a flag alerting everyone where they were. She hesitated a lot longer.

Eden wanted to shout encouragement, but someone ran across the ground just then, and she kept her mouth shut. There was no telling whether the person was an enemy or not, and they wouldn't know who she was either. Drawing attention to herself would only cause trouble.

Finally, Helena was safely crawling on the branch, and Eden's mom was looking out the window.

Once Helena was next to Eden, she decided to look for another branch that would hold her weight. There was one two branches down, so Eden swung down to that, then turned back to watch her mom's much slower progress. Helena held out her hand and helped Eden's mom onto the tree branch.

Then, Eden's father came out, coughing and swaying dizzily so that he almost lost his balance on the roof. Someone screamed nearby, close, too close, and Eden could hardly breathe with the fear piling up in her chest. Once her family was in the tree, all of them close to the trunk but on branches of different heights, they looked at each other.

Eden's mom had her arms wrapped around the tree trunk and her eyes closed.

Eden suddenly remembered something about her mom having a fear of heights. She had been told that so long ago, and Eden hadn't even considered it tonight. Still, it wasn't like they had had many options.

"What do we do now?" Helena asked.

Eden was surprised to see both of her parents *and* Helena looking at her like she had all the answers. "We should wait here," she said, her voice a little below its normal tone. "I don't think anyone will find us here." Besides, if they went down to the ground, then she would really have no idea where to go, not with people with guns running around.

The gunshots were louder now, and Eden wondered if she had made the right decision, forcing her family out of their safe hiding spot.

She closed her eyes and prepared to wait out the night in the tree.

A few hours later, Eden felt herself falling sideways with exhaustion and catching herself just before she fell out of the tree. She gripped the rough bark tightly and watched as the world around her slowly lightened. At some point as she had fought sleep, the noises around them had slowed down. As the sunlight showed her the scene below, Eden realized that she hadn't heard a gunshot in at least a couple of hours.

She stretched backward in the tree, her legs aching from holding on so tightly, and made eye contact with her mom, her dad, and Helena. Her dad had dark circles around his eyes, but her mom's eyes were wide. She probably hadn't felt sleepy at all.

"Should we…" she started to suggest, and her father motioned for her to stay put. Then, his own limbs creaking more than the tree's, her father started a slow descent downward. Eden bit her lower lip, wondering what Xander was doing right that moment. Was he hurt or…no, she couldn't think about the worst option. Just thinking about it made her feel sick.

With a thump, her dad landed on the ground and began walking toward the corner of their apartment building. Just as he reached the edge of the building, he froze, remaining in the same place for too long as Eden held her breath and traded worried looks with her mother.

Then, he moved again, disappearing from view.

She couldn't keep her worries in then. "What do you think's going on?" she asked.

Her mother opened her mouth to answer, but Helena cut in practically, "We should stay quiet," she said.

Eden nodded and turned toward the place where her dad had disappeared. None of the three of them moved as they waited for his return. The minutes ticked onward, though, with no sign of him returning.

Some noises came from the apartment building, which Eden suddenly realized had been silent for too long. "I *have* to get down from here," she finally said, the burning in her legs and butt more painful than the fear of anyone attacking her.

Despite her mother telling her not to go down, Eden started a slow climb down, her knees cracking as she followed the path her dad had taken.

Just as she reached the ground, a figure appeared around the corner of the building. Eden stumbled backward and almost fell, her legs stiff from the night in the tree. It was her dad.

She moved toward him, embracing him, but he didn't revel in her hug. "We should get out of the tree and get away from here," he told her. He started climbing back up, and Eden realized he was helping her mom. Helena made her way down by herself, and soon, Eden and her friend were watching as her dad helped her mom down the tree step by step.

When her mom was on the ground again, she once again looked more like the confident, self-possessed woman that Eden knew she was.

"What did you see?" Eden asked. She wanted to ask about Xander, but she knew it would be pretty much impossible that her father would have any information on him. As Xander once again popped into her head, she remembered Simon. She hadn't thought of him once during this whole fiasco. If that didn't tell her what she should do about the future, then what would?

"There was...a lot of death," her father answered.

Eden swallowed and looked around. "Is the apartment not safe anymore?" she asked.

"It's going to take some cleaning up before we can live in it. It looked like some sort of gas knocked people out before they were shot. Lots of things were destroyed," her father said. "I want to get somewhere with some officials, so we can figure out what's going on."

As the sun rose completely over the rocky hills, Eden and her family trudged toward the nearest officials' station, and Eden hoped they would be able to get some answers.

Chapter 32

Xander had passed out from the pain. He knew it as soon as he felt the beginnings of it prick his consciousness.

The face he did not expect to see bending over him was Greg. Xander blinked and looked around, trying to quickly get an understanding of the safety of his surroundings.

"You're lucky you're alive," Greg said. "Get up."

Xander opened his mouth and let out a silent scream as he tried to move. His back was on fire, and he felt black etching at the edges of his vision like a warning.

"Can't move," he said, falling back onto the ground. The softness of the ground made him realize that he was still lying on the parachute. He stretched his hands out to the left side, but the other person, the Alaskan, was no longer there. He turned his head to confirm, but the parachute was smooth.

"I'll send some help out for you," Greg said gruffly. "It might be a few hours. They're picking up the pieces everywhere. Take this for now." He handed Xander a bottle of something, and Xander brought it to his lips without thinking about it. Then, he smelled the contents and realized it was liquor. His stomach turned over, and he tried to hold his breath as the liquid burned its way down to his stomach.

He handed the bottle back to Greg, and Greg hurried away, gun out and ready. Even though the streets were mostly quiet, Xander wondered if he was safe here. He reached for his gun, but it was no longer in the holster. That was when he remembered losing his grip on it the night before. That whole night had been a disaster. Xander had hesitated too much when dealing with the enemy. All he wanted now was something to take this pain away and to find Eden again.

Greg had said it might be hours, but it didn't feel too long before a familiar-looking bus came chugging down the road, bumping unceremoniously over a body. Xander winced as he raised his hand so they wouldn't bump over *him* like that.

The bus rolled to a stop, and someone hopped out before the bus had even stopped moving. Xander didn't recognize him, but he recognized the uniform of an official. The man walked up to Xander. He opened his mouth to say something, but Xander just pointed at his back, and the man got to work. He stuck a needle in Xander and pumped in some sort of liquid, then started doing a quick clean and wrap right there.

"What's happening?" Xander asked. "Did we get them?"

"We won!" the man responded cheerfully.

"What?" Xander asked, unsure how something like that could happen overnight.

"We're just cleaning up the mess, but our officials in Alaska found their weapons hold and took it over. They thought we would all be here, defending our own territory, but we surprised them."

"That's it?" Xander asked, wincing as something that burned more than the bullet wound sunk into his skin. He gritted his teeth and didn't hear the official's first answer. He had to ask him to repeat it as the pain started to fade away.

"Well, we'll be keeping them in their place," the official said, "but they're not going to be able to attack again anytime soon. They lost over three hundred last night."

Xander was helped to his feet, and a strange, light feeling took over, like he could do anything. He smiled at the man and patted his arm. He was so helpful.

When he climbed onto the bus and lay on one of the benches, he heard laughter in the back of the bus. Xander joined in for no other reason than that it felt good to laugh about something, even if he didn't understand the joke.

The official at the front of the bus rolled his eyes. "Come on, keep going, two streets up, we've got two," he told the driver.

Xander laughed as he touched the leather backing of the seat in front of him. He wished he could stay here forever, surrounded by all this happiness.

By the time Xander was in the hospital that had miraculously remained untouched, the medicine was starting to wear off. Things weren't quite as funny anymore, and the fire in his back had come back with little flames licking their way across his skin.

"You're lucky," someone in a nurse's uniform told him. "The bullet passed right through your muscle. No surgery needed."

Xander had trouble connecting the word "lucky" to himself right now.

"We'll just get it cleaned and wrapped up better and get you something for the pain." The nurse muttered something before shoving Xander on a couch instead of a hospital bed. There weren't enough of those, apparently, which told Xander just how badly everything had gone.

"Hey, do you know if someone named Connor Abbott is here?" Xander called after the nurse, hoping his friend hadn't been hurt.

"I don't know," she said. "We're working on fixing people up, not socializing."

A minute later, someone hobbled into the room and was helped onto the hospital bed which was shoved into the corner to make room for one more bed.

Xander watched the bustling activity patiently for a few minutes. Clearly, the nurses were busy trying to help everyone, attending to the loudest before the rest of them.

A lot of the people passing by Xander's doorway were in the official uniform, but a good amount of them weren't. Xander wondered if they were volunteer officials like him or just regular civilians who had gotten hurt. He was sure that Eden had made it home, but he wondered if she had been safe in her apartment.

A nurse peeked her head in the door, scribbled something across a tablet's face, then hurried away before anyone in the room had a chance to ask her questions.

Xander remained patient for the first two hours, but then, the pain in his back had increased too much. He couldn't wait any longer for some attention. "Hey!" he said when the purple uniform of a nurse passed by. The nurse didn't even pause.

Xander forced himself to sit up, then get off the couch, a hand pressed to his back in an attempt to push some of the pain away. Once out in the hall, the level of activity around him doubled. Nurses shouted back and forth some codes and names. They never seemed to stop moving, and Xander almost felt sorry for how busy they were.

He approached the desk where one lone nurse was rapidly tapping and typing various things onto a screen.

"I just need some painkiller," Xander said to the nurse.

She didn't even look up at him. Another nurse shouted a name and a code, and the nurse in front of Xander tapped it into the screen in front of her. "I don't have access to any drugs," she said.

"Who does?"

"I'm not sure. I'm trying to get all of this information in here correctly, and it's harder when someone's talking to me." She glanced up at Xander just for a second, and Xander saw that she couldn't be that much older than he was. He didn't recognize her from his Olympics, but he could tell that she was overwhelmed by everything that was happening. Even though he could empathize with her, the pain in his back made him unreasonable.

"No, no," he muttered, leaning forward against the counter, losing the ability to move for a moment. When he finally felt a little strength returning, he straightened and hobbled back to his couch. But when he reached it, a new patient was lying there. This one writhed around like he had poison running up and down his veins, and he shouted loudly.

Xander backed away, stumbling down the hallway and almost running directly into a nurse.

"Where do you belong?" the nurse asked, grabbing Xander's arm and stopping his forward movement.

"Someone else is on my couch," Xander muttered. He wasn't bitter, just stating a fact.

"Let's find a place for you to lie down," the guy said, leading Xander forward slowly as he peered in the passing rooms. "We've made a few pallets on the floor," the nurse said. "You'll have to take one of those."

Xander saw rectangles of blankets being placed at regular intervals down the hallway. He settled onto one, leaning forward. If he didn't get something for the pain, he was going to pass out again. He leaned forward and absorbed the pain, swallowing each passing minute and counting it an accomplishment.

Finally, a nurse bent next to him with a screen, asked his name, and stuck something in his back just above where he was shot. This painkiller wasn't as strong as the first one had been, but the relief was almost immediate. Xander's shirt was ripped off, and the nurse quickly tended to his wound.

"Is it bad?" Xander asked. "How long will it take to heal?"

"I can't see into the future," the nurse responded. "We just need to keep it clean. I'm going to stitch it up right now, and then, you'll be responsible for cleaning it and changing the bandages twice a day."

"I don't know how to do that."

"If you wait around for one of us to do it, then you won't get them switched for a while. I'll give you a few painkillers, but I suggest you find some regular Tylenol and take a few at a time."

Xander's eyebrows shot up. He tried to turn his head to see what the nurse was doing, but she forced him to face forward again.

"You can't feel anything right here, but I don't need you to watch me stitch you up and get scared."

Xander stared straight ahead until the nurse patted his shoulder.

"You'll probably have a scar. That's the first time I've done that," she admitted now that she was done.

Xander stood, testing the strength of the medicine. "Thanks. I know you guys are busy."

The nurse shoved a small pile of bandages into his hands and a couple of rounds of antibiotics, and Xander decided to make his way home before the painkiller wore off. His mom might be sick, but she would be able to help him through the worst of the pain.

Xander stumbled out of the hospital, holding the bandages close to his bare chest when someone lunged for them like a starving person would lunge toward bread.

The hospital waiting room was filled with people. One of them shouted at him. "Have you seen Vivian Mercer? She's an official- long, red hair?"

As soon as those in the waiting room identified him as a released patient, others started asking him similar questions so that Xander couldn't focus on any one of them. He pushed his way out of the crowd and stood outside the overhanging hospital roof and stared up the road ahead. On his bike, he could get to his apartment in ten minutes. Walking with his back like this, he had no idea how long it would take him.

"Xander!" he heard, and he turned just in time to see a speeding bullet of a person rush toward him.

Chapter 33

"You're alive!" Eden said, wanting to throw herself on Xander. She could tell that he was in pain, though, and even though she couldn't see a wound, she forced herself to stop in front of him, quivering with the urge to hug him. "What happened to you? You're hurt? Where?"

Xander smiled at her, and the smile was so familiar that Eden wanted to start crying right there.

She hurried on, "The officials told us that it's over. Alaska isn't going to attack again. They said too many of them were killed, and...what happened to you?" She circled back to her original question.

"I need to get home," Xander said, his face solemn.

"Okay, I'll go with you. My family is still at the official's station. Everyone in my..." she swallowed, still not believing the news even as she said it, "in my building was killed. They tossed in the gas bombs that kill. And the people who ran out their front doors were shot."

"How did you get out?"

"We spent the night in that tree outside my window. You remember the tree I pointed out that one time, how it would be the one I would use to escape if I was *that* kind of girl?"

Xander nodded.

"Yeah, that one. It's crazy. If I hadn't acted quickly enough, then we might not be alive. I'm not saying that to brag. It's just that I can't believe it myself."

She reached for Xander's hand and took the bandages, trying to be helpful. Her thoughts turned to the report she had caught sight of on one of the official's screens. Hungry for information, she had scanned the names and seen Xander's at the hospital. But below him, a few lines down, just as she had been turning away, she had seen Simon's name. It had listed him as alive and heading toward the Sisimiut research base. He must not have been hurt.

Eden had blinked and wondered why she cared at all. She knew what she wanted for herself and her life. But despite that, Simon was still her friend. Maybe she would get the chance to check in with him later, but her first priority had been finding Xander.

Xander winced, and Eden focused back on the here and now. She leaned toward the spot that Xander was rubbing and got a view of his back with a white bandage taped into place, right where he had gotten stabbed by a knife.

"Did you get stabbed again?" she asked.

"Shot," Xander said. "The pain is a lot worse, but apparently, I'm lucky because the bullet passed right through."

Eden gritted her teeth as she remembered the sound of the bullets ricocheting in her building last night. One of them had hit Xander. Still, even though she could tell it was affecting his movement, she couldn't help but be happy that he was alive. She switched the bandages to her other hand and grasped his upper arm, dangerous words hovering at the edge of her mouth.

Xander cleared his throat, and the spell was broken. Of course she wouldn't say it to him yet. She might feel a sudden rush of emotion because he was alive, but that didn't mean she needed to rush their relationship. Now that they were both back on Earth, they had their whole lives in front of them.

"Have you...found Simon now that everything is settled?" Xander asked.

Eden winced at his name and realized she probably should have asked after him at the hospital. She had been so excited to see Xander upright and moving that she hadn't even thought of anyone else, including the names Helena had asked her to search for. Oops.

"No, I, well, I just wanted to see you, to be honest. Xander, look, I know that I liked Simon and everything, for a little while," she added to make it clear that the way she had felt about Simon was nothing in comparison with Xander. "But when everything was happening last night, all I could think about was if you were safe or not. And, Simon might be a friend, but you're...more than that."

Xander found her hand and squeezed it. Then, he didn't let go as they continued to stroll slowly up the hill toward Xander's apartment building.

"I'm going to stay with you while you're getting better," Eden promised when Xander didn't say anything. "And once you're better, we can both get jobs, and...it will be great."

Xander laughed and squeezed her hand again. "Right now, all I can think about is how long this pain medication is going to last. But, I don't know if I can just relax and accept that we both get normal, adult lives with jobs. I keep feeling like someone will come and tell us it was all some joke just to get us to volunteer."

"They won't," Eden told him. "I won't let them."

"Well, now that you're going to put them in their place, what have I even been worrying about?" Xander asked.

Eden could tell he was teasing her, but she couldn't let her anxious side take over and start telling her that it would be impossible for them to have the lives she had always wanted. She had to believe that there was still some good and that at least some people would follow through on their promises.

Eden opened her mouth to ask about Xander's mom, but shut it again. They would find out how she was doing, if she was doing, soon. Squinting against the unexpectedly bright sun, Eden saw Xander's apartment building only five more minutes away.

"I feel like we've won something," she said, "and I mean more than just against Alaska. I feel like we've won, because we're still alive even though we shouldn't be."

"Don't say that too loud or fate might come find us and decide to fix things."

"Well, I'm just saying it because I feel like we fixed something, changed something, but we really didn't. I mean, the Olympics are still going to take place again next May, and the planet is still sick. There is no long-term plan for dealing with global warming." The weight settled heavily onto Eden's shoulders, and she looked for some reassurance from Xander.

He continued forward at the same, steady pace. Finally, he said, "You're right. None of that has changed, but they're letting the eliminated live. That's something." He remained quiet after that, and Eden could tell he was thinking. She wanted to get inside his thoughts, but didn't know the right questions to ask.

Finally, they were in front of the bike racks at Xander's apartment building. He leaned on the closest rail and took a few deep breaths.

"Are you okay?" Eden asked.

"Yeah, but I think my medicine might be starting to wear off," Xander said. He reached back and gingerly felt around the edge of the bandage. Eden pulled his hand away from it.

"Don't," she urged. "You'll just get the germs from your hand in the bandage."

Xander smiled. "Thanks, Ms. I Won a Science Medal."

"Oh please, like that even matters anymore."

Xander squeezed her hand and pulled her toward him just a little. "Before my medicine wears off," he said, "I want one good kiss."

Eden smiled, her cheeks flaring a red that had nothing to do with the sunburn she had gotten yesterday. "Sure you don't want two bad ones?"

"You couldn't give me a bad kiss," Xander flirted right back. He leaned forward, and Eden closed her eyes, feeling the touch of Xander's lips on hers.

Then, a *bang* sounded, and Eden's eyes flew open. The door to one of the apartments opened, and Xander's mother suddenly stood on the porch above them. For a sick woman, she sure moved fast.

"Xander! Oh, thank God you're alive. Eden, come on up, you two!"

Eden took Xander's hand and led him up to his apartment, full of hope for the future.

Epilogue

"I'm sorry, Colt," Xander apologized, feeling like a failure. It was his fault that he hadn't returned to the space station in time. He had dangled Emily in front of Colt like a prize, but she had been dead by the time Xander had arrived at the space station to rescue everyone.

Colt rubbed his new pair of glasses against his shirt. He didn't make eye contact. "I understand that you could not have foreseen the current situation of the space station. I do wish I had had the chance to behold Emily once more. However, I shall move forward nevertheless."

Xander patted his friend on the shoulder. He knew it bothered Colt more than Colt would admit, but all Xander could do was be there for him.

Right now, though, he had other things to worry about. The board members were waiting for him beyond that door. He wished that Colt could attend the meeting with him, but he had Colt's calculations tucked under his arm. When the board members requested to see one person only, that's who they got to see.

With another deep breath, Xander strode forward, trying to convince himself that he felt confident. He pushed open the doors to the meeting room and stood in front of the board members of the Olympics.

There were fifteen in all, five originating from each country, and most of them looked to be at least seventy years old. In fact, Xander was the only one in the room without a beard.

"Go ahead," the board member closest to Xander said. "Tell us about your experience in the space station."

But Xander's real purpose in meeting with the board members had nothing to do with complaints about the space station. "I am the one who used the spaceship to get back to the space station and brought most of its occupants back here to Earth."

"Despite the fact that they had been eliminated," one of the men clarified in an accusing tone.

"Despite that," Xander agreed with a nod. "The fact that I found interesting is the amount of resources that you seem to have." His anger at the fact that the board members seemed to be using the Olympics as a way to control people rather than to actually keep too many people from living on Earth burst out in angry accusations. "Suddenly, if the people from the space station are willing to fight, then they can stay. Resources were never even mentioned. It was just an accepted fact that there would be enough food and housing for them. How is that possible if resources are really as limited as you claim?"

The board members were all silent for a moment, throwing each other looks that Xander couldn't quite interpret. He wished he had Colt by his side, but he just had his calculations.

"Based on the square feet needed for healthy habitation of this land, our population could double, and we would still have enough space."

"Clearly, you came here with an agenda," one of the board members said instead of addressing his claims.

"I don't mind speaking to him," another said. He stood and clasped his hands in front of a stomach that clearly demonstrated access to plentiful resources. "Address your questions to me."

Xander started, "How can you kill eighteen-year-olds every year if there is enough space for them?"

"If we were allowing every single resource to be allocated to someone, every liveable space on this Earth to be inhabited, then we would have to kill *everyone* due for the Olympics the next few years. At least this way, there is a steady population increase, rather than maxing out our space and having to wait until enough people die of old age to allow more young people to live."

Xander shook his head and brought out his next accusation. "How come none of you have had your children or grandchildren eliminated?"

He waited for them to shake their heads, to deny what his and Colt's research had discovered. But they didn't.

"It's part of our reward for serving on the board. We are not paid any more than any other profession. However, we have dedicated our lives to creating a successful society, something that many people before us have not been able to do."

Xander stared at the man for a few moments. "So you're still going to hold the Olympics in May this year?"

The white-haired man nodded. "We will. Everything changed when Alaska attacked Greenland a few months ago. However, it does not mean that we are unwilling to continue working together. We must keep things predictable for everyone while we figure out a solution to the global warming problem."

So nothing had changed. Xander felt like he had tried so hard, given so much of himself, but it hadn't made a difference after all.

"Now," the man said, sitting down with a sigh. "Let's hear about your experience on the space station."

Xander settled in to recount the details of his life on the space station as he realized that he *had* made one difference. To each of the people who had been eliminated and had become resigned to living life on the space station, he had given another chance at life on Earth. All that had returned had been given jobs and the right training, and even though some of them had had slow starts, they had all contributed to society in some way. At least he had made a difference for all of them. He couldn't expect to make a difference for everyone on Earth. At least not yet.

About the Author

Laurel Solorzano has enjoyed writing since she was in middle school, exchanging manuscripts for years with her best friend. After traveling the globe for a time, Laurel set her goal to become a published author. As she works teaching English and Spanish, she writes stories in her free time. Laurel currently lives in Raleigh, North Carolina with her husband, Yader.

Read more at https://www.laurelsolorzano.com.